ALSO BY DONNA ANDREWS

Dashing Through the Snowbirds

A Meg Langslow Mystery

Donna Andrews

St. Martin's Paperbacks

This is a work of fiction. All of the characters, organizations, and events portrayed in this novel are either products of the author's imagination or are used fictitiously.

Published in the United States by St. Martin's Paperbacks, an imprint of St. Martin's Publishing Group.

DASHING THROUGH THE SNOWBIRDS

For information, address St. Martin's Publishing Group, 120 Broadway, New York, NY 10271.

www.stmartins.com

ISBN: 978-1-250-89593-6

Our books may be purchased in bulk for promotional, educational, or business use. Please contact your local bookseller or the Macmillan Corporate and Premium Sales Department at 1-800-221-7945, ext. 5442, or by email at MacmillanSpecialMarkets@macmillan.com.

Printed in the United States of America

Minotaur hardcover edition published 2022
St. Martin's Paperbacks edition / October 2023

10 9 8 7 6 5 4 3 2 1

Dashing Through the Snowbirds

Chapter 1

"Blast! You scared it away!"

My grandmother Cordelia turned around and frowned at me. She held a pair of binoculars and stood in front of one of the kitchen windows, so I deduced that my arrival had startled some rare bird into flight.

"And a Merry Christmas to you, too." I strode over and gave her a hug of greeting in spite of the frown. "Did you just get here?"

"Sorry," she said, hugging me back. "It's just that we were so hoping . . . ah, well. Either it was or it wasn't."

"But unless you see it, you won't be able to add it to your life list," I said. "What unique and fabulous feathered creature did I deprive you of seeing?"

"Nothing rare," she said. "I've seen thousands of *Junco hyemalis* in my life. It's just that it would be encouraging to see one here today."

"Why?" I asked. "Is the dark-eyed junco in danger of extinction?" I was rather proud of myself for being able to come up with the common name, but Cordelia took my knowledge for granted.

"Of course not," she said. "At least no more than any other common songbird. But they're well known to be harbingers of snow. You know how much your mother is hoping for snow—I gather it would make these Canadian guests of yours so happy."

"It's going to take a lot more than a little snow to make the Canadians happy." I sighed at the notion, and the flicker of holiday cheer that had started to grow vanished.

Cordelia didn't say anything for the moment—she was busily tucking up the evergreen garland that swooped down gracefully over the window, blocking a fair portion of the glass. I'd been meaning to mention that garland to Mother, since it broke one of our unwritten but well-understood rules about her Christmas decorating: nothing should cover more than a tiny bit of the back windows. I suspected the offending garland had been the bright idea of one of Mother's overeager volunteer helpers, but I was still glad to have it fixed. Apart from wanting to let in as much sunlight as possible this time of year, I didn't want anything that would obscure my view of what the kids, dogs, cats, llamas, and visiting relatives were getting up to out in the yard.

"That's better," Cordelia said when she was finished. "It was like peering out of a thicket. So explain to me why the Canadians are here in the first place. Your mother told me quite a lot about how much of a bother they are, but she never did get around to explaining why your brother invited a dozen Canadians to stay here with you over the Christmas holidays."

"Most of them aren't that much of a bother," I said. "And it's not really Rob's fault they're here. They're with a Toronto-based company that Mutant Wizards is doing a rush project for."

"An exciting new game?"

"No," I said. "Remember, Rob's company does a lot more than games these days."

"But the games are the interesting part," Cordelia said.

Yes, and since Rob's company had started out by developing computer games—including the legendarily successful *Lawyers From Hell*—most of the world still thought of them that way.

"Actually, this is kind of an interesting project," I said. "The company's called AcerGen. They've been around for years doing genealogy-related stuff, like letting you research your ancestors and put them into an online family tree."

"Not exactly a new idea." Cordelia sat down at the kitchen table and studied another of Mother's new decorating notions—a centerpiece of holly and red ribbon that concealed a tiny electric potpourri dispenser. "There are already a couple of big commercial sites doing genealogy—Ancestry.com, for example."

"Yeah, AcerGen is kind of a wannabe Ancestry.com," I said. "More focused on the Canadian market. And they recently branched out into genetics. You take their DNA test, and then you can connect with any other AcerGen members you share genes with."

"The big commercial sites do that, too," Cordelia said. "And I bet they have a lot more people you could connect with than some company that I, for one, have never heard of."

"AcerGen has figured that out," I said. "So they've hired Mutant Wizards to come up with a lot of cool bells and whistles for their website, in the hope of luring enough people to join them instead of the big sites. Or more likely, in addition to the big sites."

"None of which explains why they have to work on this new website here in Caerphilly during the holiday season." Having contemplated the potpourri-emitting centerpiece from close range for a few minutes, Cordelia picked it up and, after a few moments of study, found its off switch. "Or why Rob had to inflict them on you and Michael while they're doing it."

"Good question." I glanced over my shoulder to make sure I wasn't going to be overheard when I answered it. "Apparently AcerGen's president has promised his board of directors that they'd have the new, improved website operational by New Year's Day. And he doesn't seem to understand the concept of working remotely. So a few days ago he dragged all his key managers and programmers down here. Without even trying to make reservations for them to stay anywhere— never mind the fact that this time of year you can't even get on the waiting list at the Caerphilly Inn or any of the bed-and-breakfast places. They all showed up with their suitcases and briefcases and no place to stay, so we took them in."

"Rather an imposition on you." Cordelia looked disapproving.

"Well, we're billing AcerGen for their room and board," I said. "And with them here, we can at least try to keep their morale up. Which is—"

I heard footsteps behind me and turned to see a tall and slightly pudgy figure slouching into the room.

"Speak of the devil," I muttered. And then I went on, more loudly. "Morning, Ian. This is Ian Meredith, the president of AcerGen. Ian, this is my grandmother, Cordelia Lee Mason."

"How do you do?" Cordelia made a motion as if to extend her hand, then checked it. Probably wise. Ian looked snappy when he put on a suit to give his investors a show, but the morning Ian, unshaven and unshowered, didn't exactly look like someone you wanted to be in the same room with, much less touch.

"Uh . . . hey." Ian looked startled and sounded surly. He frowned and looked around. "No one's cooking."

"It's ten thirty," I said. "Rose Noire stops cooking breakfast at nine. There are still a few packed lunches in the fridge. Have one of those."

He sighed heavily. He glanced at Cordelia, as if wondering whether she could be induced to fill in for my cousin as cook. Her cool, assessing gaze seemed to discourage him. And he already knew better than to ask me. He dropped something onto the kitchen table—another of what I thought of as his fidget toys. In this case a pair of V-shaped gadgets that you squeezed to strengthen your grip. I'd never actually seen Ian completely empty-handed. Then he shambled across the kitchen, flung open the refrigerator door, and stood staring inside. Eventually he located the packed lunches and began peering into the bags and poking their contents.

"Getting back to the juncos—they're ground feeders," Cordelia said. "You might have more luck attracting them if you spread some seed in your backyard."

"Rose Noire does, every morning, when she feeds the chickens," I said. "But I'm sure all the girls would love it if you spread some more. Just don't expect them to leave it for the juncos."

"I hadn't thought of that."

"And anyway, are we really trying to attract juncos? Or are we hoping for snow, so we can all have a white Christmas? It's not as if the juncos magically produce snow—they just signal that it's coming. Maybe we should get Rose Noire to lead us in a snow dance."

"True." She lifted her binoculars back to her eyes again. "Count me in for the snow dance."

Just then a loud scraping noise made both of us wince. I turned to see that Ian had carelessly shoved a kitchen chair out of his way, managing to leave a long, unsightly scratch on the kitchen floor in the process, and was shuffling down the hall with his exercise toys hanging out of his back pocket and his hands full of food. Food he'd scavenged from four—no, make that five—packed lunches. The scorned remnants were scattered across the kitchen table.

"Jerk," I muttered. I tossed the two sandwiches Ian had pried open and handled—did he not notice the labels that spelled out the contents of each bag? I managed to assemble two unspoiled lunch kits using ingredients he'd rejected, tossed a few apples and bags of salad back into the fridge, and marked down what he'd made off with in the ledger I'd use when I billed AcerGen for this week's meals. I looked up to see Cordelia frowning at the door through which Ian had disappeared.

"Are they all that rude?" she asked.

"No, the rest of them are just as nice as you'd expect. Polite, considerate—not as cheerful as I'd like, but then you have to make allowances for the fact that they're all homesick, over-worked, and mortally embarrassed at everything Ian does."

"How long have they been here?"

"Five days," I said. "Seems like longer."

"I can imagine." She turned back to scanning the back-yard with her binoculars. I pulled out my notebook-that-tells-me-when-to-breathe, which serves as my calendar, planner, and to-do list, and began planning my day. I often zone out while communing with my notebook, so I didn't even notice when someone else entered the room.

"Meg, dear." I turned to find my mother frowning at me.

"Sorry." Sometimes a preemptive apology wards off a lot of trouble. A preemptive apology and a distraction. "I didn't mean to scare off the bird that might have been a junco."

"Oh!" Her face lit up and she turned to my grandmother. "Have we spotted juncos?"

"Not definitively," Cordelia said. "Possibly a few early out-liers, but they're easily spooked. And it's not as if I can ask everyone to stay out of the backyard all day so we can see if the juncos have arrived."

I could tell from Mother's expression that she considered this a perfectly reasonable request, and for that matter she'd be making it an order, not a request.

"It won't really be significant until we see them in flocks," Cordelia went on.

"And all the construction noise doesn't help, does it?" Mother sighed in a manner intended to suggest that her last nerve was rapidly fraying.

"Construction noise?" Cordelia looked puzzled.

"Back there." Mother waved toward the kitchen window. "That's why I came in here. Meg, dear, do you know what in the world your father is *doing* in your backyard?"

"Technically not in our backyard," I said. "In the back pasture."

I glanced out the nearest window. At the far end of our yard a barbed-wire fence separated it from one of the fields that belonged to Mother and Dad's farm. Some years ago Dad fenced off the half acre that adjoined our property so Rose Noire could plant her herbs there. Beyond that was the back pasture, a sort of grassy cul-de-sac between the herb fields and the surrounding woods, out of sight from the main pasture but fully connected to it. Thanks to all the towering oaks nearby it was shadier than the main pasture, so Dad's cows and sheep often took refuge there on hot summer days. In the winter, though, they tended to stay in the sunnier areas closer to the barn, so according to Dad they wouldn't mind that most of their summer hangout was currently surrounded by the eight-foot privacy fence the Shiffley Construction Company had erected to help keep Dad's project secret. The fence wasn't exactly an eyesore.

"But highly visible from the back of your house," Mother

said, as if reading my thoughts. "And what if whatever he's having built spoils your view?"

"According to Dad, it's only temporary, and will barely be visible from the backyard, and if Michael and I hate it he'll take it away," I said. "And no, he hasn't told me what it is. He hasn't told anyone."

With luck she wouldn't notice that I hadn't answered her question. No, Dad hadn't told me what he was up to. But yes, I knew. I'd sneaked back there to spy on his project. But I wasn't sharing that with anyone but Michael. I tried not even to think about it around Mother. Not that I still believed her to be a mind reader, but old habits die hard.

"And they were a little noisy the first two days," I went on. "But they've been very quiet today."

"Too quiet," Mother muttered. "If you find out what he's up to—"

"The minute he tells me, I'll call you." I held up my cell phone as if making a pledge. "And I assume you'll do the same."

"Of course, dear." Mother took a step and looked up in annoyance as a low-hanging garland caught in her hair. I'd been meaning to mention that, too. The unwritten rules also called for nothing that would whack Michael in the head— and at six foot four, he was a good six inches taller than Mother. I suspected that this annoyance would also turn out to be the fault of a well-meaning volunteer. Mother took out a pocket memorandum book, penciled a neat note in it, and tucked it away again. Soon a cousin or two would turn up with a stepladder, and the wayward garland would find itself much closer to the ceiling.

Mother took a moment to survey the rest of the decorations. She'd done the kitchen less elaborately than the rest of the downstairs, since it was, of course, a workspace—more so than usual at the moment, with so many visitors to feed.

Evergreen garlands festooned with red bows looped around the walls near the ceiling, with a few outlying strands criss-crossing overhead, and some of the red bows boasted little sprigs of herbs spray-painted gold—rosemary, bay leaves, and tiny little allium flowers. A soft instrumental version of "What Child Is This?" drifted down from the tiny speakers hidden in the garlands. Mother sighed softly, and I knew she was still regretting that I'd vetoed the tiny wreaths she'd wanted to hang on every cabinet door.

She turned back to Cordelia. "I'm so glad you're here. I'm running out of ideas for entertaining those poor mistreated Canadians. I thought tonight we'd serve them a nice cassoulet with a green salad—I've found some lovely arugula. And thank goodness Cousin Nora has arrived, so she can make baguettes—I think a real, authentic-style baguette will go a long way toward making them feel more at home. Let's go sit by the fire and talk menus."

The two of them headed for the living room, talking airily of coq au vin and croissants. I sighed and closed my eyes for a few seconds. Perhaps Cordelia could help me convince Mother that she was focusing too much on food and not enough on the Canadians' other wants and needs. And for that matter, focusing too much on the three Québécois employees and ignoring the needs of the rest. Surely at least a few of the remaining nine had grown up eating food more influenced by traditional English fare than Parisian haute cuisine. For that matter, I suspected a few of the young programmers would be just as happy with pizza and hamburgers.

Then again, maybe Mother was focusing on food because so far it was the only way she'd been able to think of to show the Canadians our hospitality. With the exception of Ian, who seemed to find our dining room much more convenient than the guest office Mutant Wizards had given him, the Canadians got up early, worked long hours in town, and came home with little energy for anything other than dinner and an early bedtime.

"Of course, they're much too polite to complain," Mother had said, after yet another attempt to entertain a brace of tired-looking young programmers. "But they're not happy. You can see it on their faces. We need to find ways to boost their morale."

And then she'd spotted Claudine, AcerGen's Québécois project manager, wincing slightly as she contemplated the breakfast buffet—and in particular the plate of store-bought croissants that clearly didn't measure up to her standards. Well, they didn't measure up to mine, either, but I'd thanked the cousin who brought them anyway—thanked him, and hinted that while of course Mother loved all croissants, she was particularly fond of those baked by the Caerphilly Bakery.

Mother's reaction to Claudine's disappointment was to escalate our culinary efforts to full-bore French haute cuisine. Luckily she'd managed to entice Cousin Nora, whose cooking skills were legendary, to come and take charge of our kitchen for the duration of the Canadian infestation. Once Nora arrived sometime later this morning, I could stop worrying about my cousin Rose Noire. She normally did most of the cooking for our household—but our household didn't normally include an extra dozen people.

But unless Nora's meals turned the Canadians into cheerful, smiling optimists, Mother would soon be trying to think of other ways to cosset them. She was already hinting that I should Do Something about our visitors' morale.

I'd enlist Cordelia's help with this later. For now—

Just then my phone rang, and I pulled it out of my pocket. It was my cousin Festus Hollingsworth.

"Meg? Are you busy?" he asked.

"Define busy," I said.

"Okay, let me rephrase that—I know you're swamped, but I could really use a small chunk of your already overbooked day. Can we talk?"

"Drop by anytime." Talking to Festus was bound to be more entertaining than anything else I had planned. "I'll be in the kitchen, at your disposal."

"Actually, can we talk in your office? I'll explain when I see you."

"Okay," I said. "When?"

"I'm just parking my car. Maybe five minutes."

Should I worry that our family attorney wanted to see me ASAP?

"Five minutes it is."

Chapter 2

Festus and I hung up, and I stood for a second, wondering what in the world he wanted to talk about.

Festus had watched *To Kill a Mockingbird* at an early, impressionable age and developed such a case of hero worship for Atticus Finch that he refused to consider any career other than the law. Fortunately he'd turned out to be very good at it. And I was pleased that his career consisted largely of what he laughingly called "tilting at windmills"—suing rapacious corporations for their financial or environmental sins and defending people who'd been unjustly accused. He'd brought down a lot of evil windmills. His career was going so well that a few years ago he'd bought a large farm here in Caerphilly County and was spending much of his time on pro bono work, including not just environmental causes but a growing number of wrongful conviction cases.

He also took care of any legal problems Michael and I had—for that matter, he was the go-to attorney for any family member in need of one. But we didn't have any legal problems at the moment—not that I knew of, anyway—and yet that had definitely been his professional tone of voice.

Whatever he wanted, I wasn't going to get any wiser fretting about it. I put on my wraps—that took most of the five minutes. Then I grabbed a kitchen chair, since my office didn't have any guest chairs, and headed out the back door toting it.

I saw Festus in the yard—he had stopped to greet Skulk, the larger of our two feral barn cats, a gray-striped behemoth who was probably at least part Maine coon cat. Apart from me, Festus was the only human being Skulk and Lurk allowed to get anywhere near them—and I suspected if they had a choice between Festus and me, they'd pick him.

I waved and went inside, unlocked my office door, set down the chair, and shed my wraps. I had just plopped down in my desk chair when Festus strode in.

"I see you don't let your mother in here," he said as he shut the office door. "Not even a sprig of evergreen."

"Out here, I honor Christmas in my heart," I said, quoting the reformed Ebenezer Scrooge.

"And try to keep it all the year?" Having just seen Michael's annual one-man dramatic reading of *A Christmas Carol*, Festus could easily complete the quote.

"Only in the proper season," I said. "So just why do you need to meet with me? I mean, I'm always glad to see you, but you made it sound as if this was a business meeting. And even if you are my cousin, the idea of a business meeting with a lawyer makes me just a wee bit anxious."

"Relax." He began shedding his coat, gloves, hat, and scarf, revealing that he was wearing a red-and-green plaid tie with his customary well-tailored three-piece suit. "It's not really about you—it's about Mutant Wizards."

"Still involving me, then." I shoved the kitchen chair in his direction. "I'm on the board of directors, remember?"

"I remember," he said. "I wanted to meet with Rob about something, and I also wanted to make sure someone else from the board was there. Someone who . . . er . . ."

"Someone with at least a minimum amount of common sense," I said.

"Yes." He nodded firmly. "And also someone who doesn't panic easily."

"I thought you wanted me to relax. What's this about not panicking? And why are we meeting in the barn, anyway?"

"In your office," he said.

"Which is in the adequately but not brilliantly heated barn. And requires me wrapping up like a polar explorer and braving the near-record cold temperatures to reach. I mean, why not the library, or Michael's office, or the living room, where there's a lovely fire going right now."

"Two reasons, actually." He sat down and tipped his chair back to lean against the wall of my office. He didn't look like someone bearing news that should provoke panic. "One is that I wanted to make sure we weren't overheard, and your office is a bit more private."

"A lot more private than the house is with all the Canadians coming and going, plus family members starting to show up for the holidays."

"And they're the second reason—all those AcerGen employees. One of them might recognize me."

"How would they recognize you?" I asked. "And why would that be such a bad thing?"

"It's no secret that I'm the Mutant Wizards outside counsel," Festus said. "And if they're paying attention, the staff should have figured out by now that AcerGen is heading into some rough waters."

"Rough legal waters? That could also affect Mutant Wizards?"

Festus nodded.

"How bad is it?"

"We should be fine," Festus said. "Providing you and the rest of the board can help me get through to Rob what needs to be done and make sure he does it."

"And what needs to be done?"

"Well, I hate to say this, but I think we're going to need to terminate that contract with AcerGen."

"Damn," I said. "Fill me in on exactly what the problem is."

Festus glanced down at his vest, then pulled out his cell phone and looked at it.

"Well, I was hoping to explain it to you and Rob at the same time," he said. "But Rob just texted me asking if we could meet tomorrow instead of today. So how about if I explain it to you, and you figure out a way to brief the rest of the board. And then we'll tackle Rob as a united front. Hang on." He tapped briefly on his phone—agreeing to Rob's postponement request, I assumed—and stuck it back into his pocket.

"Ironic," I said. "I bet Rob's rescheduling because of something related to AcerGen."

"Yes."

"So why do we need to break the contract?"

"Please!" Festus winced, and unleaned his chair, so all four of its legs were resting on solid ground again. "Terminate the contract. Breaking the contract would imply that we failed or refused to live up to our obligations. Terminating means we're ending it, not only for a good reason but in full compliance with the terms of said contract."

"Terminate not break." I nodded. "I'll work on remembering that. So why the termination?"

"Okay. You know the background. AcerGen originally focused on the Canadian genealogy market, and used to be the best place to go for information if your family tree was mostly in Canada."

"But then the big commercial American sites began making inroads on their market," I said. "And AcerGen figured maybe home DNA testing was the way they could gain back the ground they'd lost. Which was ambitious, and probably unrealistic, since the big sites already dominate the market and have a lot more subscribers."

"Millions, last I checked." Festus sighed. "AcerGen's got a long way to go to catch up. And unfortunately, about the time they decided to hang their hopes on DNA tests, the company's founder and longtime CEO developed serious health problems and handed the reins over to his son and heir."

"Ian Meredith?"

Festus nodded.

"Well, that finally answers one of the things I've been wondering about," I said. "I couldn't imagine any sane company promoting Ian out of the mailroom."

"AcerGen's still family owned," Festus said. "And unfortunately the senior Mr. Meredith hasn't yet figured out that his son's a doofus."

"I don't think we figured it out until we'd already signed the contract," I said. "I could have sworn his father was involved in the negotiations."

"They trot him out when they need to make a good impression," Festus said.

"And unless I've got it wrong, the idea of getting the drop on the competition by adding a lot of really cool features to their website came from Ian. Are you thinking that's not going to be enough to turn the tide?"

"Well . . ." Festus looked thoughtful, and I suspected I wasn't going to like whatever he was about to say. "It might be enough for a company with competent management and a sensible business plan, if that company were financially sound to begin with."

"But AcerGen has Ian," I said. "And what are the odds that

any business plan he came up with is sensible. You heard why he was so gung ho to have his staff work here in Caerphilly, didn't you?"

Festus shook his head.

"He thought Virginia was next door to Florida," I said. "And didn't seem to realize that Caerphilly's not on the coast. He saw himself sitting on a beach under a palm tree, drinking fruity drinks with parasols while his employees slaved away."

"I suppose they don't teach much US geography in the Canadian schools." Festus looked pained.

"You can't blame Canada for Ian," I said. "All of his employees know perfectly well where they are. Ian's the only one suffering weather shock. He's actually not a native Canadian. He was born and raised in the US—on the West Coast somewhere. Getting back to AcerGen—you said 'if that company were financially sound.' Sounds as if you think AcerGen isn't."

"I'm looking into that, but I'm afraid it may not be. When I was here a few days ago for the big welcome party, I overheard a couple of the AcerGen employees complaining about delays in their paychecks."

"That's not good." My mind conjured up the very large amounts of money AcerGen was supposed to be paying Mutant Wizards under the contract. Those large amounts weren't profit—especially in this early stage they mostly represented the salaries of the legions of programmers and techies working on the project.

"I asked the Mutant Wizards CFO to let me know if AcerGen made the first scheduled payment on time," Festus said. "They didn't. They were two days late. Which might not be significant—"

"But maybe it is," I said.

"It suggests they're having a cash-flow problem," Festus said. "Which would be highly unlikely if the information they provided during the contract negotiations were accurate.

They represented themselves as being financially sound, with solid profits and a steadily growing customer base. I suspect none of that is true."

"They lied," I said. "They thought the project with Mutant Wizards was going to save them and they lied to make it happen. What can we do?"

"First of all, we brief Rob," Festus said. "All the safeguards I built into the contract won't save us if Rob digs in his heels and insists on continuing the project."

"His board of directors could overrule him," I said.

"But that would be messy and unpleasant and definitely something to be avoided," Festus said.

"True," I said. "Since three of the board members are family members and the other two family friends."

"Exactly." Festus pretended to shudder. "Your mother will never forgive me if I set off a family feud in the middle of the holiday festivities. So we need to convince Rob. Especially since we also need him to strategize on how to minimize the negative impact on Mutant Wizards if AcerGen is about to fail."

"For that, we convince Delaney," I said. "Remember, Rob's one outstanding talent is coming up with brilliant game ideas. If there's strategy involved, you need Delaney."

"His other talent seems to be hiring excellent employees and then managing to fall in love with and marry one of the best." Festus smiled. "Is Delaney heading up Mutant Wizards' part of the project?"

"I have no idea," I said. "But she'll know who is, and how to deal with this. Especially if she puts her head together with a few board members, like Mother and Caroline."

"And you." Festus grew serious again. "It's going to be a difficult thing to finesse, because obviously for the time being we have to make sure Mutant Wizards fulfills all its responsibilities under the contract. And I could be wrong. I'm still gathering facts. And until I'm sure I've got the goods, Rob's people need to keep doing whatever is necessary to make the project succeed."

"But if anyone in the project suddenly comes up with a brilliant new idea that will cost the moon, we stall," I said.

Festus nodded.

Someone knocked on my office door.

"Want me to get that?" Festus asked.

I nodded. Festus opened the door to reveal Stanley Denton—a family friend, and also Caerphilly's leading private investigator. Actually, as far as I knew, Caerphilly's only private investigator. I had the sinking feeling he was here in his professional capacity.

"I retained Stanley a few days ago," Festus explained. "As I said, we're still gathering facts. He's been looking into some aspects of the AcerGen situation. I asked him to join us today. Rob can't make it," he added to Stanley.

"Maybe better to fill Meg in and let her decide what we tell Rob. And how." Stanley sat down on one of the several sturdy wooden file boxes that littered my office and set his briefcase on another. One of these days I'd either weed out the files or banish the boxes to the attic, which would make room for a couple of guest chairs. Not this month, though.

"I gather you've found something interesting," Festus said.

"Very." Stanley turned to me. "I've been hanging around the Mutant Wizards office. Officially, I'm conducting a safety and security audit. Had a few discussions in the hallway with various officers about whether the locks on the file cabinets need to be replaced and things like that. Had a lot of conversations with the staff about whether they feel safe and whether they've had anything stolen and such."

"Including the visiting Canadians?" I asked,

"Especially the visiting Canadians. Although it was one of

the regular Mutant Wizards staff who told me about an interesting incident that happened in the parking lot yesterday. Involving Mr. Ian Meredith."

Festus and I both nodded and leaned forward to hear.

"Woman came up to him in the parking lot and handed him some papers," Stanley went on. "Or tried to—he glanced at them, then tossed them down, elbowed her out of his way, and hopped into his car. Ignored her knocking on his window. Eventually she left the papers lying on the asphalt beside his car, got into her own car, and drove off. After which Mr. Meredith got out of his car, picked up the papers, tore them in two, threw them down, and jumped up and down on them a few times. From the way his mouth was moving my informant was pretty sure he was cursing a blue streak. Then he got back in his car and drove off, going way over the speed limit, as if he was in a temper."

"Sounds like the way some people act when you serve a subpoena on them," Festus said.

"Struck me that way, too," Stanley said. "And the description of the woman sounded familiar, so I showed the employee a picture of a PI I know from Mechanicsville who occasionally does process serving here and in Clay County for out-of-town law firms. It was her."

I was pretty sure I knew the PI he was thinking of.

"How did you happen to have a picture of Bridget on you?" I asked.

Stanley started slightly before answering.

"Had some group pictures from last year's PI association holiday party on my phone," he said. "How do you know her?"

"That's right—you were off on a case this time last year," I said. "Long story—I'll fill you in later. So does it help that we know she was serving a subpoena on Ian?"

"Not a whole lot unless we know what the subpoena is all about," Festus said. He looked back at Stanley. "Do you suppose you could find out anything else? If not what the case is about, then at least the name of the law firm involved?"

"Maybe," Stanley said. "Of course, she might want to know why I want to know."

"You could tell her some Mutant Wizard employees were worried and you'd like to be able to reassure them that it doesn't have anything to do with their company," I suggested.

"Might work," Stanley said. "But Bridget's sharp. She might tell whatever law firm she's working for that I asked."

"We'll think of something else, then." Festus shook his head.

"Wait," I said. "Ian just drove away and left the papers lying in pieces in the parking lot?"

"They aren't still there," Stanley said. "I already looked. Not surprising, since it happened yesterday and I only heard about it today."

"Amazingly irresponsible," Festus murmured.

"Odds are he came back when he got his temper back," Stanley said.

"But if you'd seen what the employee saw, wouldn't you have gone out to see what made Ian so mad?" I asked. "I would. I'd have looked at the papers—maybe even taken them away."

"Not sure everyone would, but it's a good point," Stanley said. "I could ask around."

"No need," I said. "Let me make a call."

"To whom?" Festus asked.

"Rumor Central," I said. "Don't worry—I'll be discreet."

I pulled out my phone and called Kristyn, one of Michael's drama grad students who was working part-time as a receptionist at Mutant Wizards. While her phone was ringing, I put mine on speaker and put my finger to my lips.

"Hey, Meg, what's up?" Kristyn said.

"I'm calling because you always know everything that's going on," I said. "Is it true that the Sasquatch had a run-in in the parking lot with a redheaded woman yesterday?"

"The Sasquatch?" Festus murmured, though not loud enough for Kristyn to hear.

"It wasn't a woman." Kristyn's low tone suggested that she was taking care to avoid being overheard, "I mean, yeah, it was a woman, but she wasn't just a woman—she was a process server!"

"No!" I exclaimed. "Seriously? How do you know?"

"Because Ash saw the whole thing in the parking lot. The woman tried to hand the Sasquatch some papers, and he tore them up and threw them at her and drove off. And you know how Ash is about littering."

Yes, I'd seen Ash picking up other people's cigarette butts in the parking lot.

"Ash picked up the papers and brought them in," she went on. "And handed them to me to throw away, but when I saw what they were, I stuck them in my desk drawer instead. I figured the next time I saw you or Delaney I'd ask what to do with them. I mean, I could try to give them back to the Sasquatch, but not if he's going to bite my head off. And he did throw them away. And hasn't asked about them—at least not yet."

"I'll tell you what," I said. "Can you take some pictures of the papers and text them to me?"

As if they'd rehearsed it, Festus and Stanley simultaneously did a fist pump while hissing "Yes!" in a barely audible tone.

"No problem," she said.

"And if they turn out to be something he might need, I'll figure out a way to get them back to him without you having to deal with him," I went on. "So put them in an envelope and seal it and write my name on the front. I'll either drop by to collect it, or maybe send someone."

"If you send someone, make sure they know the secret password. The pellet with the poison's in the vessel with the pestle."

"The chalice from the palace holds the brew that is true," I answered. "Oh, and keep this to yourself."

"You bet!" With that she hung up.

"I thought the pellet with the poison was in the flagon with the dragon," Festus said.

"She'd probably accept that," I said.

"Is this a family thing?" Stanley asked.

"Old movie quote," Festus said.

"*The Court Jester,*" I explained.

"Starring Danny Kaye," Festus added. "Old movie from the sixties."

"Fifties," I said. "And don't forget Basil Rathbone and Angela Lansbury."

"You might need to write that secret password down for me if I'm the one doing the picking up," Stanley said.

"Let's send someone who isn't a private eye," I said. "Or a lawyer. Ah! Here come the pictures."

"Share," Festus said.

So as Kristyn's pictures of the subpoena appeared on my phone, I re-texted them to Festus and Stanley. But it only took the first picture to astonish them both.

"Oh, my God," Stanley said. "Is this what I think it is?"

"It's Cyrus Runk!" Festus exclaimed.

Chapter 3

"Okay, guys," I said. "If you want me to share any more pictures, you need to tell me what Cyrus Runk is."

"It's a who, not a what," Stanley said.

"Cyrus Runk was convicted of a particularly nasty murder in southwest Virginia," Festus said, without taking his eyes off his phone screen. "Unfortunately, the prosecution made a procedural error during his trial, and his conviction was overturned."

"Unfortunately?" I said. "I thought you were big on overturning wrongful convictions."

"I am," Festus said. "His wasn't wrongful. They had him dead to rights with DNA and two eyewitnesses."

"Then how did he get his conviction overturned?"

"He didn't," Stanley said. "Fancy Richmond law firm by the name of Mason, Morgan, and Friedman managed it."

"Yeah, he'd need someone like them," Festus said. "The Innocence Project turned Runk down flat, so I'm not the only one who thought the jury got it right."

"I gather you don't think much of this Mason whatever law firm," I said.

"Most of us work to overturn a conviction when we believe in someone's innocence," Festus said. "Bill Morgan does it just because he can. Doesn't care if he's turning a psychopath loose to prey on society. If you ask me, he mainly wants the publicity. Mason, Morgan, and Friedman has aspirations of building an image as a prestigious white-shoe law firm."

"And they're not one now?"

"More like a brash young upstart," Festus said. "With the manners to match." Stanley nodded.

"How'd they get Runk out?" I asked.

"Brady violation," Festus said, rather absently, since he was squinting at his phone again.

"Enlighten me," I said. "What exactly is a Brady violation? Kevin and Casey throw the term around a lot on their true crime podcast, and I keep intending to look it up, but I haven't."

"A Brady violation is when the prosecution has evidence that might help exonerate the defendant and doesn't turn it over to the defense," Stanley explained. "In this case, the prosecution didn't tell the defense that someone else had confessed to the crime."

"Oops," I said.

"A perfectly understandable omission," Festus said, "considering that the guy who confessed had also confessed to dozens of other crimes over the past decade. Including the Kennedy assassination, which would have been a neat trick since he wasn't even born until 1981."

"Maybe he recalls doing it in a past life," I suggested.

"And then there's the fact that Mr. Confessions-R-Us was in jail on a bum check charge when the murder happened," Stanley added. "I still don't get it—a well-known liar with an airtight alibi gives a provably bogus confession and they overturn Runk's conviction? What do you suppose the Court of Appeals judges were smoking that day?"

"If anyone can pull the wool over their eyes, it'd be Bill Morgan," Festus said. "But he knows that if he can't find some compelling new evidence, Runk's second trial will probably go the same way as the first. And now I know what he plans to do."

"What?" Stanley and I said in unison.

"He's going to challenge the DNA," Festus said.

"Good luck with that," Stanley said. "I think most juries believe in DNA these days."

"They believe in it a little too much," Festus said. "And seem to think the police are falling down on the job if a case doesn't include DNA. No, Morgan is going to try to get the DNA thrown out entirely."

"How?" I asked.

"They found DNA at the crime scene, but came up empty in CODIS," Festus said. "That's—"

"The FBI's Combined DNA Index System," I said. "Kevin and Casey have explained that."

"Evidently Runk had never been caught committing any of the kind of crimes that would have gotten his DNA into CODIS," Festus went on. "And nowadays habitual felons are curiously disinclined to take home DNA tests. So the police expanded their search to include familial DNA and Acer-Gen gave them a hit on a guy who turned out to be Runk's first cousin. That was a close enough match that it gave them probable cause to get a sample from Runk."

"Sounds like the way it's supposed to happen nowadays," Stanley said.

"It is," Festus said. "But Morgan's going to claim AcerGen invaded Runk's privacy by giving his cousin's DNA to the police."

"Is that going to work?" I asked.

"Impossible to predict," Festus said. "The courts have only

just begun sorting out the legal issues around DNA and privacy. We're seeing a lot of cases around the country, not to mention that a couple of states have introduced or even passed legislation that could have a profound effect on how law enforcement is able to use DNA. And on a more immediate and practical note, there's the very sticky question of whether AcerGen's terms of service gave it permission to share their users' DNA. Most of the big players in the home DNA testing market say they won't unless it's in response to a subpoena from law enforcement, and even then they fight it. But from what I've seen of AcerGen's legal department, it wouldn't surprise me if they didn't think about that."

"But that's AcerGen's problem, not ours—right?" I asked.

"Could turn into a financial problem for Mutant Wizards if Runk sues AcerGen in civil court for violating his privacy," Stanley said, "and takes every penny they have. I don't get the idea they're wallowing in dough."

"True," Festus said. "And if AcerGen hasn't thought out the impact of privacy concerns, right now it's their problem. But once that website Rob's people are designing for them goes public, it could turn into Mutant Wizards' problem, too."

"Great," I said. "Terminating the contract is starting to sound better and better. And not just because I'm tired of having Ian and the Canadians underfoot. Well, mainly Ian. I don't really mind the others. So does the whole Runk thing give you more ammo for terminating AcerGen?"

"Alas, no," Festus said. "It merely makes termination all the more imperative. If Ian's actions lead to Runk's conviction being overturned, it will be a PR nightmare for AcerGen and anyone connected to them. And will probably drive them that much closer to financial disaster."

"So we need to prove they lied so Mutant Wizards can cut its losses and kick AcerGen loose before that happens," Stanley said.

"Exactly," Festus said. "We're relying on you to get the goods on them."

"Can do," he said. "I guess you want to find out if a big lawsuit will send them under."

"More than that." Festus leaned his chair back again and a satisfied smile crossed his face. "Remember their legal department is pretty bush league. I managed to get everything we needed to protect Mutant Wizards into the contract. Including a clause that lets us terminate if any of the material information they provided proves to be false. And that material information included their financial statements—which I am beginning to suspect may have been heavily massaged." His face grew serious again. "But we need to have rock-solid evidence to prove it."

"Makes sense," Stanley said. "It'll go a lot faster if I get a Toronto PI working on it. One who understands financial stuff. I know someone good."

"Make it so," Festus said. "Meanwhile, I'll see what else I can find out about the suit Mason, Morgan, and Friedman is filing against the Sasquatch."

"And I gather I should brief Delaney and as many of the board members as I can round up about the possibility that we might need to terminate the contract," I said.

"Make that *probability*," Festus said. "And yes. And while you're at it—you seem to have excellent sources of information inside Mutant Wizards. Share anything you find, no matter how trivial you think it is."

"Will do," I said. "And I can get Kristyn to help—without letting her know why, if that worries you. I already had her create a cheat sheet for me—it has all twelve of the pictures we took of the Canadians for their temporary Mutant Wizards IDs, labeled with the names, so I could start sorting them out. If I tell her that as a hostess I want to work on making them happier, and need to know as much as possible about their likes and dislikes and hobbies and anything else, she can probably come up with an amazing amount of information. I'll pass along anything that even looks remotely interesting."

"As long as you trust her not to gossip about it," Festus said.

"She's completely reliable," I said. "Not to mention the fact that at the office, she has so successfully adopted the persona of a cheerful airhead that people will say just about anything in front of her—they all assume that even if she's listening she either won't get it or won't remember. Sooner or later she hears all the secrets."

"A useful source indeed," Festus said. "By the way, speaking of secrets, has your father dropped any hints about what he's having built in your backyard?"

"Not a word," I said.

"I have some suspicions," Stanley said.

"So do I," I said. "But I'm ignoring them so I can let Dad have his big reveal."

"That's what I was planning," Stanley said.

"So you'll have to wait for Christmas," I said to Festus.

"I'll be too busy to worry about it." Festus assumed a sad, put-upon expression, and then dropped it because he knew neither Stanley nor I would buy it. We both knew perfectly well that Festus loved nothing more than a good legal battle—especially one that promised to involve both clandestine maneuvers and tense, adversarial negotiations. Only the prospect of a dramatic trial would make him happier, and if he foresaw that I hoped he'd keep it to himself for a while longer. Like until after Christmas. Better yet, after New Year's.

I let the two of them out the barn's small, human-sized back door and they set out for the woods that came nearly up to the fence on that side of the yard. In theory this should reduce the odds of being seen from the house by Ian. Or by other AcerGen employees who might have returned from town for any reason. But if Festus and Stanley were spotted, wouldn't the fact that they were creeping furtively through the woods make their departure more suspicious?

Not my problem.

I shivered—had the temperature dropped while we were in the barn?—and turned to go back inside. Then I caught sight of the privacy fence surrounding Dad's surprise.

Was it crazy that I'd taken to calling it "Dad's surprise," even in my thoughts? Mother sometimes gave the impression that she could read minds, but I didn't really believe in psychic phenomena.

"Let's call it what it is," I said to myself. "Dad's backyard ice rink."

Chapter 4

I had no idea what had inspired Dad to install a portable ice rink in the back pasture. And it was only portable in the sense that it was supposedly easy to assemble and disassemble, so you could take it down in the spring and reinstall it in the fall—according to the research I'd done online once I'd figured out what Dad was up to.

But unless Dad knew something about our future weather that I didn't, the ice rink wasn't going to be useful all that much of the time, since even in the winter months the average daytime temperatures here in Virginia were above freezing.

Unless he'd also shelled out for a refrigeration system. I suspected he had, even though it would have significantly increased the cost of the project—not to mention the cost of hiring some of Randall Shiffley's workmen to set it up now and take it down again in the spring.

But if setting up a home ice rink made Dad happy, I wasn't going to complain.

I did wonder if Dad had given any thought to the fact that unveiling his surprise would probably set off a mad county-wide search for ice skates. We sometimes went all winter without the local ponds and creeks freezing, and the nearest ice-skating rink was an hour away in Richmond, so not every household in town owned skates. Even if they owned any, the family members arriving from out of town would have had no reason to bring them. And the same went for the Canadians, of course.

Michael, the boys, and I had some, and I'd dragged them out of storage and made sure they were ready—I'd sharpened the blades, and the boys' still fit, although just barely. When I'd had Josh and Jamie try them on, I'd explained that given the prolonged cold snap, nearby Caerphilly Creek might freeze. For that matter, so might the pond across the street in Seth Early's sheep pasture. The four of us might be almost the only people in town poised to take advantage of Dad's surprise.

"Not my circus," I muttered. "And not my monkeys."

I went back inside, locked up my office, and headed toward the house. On my way I waved at Rose Noire, who was heading for her combination greenhouse and herb-drying shed. Good. She had been looking frazzled. A few minutes of breathing in the scents of the herbs and flowers—and maybe a short session of yoga or meditation—would do her a world of good.

I hurried toward the back door, eager to return to the warmth of the house. In the kitchen I greeted Cousin Nora, a plump, cheerful woman in her sixties who already had smudges of flour on both cheeks. She was humming along with "Good King Wenceslas" while rolling out dough and making pie crusts.

"You're running low on butter," she said.

"Roger." I pulled out my phone and added butter to my grocery list. "Do I need to go now?"

"No," she said. "We have enough for today. But soon."

I nodded and went out into the hall, stopping at the foot of the stairs. Something had changed. Something about the decorations. No matter how many times Mother declared that the decorations were done, she never stopped trying to tweak them. The hall had the same elaborate evergreen garlands, with the same red bows and tiny golden bells, and thanks to the hidden speakers they emitted the same soft version of "King Wenceslas" I'd heard in the kitchen. In one corner was a tree—a tree whose tall, narrow size was chosen deliberately to minimize interference with all the people who would be coming and going and throwing on wraps in its vicinity. It was decorated with leaves spray-painted gold.

Spray-painting natural objects with metallic gold paint appeared to be the leitmotif of this year's decorations. Just after Thanksgiving, Mother had recruited a few willing cousins and set up a regular production line, spray-painting vast quantities of a wide variety of objects—leaves, twigs, branches, nuts, fruit, shells, seed pods, interestingly shaped rocks, and—accidentally—two of the Pomeranians, who'd gotten loose and run over to investigate. A quick trip to Clarence Rutledge's veterinary clinic reassured us that the Poms were unharmed, and the paint had all landed on their fur, which could be trimmed off, instead of the skin. The two canine skinheads, as we now called them, had developed an understandable aversion to anything spray-painted gold, which was unfortunate, because there was such a lot of it about this year.

In addition to gold oak, holly, dogwood, and tulip poplar leaves, Mother had recently added maple leaves, in honor of our Canadian guests. But those had been there a couple of days. What else had changed?

Aha! Hanging from the light fixture, already laden with evergreen and velvet ribbon, was a pomander ball—a large clove-studded orange. I couldn't quite remember what it had replaced—a sprig of mistletoe, possibly, or perhaps a cluster of red holly berries. A nice touch, though I wondered if it was purely decorative or if she'd decided that a hint of perfume was needed with so many coats and boots always drying in the hallway.

I could hear Mother and Cordelia talking in the living room. I glanced in and saw that they had pulled chairs close to the hearth and were sitting with their feet outstretched to the fire, each holding a half-grown Pomeranian in her lap. Several other Pomeranians curled around their feet, along with Tinkerbell, my brother's Irish wolfhound, and Spike, the small furball who tolerated me only because I had provided him with his beloved Jamie and Josh. It made a charmingly domestic picture. I was half tempted to join them. On a more practical note, I decided I should go in and ask them if they had any requests for the shopping list. But I found myself staring at the closed door to the dining room. Evidently Ian was still there.

Instead of heading for the living room, I turned, quietly climbed the stairs, and went into Michael's and my bedroom.

One of the charms of living in a Victorian-era house was its wide selection of odd nooks and crannies: The windowed turret off the attic that the boys still claimed as their sanctum. The built-in glass-fronted china cupboards in the dining room. And the dumbwaiter. It led from the dining room down into the basement and up to the master bedroom. I surmised that the house's original occupants had exiled their kitchen to the basement and were fond of having breakfast in bed sent up via the dumbwaiter.

Although the boys no longer used the dumbwaiter quite so often to play pranks on Michael and me—possibly because we'd installed a good lock on the small doorway in our bedroom—they still kept its moving parts in good condition and well oiled, just in case. And while a claustrophobe couldn't have managed it, I had no anxiety about crawling into the dumbwaiter and hauling myself down to the dining room level.

And also no qualms. Ian could be up to something.

I lowered myself hand over hand with the rope and pulley until the dumbwaiter was at the level of the hatch in the dining room. I was counting on the ambient Christmas carols to cover any slight noise my descent made—Mother had, as usual, hidden little speakers in wreaths and garlands all over the ground floor.

Light leaked in around the edges of the hatch door, making it easy for me to anchor the dumbwaiter to a large screw-eye in the door frame—with a slip knot that I could untie quickly if anyone suspected my presence and came over to open the door.

"When did this happen?" Ian's voice was loud enough that I could probably have heard him just as well by putting my ear to the dining room door—but of course I didn't want anyone to know I was eavesdropping on him.

And it occurred to me that if he said anything interesting, it might be useful to have a record, so I pulled my phone out of my pocket, turned on its voice recorder app, and held it up to the crack in the door

"I don't understand why they're going out of business," Ian was saying. "They should be making money hand over fist with all the work we've been sending them. . . . well, yeah, but they could have raised their prices quite a bit and still be cheaper than the big, expensive places. . . . Whoa! Actually indicted? Where did you hear that? . . . Can you send me a link?"

I wondered, just for a moment, if I should ask Kevin to install a few hidden cameras in the dining room—since that seemed to be Ian's favorite haunt. What was the use of having a tech guru living in your basement if you didn't occasionally take advantage of his superpowers? Of course, a hidden camera probably wouldn't have let me see whatever link someone was sending Ian. Unless it had a pretty powerful ability to zoom and we could figure out where Ian was in the habit of sitting. We'd need something more like a drone camera. And even Ian would probably notice one of those buzzing around him.

"Damn." Ian's voice interrupted my thoughts. "Talk about a nasty headline. 'Fraud Uncovered at Medical Testing Firm'— shouldn't they be saying 'alleged'? Is the rest of the article that bad? Does it mention us?"

My fingers itched to search for an article with that headline, but I wasn't sure if doing so would interfere with using my phone as a recording device, so I repeated the words to myself a few times—silently, of course—and went on listening.

"Yeah. See what you can find out. Maybe they won't actually go out of business. Maybe they'll just lie low for a while and start up again soon. . . . well, yeah, but they can always apply to have it unrevoked. Let's not panic yet. . . . yeah, I'll work on that."

The idea of Ian actually doing anything that resembled work amused me, but I restrained the impulse to giggle.

"At least it gives us a solution to that other problem," he went on. "We tell her the lab screwed up and they're not related. And if she wants to sue someone, she can sue the lab."

I hoped he'd continue—this sounded like the start of another interesting story. But instead he ended his conversation and began pacing up and down the room, muttering "Damn!" at intervals. I stopped recording him and figured out how to send the resulting audio file to Festus and Stanley.

Ian obligingly waited until I'd finished doing that before throwing himself into a chair—if the man broke one of our dining room chairs he'd be getting a very large bill—and starting another conversation. I turned on my phone's recording app again.

"Clive? It's me. We've got a problem. DNA Gnostics is in big legal trouble and they're shutting down. We need to find someone else to process the DNA kits."

"There is no one else," came a fainter voice. I realized, to my delight, that Ian had put his phone on speaker—probably so he could continue obsessively squeezing his hand exercisers.

"C'mon," Ian said. "There must be a bajillion companies getting into the DNA biz these days. Just find one."

"It's a heavily regulated business," the other voice said. "And getting into it requires a steep investment in equipment and highly trained personnel. So no, there aren't a bajillion companies getting into it, and even if they were, it wouldn't take them long to figure out that we suck when it comes to paying on time. That's why Quest and LabCorp no longer want to have anything to do with us. And if we find anyone else as cheap as DNA Gnostics, they'll probably have the same quality control problems."

Ian muttered a few words that would have gotten the twins' mouths washed out with soap if they said them in my presence.

"Just keep trying, okay?" he said.

"Yeah, right." I suspected the voice wasn't going to do any more trying than he could help. "What are we going to do about all the tests DNA Gnostics is still sitting on?"

"I'll see what I can do," Ian said. "You keep working on finding a place to send them when we get them back."

"Yeah, whatever." Definitely the voice of a man who had a lot of résumés out in the world.

"Later," Ian said.

I turned off the recording app, but kept my phone handy, in case he made any more interesting calls. But I heard nothing for several minutes. I carefully shifted until I could peek through the crack at the top of the hatch door. Ian was sitting slumped in a chair with his feet on our dining room table, slowly and absently squeezing his hand exercisers.

I fought back the impulse to leap out of the hatch door and order him to get his muddy shoes off our beautifully polished Stickley dining table. With any luck, Mother would catch him doing it, and then maybe we wouldn't need to terminate the contract. She'd terminate Ian—with extreme prejudice. Or at least kick him out of the house. She was already quite annoyed that his use of the dining room had forced her to cut back on her decorating there. The customary evergreen garlands graced the walls, of course—much more elaborate ones than in the kitchen, featuring not only red velvet bows but also gilded faux fruit and tiny golden bells that tinkled softly at the slightest breeze. But usually the sideboard would have featured a small live Christmas tree decorated with gold food-themed ornaments. She'd whisked that away after she'd realized Ian was using it as a hat rack. She'd also locked up the festive red-green-and-gold Christmas dishes after she'd found Ian flipping quarters into the soup tureen and spitting his pistachio shells into the teapot.

I reminded myself that with luck he wouldn't be around much longer. As soon as we terminated the contract, we could send him home to Toronto and Mother could return the dining room to its usual over-the-top glory. Meanwhile I focused on emailing the second recording to Stanley and Festus.

Eventually Ian opened up his laptop and put on a pair of reading glasses. He clicked buttons. I waited, not very patiently, hoping for another phone call. Something he saw seemed to alarm him, and he leaned in to peer at the screen. Then his features relaxed into a broad smile.

"Fooled you, Boyd," he muttered. Or was it "fooled you, boys?" Probably the latter. Crisp diction wasn't one of Ian's traits.

He leaned back and continued to tap on the keyboard and move the mouse. I couldn't see the computer screen, but after a few minutes of studying its reflection in his lenses, I figured out that he was playing Spider Solitaire.

However amusing he might find his game, watching him play it was starting to make my eyelids feel heavy. At the moment, the house was remarkably quiet—evidently someone had even turned off the Christmas carols that would normally have been playing throughout the ground floor. But sooner or later someone would make some noise I could use as cover, and when that happened I'd make my retreat.

In fact—was there some way I could use my phone to start up the Christmas carols?

But before I began trying, someone else must have noticed their absence. An instrumental version of "Do You Hear What I Hear?" started up in mid-chorus, emerging from someplace near the dining room ceiling. Ian looked up, rolled his eyes, and returned to his game.

I was just reaching for the rope to set the dumbwaiter in motion when Ian's phone rang. He glanced at it, then craned his head to see around his laptop screen. Checking to make sure the dining room door was closed, I'd bet. Then he answered the phone and—bless his heart—put it on speaker. Probably so he could hear over the violins. I started my recorder app again.

"This better be good news," Ian said.

"I wish," the voice said. "She won't settle."

"Damn," Ian said. "Can't you just scare her so she backs off, like you did with the other two?"

"This one has witnesses," the voice said. "Witnesses who don't work for you."

"Probably have it in for me, or they wouldn't claim sexual harassment over a little bit of innocent fun."

"Innocent fun?" the voice said. "Ian, you grabbed her by the—"

"Yeah, whatever," Ian said. "You said you could make it go away."

"I said I'd try to arrange a discreet settlement," the voice said. Obviously a lawyer. And maybe it was my imagination, but the lawyer's tone suggested that he wasn't exactly a big fan of this particular client.

"Pop will have a cow if he hears about this," Ian said.

"Maybe you should have thought about that a little earlier," the lawyer said.

Exactly what I was thinking. I could get to like this lawyer if it wasn't for his bad taste in clients.

"So what happens next?"

"I'll be working on drafting a response to the complaint they filed," the lawyer said. "So if you can think of any possible mitigating circumstances, now would be a great time to mention them. And for your information, neither 'I was kidding' or 'she led me on' will help your case."

"Yeah, right." Ian sounded more petulant than penitent.

"I'll let you know when I have a draft for your review." The lawyer hung up. I let my imagination loose to conjure up a picture of an earnest young attorney storming down the hallway of his white-shoe law firm and demanding to be assigned to some other client. Any other client.

Ian stared glumly at his phone for a few seconds, then began to mutter a string of obscenity-laced imprecations. Judging from the pronouns he used, he wasn't any happier with his attorney than with his accuser.

Then he slouched down in his chair again and went back to Spider Solitaire.

I emailed my latest recording to Festus and Stanley. Then I put my phone in my pocket and carefully hauled myself back up to the master bedroom. When I was about to open up the hatch door and step out, I heard sounds in the room and froze, listening. Footsteps. They sounded like Michael's footsteps, but just to be careful I waited a few more seconds. Then I heard humming. Almost certainly Michael, humming "Sing We Now of Christmas," currently his favorite carol. I popped out of the hatch.

Michael started when I appeared, and dropped the stack of presents he was holding.

"Sorry," I said, as I helped him pick up the boxes. "Nothing breakable in any of those, I hope."

"Anything breakable was well padded, and if that's an attempt to find out what's in the one addressed to you, my lips are sealed. I was wondering where you'd gone. Just keeping in practice, or are you actually doing a little light holiday espionage?"

"Not that light, actually," I said. "Shut the door, and I'll fill you in."

While he strode to the door I stole a glance at my phone. I had texts from both Stanley and Festus. Festus just said, "Fantastic!" Stanley said, "Any chance I could talk you into giving up this blacksmithing gig and going into partnership with me?"

I was smiling when Michael returned from the door.

"Nothing serious, then," he said.

"Actually, it could be incredibly serious."

"Spill."

He sprawled on the bed, and reached over to turn on our new electric mattress warmer—a Christmas present from him to me that he'd decided to have me open early, given the weather forecast. We lounged together in toasty comfort while I filled him in on what Festus and Stanley had told me about Ian and AcerGen and what I'd just overheard from Ian.

"I feel sorry for our guests," he said when I'd finished. "I mean, apart from Ian. They're working their hearts out for the good of a company that could go bankrupt and kick them all to the curb, if Festus and Stanley are right about what's going to happen. Not to mention having to work for someone who's at best a jerk, and maybe even a sexual predator."

"I know." I pulled out my notebook-that-tells-me-when-to-breathe and began jotting in it. "Just making a note to suggest to Delaney that if any of the Canadians are turning out to be really useful colleagues, they might eventually be available for direct hire. And to keep an eye out in case he tries anything with any of our women employees."

Michael nodded. A sudden gust of wind rattled the windows, and he wriggled as if trying to sink deeper into the heat from the mattress pad.

"Aren't you glad I suggested opening this thing early?" he asked, tapping the bed surface.

"Brilliant idea," I agreed. I had a feeling he was also going to love the electric towel warmer he was getting from me. The weather had definitely influenced this year's Christmas shopping.

"I think there's another present that should be opened early," he said. "Your dad's big surprise. Assuming it's close to finished."

"I think it is finished," I said. "Yesterday I noticed there wasn't much hammering, and around noon I saw some of the workmen dragging a long, flexible hose across the pasture and through the privacy fence. I did a quick reconnaissance and found a big water truck parked in the lane that goes through the woods to the pastures."

"So they're filling it," Michael said. "I like the fact that they're not running up our water bill."

"From what I can tell, they finished filling it yesterday," I said. "I looked it up online, and those backyard rinks only hold a few inches of ice."

"And it can't possibly take that long for the water to freeze."

"Not in this weather," I agreed.

"But this weather isn't going to last forever," Michael said.

"Thank goodness," I muttered.

"And while I know those long-range forecasts aren't etched in stone, they're talking about a probable warming trend after Christmas," Michael said.

"He probably also got a cooling unit," I said. "To keep the ice frozen when the temperature gets above freezing."

"But I bet even that won't keep it going if the temperature gets into the fifties. If he waits until Christmas day to unveil it, we won't get all that much time to use it before it thaws."

"Good point," I said. "I'll talk to him today."

"Could be a tough sell," Michael warned. "You know how much he loves the whole tradition of opening everything on Christmas morning."

"Don't worry," I said. "I have a plan."

"Good. And I should take off, or I'll be late for my noon class." He closed his eyes for a moment, then opened them and rolled briskly off the bed. "Turn off the heat if you're leaving," he added, leaning down to give me a quick kiss before he strode out.

I closed my eyes and basked for a few seconds in the heat that was radiating up from the mattress pad. Then I hit the off switch, rolled off the bed, and headed downstairs.

Chapter 5

When I stepped out into the hall I almost collided with one of the Canadians, who was standing at the top of the stairs and peering down into the hall. She uttered a small yelp, then put both hands over her mouth and shot a glance downstairs.

"If you're looking for Ian, he's made himself at home in the dining room this morning," I said. "And if you're hoping to avoid him for any reason—"

"Why would I do that?"

I mentally called up the cheat sheet I'd had Kristyn make, and managed to retrieve her name. Rhea. She was a tall, thin young woman whose age was hard to guess. From her looks, and the fact that her hair was dyed a soft violet, I'd have said she was in her twenties, but it was always possible that she was older. She was almost always in the company of two other AcerGen staffers, Angela and Maeve, who were in their forties and fifties, respectively. It seemed like an odd friendship.

Then again, maybe it was a friendship born of being thrown together here in Caerphilly.

The faint lines on Rhea's face suggested that she normally spent more time smiling than frowning, but right now she was visibly tense and anxious.

I came to a sudden decision. I was going to stop pretending I didn't see how things worked in AcerGen.

"Why would you do that?" I echoed. "Because Ian gets cranky whenever he sees one of his employees not sitting at her desk and working like a dog. Which is a rotten way to treat people who are putting in the kind of hours he seems to expect. So if you want to avoid him, I can go down first and make sure he stays put. Distract him if he opens the door. If you leave through the library, there's no chance he'll see you."

Her face relaxed slightly.

"That would be kind of you."

I went down the stairs, noting with relief that Mother had made the changes I'd requested to the decorations there. A couple of days ago I'd come home from a long day of errands to find all the handrails thickly wrapped with garlands made of prickly holly and metallic gold ribbon. It was all quite beautiful, but completely impractical if anyone actually needed to use the banister for security or support—and this dangerous addition to the décor had appeared on the eve of the arrival of the first visiting relatives, some of whom were old enough to need the handrail. The holly garlands were now woven through the newels, with most of the prickly bits on the outside, though anyone wearing panty hose or other easy frayed clothes would probably need to keep their distance. When I reached the bottom, I stood just outside the dining room door until Rhea could scurry past me and reach the hall end of the long corridor that led to the library. I was about to head for the kitchen when—

"Um . . . could I . . . I mean."

I turned again.

"What can I do for you?" I asked.

"Ms. Langslow, may I ask you something?" Her normally pale, thin face was pink, so I deduced she was about to ask something embarrassing like, could I recommend a good local gynecologist?

"Just Meg, please," I said. "When I hear 'Ms. Langslow' I assume someone's trying to call one of my aunts. What's up?"

"Um . . . there's a book in the library. I only went in there because Ian was there and I had a message for him, and while I was waiting for him to get off his phone I happened to notice that you seemed to have a very large collection of R. Austin Freeman's Dr. Thorndyke mysteries—including several I've never been able to find. Would you mind if I read one of them? I wouldn't take it out of the library, of course, and I completely understand if you don't want anyone handling them, and—"

"Good heavens," I said. "Read as many as you like, with my blessing. And never mind staying in the library—as long as you don't drop it in the bathtub, you're fine. We're readers, not collectors. And may I tell my dad you like the Thorndyke books? He adores them, and he doesn't often get a chance to talk to a fellow Golden Age mystery fan." Especially one who had not only heard of but liked a writer as relatively obscure as Freeman.

"Oh!" Her face broke into a slight, shy smile. "Of course. There are a couple of us who like mysteries—especially the classic ones. And I'm not the only one who's running out of reading material. For some reason our home library doesn't let us check out e-books from down here."

"Pillage our library, then," I said. "And if there's anything you've been wanting to read that we don't have, let me know and I'll sic Ms. Ellie on it—Caerphilly's head librarian. If a copy of a book exists anywhere on this planet, she can arrange an interlibrary loan. And if you want to use our local e-book collection I'm sure she'd set you up with temporary library cards—we've arranged it for visitors before. And she makes deliveries to shut-ins and people who can't make it to the library during normal operating hours—which could be useful, given the schedule Ian's got you folks on."

"That would be wonderful."

"We're very good book enablers here," I said, which produced another smile from her.

Another thought struck me.

"By the way, I've been meaning to ask—are any of your crew bird-watchers?" I asked.

"Yes," Rhea said. "Several. I'm only a duffer at it myself, but Angela and Maeve are quite passionate. In fact, that's why I asked to switch rooms with Angela a few days ago—my original room had a good view of your backyard feeders, and she was longing to be able to watch them."

"Heck, if there's anyone else whose room doesn't have a view of a feeder, I can arrange to have a few more installed, so all sides of the house are covered. Actually, I was asking because my grandfather is planning to lead a few owling expeditions sometime soon, and anyone who'd like to go would be welcome."

"He's an owl expert, then?" She definitely sounded interested.

"He certainly thinks he is. Dr. J. Montgomery Blake, the naturalist and environmentalist. You might have seen him—he shows up regularly on all the nature channels."

Her eyes grew wide.

"Oh, my!" she said. "He's your grandfather? How wonderful! And yes, I think several of us would be very interested."

"Just don't let him talk you into volunteering at his zoo," I said. "Unless you really want to. Give him an inch and the next thing you know he'll have you bottle feeding orphaned koalas."

"That actually sounds like fun," she said. "Oh!" She glanced down and patted her pocket in the familiar modern gesture of someone whose phone, though silenced, had just summoned her with a vibration. "I should run or I'll be late."

"Hope you have a good day," I said.

"Thank you!" She rushed off—but she looked a lot more cheerful than she had when we first started talking. In fact, I couldn't remember when I'd seen any of the Canadians look quite so happy. I'd probably made more progress toward improving their average morale in the last five minutes than in the whole time they'd been here.

So, while I was thinking about it, I pulled out my phone and called my grandfather.

"What's keeping Caroline?" he snapped in lieu of hello.

"No idea," I said. "I don't know if she's even arrived yet."

"From what I can see she hasn't even taken off yet, and she was supposed to be here by noon."

"Life happens," I said. "And I'm sure you wouldn't want her to leave before making sure all the animals at her sanctuary are doing well. Didn't she say yesterday that one of her leopards was off his feed?"

"She could leave that to her vet."

"She could," I said. "But she won't, and you wouldn't either if it was one of your leopards, so stop fretting. If she's here, shall I tell her you are eagerly awaiting her arrival?"

"Yes, dammit. I've got all kinds of projects I need her help with."

A good thing Caroline liked spending time over at Grandfather's zoo.

"I'll tell her," I said. "Meanwhile, are you planning on doing any of your owling expeditions anytime soon?"

"Why—are you suddenly interested in owls?"

"I'm not," I said. "Well, no more than usual, and my interest will keep till the weather's warmer. But some of our house-guests are avid birders, and I think they might enjoy one of your birding walks."

"Just as long as they're not weather wimps," he said. "Nothing worse than trying to educate people about the world around them and having them spend the whole time whining about how cold their feet are getting."

"They're Canadians, remember," I said. "They're used to this kind of weather, and know how to dress for it."

"Hmph. I hope they're more knowledgeable about birds than they are about DNA," he said. "Last night over dinner I tried to have an intelligent conversation with a couple of them about some of the new developments in the field—like using massively parallel sequencing instead of capillary electrophoresis for example—and they had absolutely no idea what I was talking about."

"Well, neither do I," I said. "Does that mean you're going to disown me?"

"I wouldn't expect you to know anything about it," he said. "You're not a biologist."

"Neither are any of them," I said. "Except for the two genealogists, they're all programmers and analysts. Computer experts. They're not analyzing DNA—they're building a website to help people understand their DNA test results and connect with their genetic relatives."

Apparently this came as a surprise to Grandfather. He was silent for a good thirty seconds—digesting the news, I supposed. Then he gave a heavy sigh.

"So when are they going to bring down their DNA experts?" he said.

"I don't think they have any," I said. "They send the DNA out to an actual lab for processing."

"Blast," he said. "And here I was looking forward to showing off some of the new things my DNA lab has been doing. Remember how Chief Burke was complaining that it takes so long to get DNA results that the police end up letting dangerous criminals go?"

"Sounds familiar." Although I wondered if Chief Burke had come up with this complaint on his own or if he'd been getting his hopes up after listening to Grandfather's diatribes about the direction forensic science needed to take.

"Well, I issued a challenge to my DNA guys. And gals. Come up with something that lets the police run a quick test so they can see if their guy's in CODIS before they let him go. I figured it shouldn't be that hard—CODIS only uses a couple dozen markers. We've come up with something that can do it in six hours."

"That's fabulous," I said.

"We need to whittle the time down, though," he said. "There's another lab out there that claims to be able to do it in four."

"Still, I bet the police can manage to keep a suspicious character around for six hours if they really want to," I said. "Of course, that only works for police departments like ours, that are within easy driving distance of your guys or the lab with the four-hour turnaround."

"No, what my crew have come up with is a gizmo that a smart forensic examiner like Horace can learn how to use right out of the police station," he said. "Kind of like a DNA testing lab built into a special computer chip. It's turning into an interesting project."

I found myself wondering how much influence Dad was having on Grandfather's forensic DNA projects. Grandfather had originally acquired his DNA technology for zoological purposes. He was passionate about rescuing endangered species and figuring out how to get them to breed in captivity so large numbers could be released into the wild. In addition to

the animals on display for the public, the hidden reaches of
the Caerphilly Zoo supported large populations of such rare
creatures as black-footed ferrets, red pandas, golden-rumped
tamarins, wild yak, several kinds of lemur, and woylies, small
Australian marsupials also known as farting rats. His DNA
lab helped him limit the dangers of inbreeding. But given
Dad's fascination with reading mysteries and helping solve
real-life ones, I should have guessed it would only be a matter
of time before Grandfather took a keener interest in human
DNA.

"Getting back to the Canadians," I said. "It's not really their
fault that they're not DNA-savvy. We still want to keep them
happy—and maybe even improve their minds. How about if
I ask Caroline to help you figure out when would be a good
time for some birding walks or owling expeditions? And then
I'll tell her you're waiting impatiently for her arrival."

"Good! I'll be in the Small Mammal Pavilion."

With that, we hung up.

"Heaven help the small mammals if he's that cranky," I murmured. I thought for a moment, then called Kristyn again.

"Hey, Meg," she said. "Still got that envelope."

"I'll be by a little later," I said. "Quick question: Are the
AcerGen staff working in that big open room on the ground
floor? The one right behind you?"

"You mean the Pit—yes, there, and in those couple of
glass-fronted offices along the side of it."

"Thanks," I said. "I'm going to arrange a little surprise to
boost their morale."

"Great," she said. "Because right now they're about as
cheerful in there as a flock of buzzards with no carrion."

I thanked her and hung up. And then I jotted an item in
my notebook. The Pit, as the Mutant Wizards staff called it,
was actually a pleasant place to work if you had no need for
privacy or peace and quiet. It was a big, double-height open

room with plenty of natural light, thanks to a wall of windows along one side. If I set up half a dozen bird feeders right outside those windows, the Pit would be a bird-watchers' paradise.

So, I'd just taken steps to make the readers and the bird-watchers happier. Which meant at least three of the Canadians—maybe more. With luck, and a little inside scoop from Kristyn, maybe I could figure out similar ways to brighten the lives of the rest of them. Make their Yuletide at least a little more cheerful.

Time to check up on what Mother and Cordelia were planning.

Chapter 6

I strolled into the living room and found that Caroline had arrived and was sitting beside the fire with Mother, Cordelia, and the dogs, discussing quiches and daubes and admiring the decorations. Which were over the top, as usual—Mother went a little overboard there to make up for all the practical limitations she'd encountered in the rest of the downstairs. Surely the Shiffleys had to have denuded an acre of trees to provide enough evergreen boughs for the garlands, and every day I expected to hear news of a worldwide shortage of red satin and velvet. The main tree was so completely decorated that you had to take it on faith there were branches beneath all the ornaments, garlands, and tinsel. The food-themed tree that usually adorned the dining room sideboard now occupied a space by one of the front windows, to such good effect that I suspected we'd have a double-treed living room for all future Christmases. Our stockings were hung by the chimney not with care but with reckless abandon. There appeared to be stockings not only for the immediate family but also for the visiting relatives, the Canadians, and an undetermined number of family friends who would probably be dropping by over the holidays. I'd forgotten what the mantel actually looked like. Even the dogs now formed part of the decorations—at least Tink and the Pomeranians. Tink, the most tolerant of dogs, wore a huge floppy red bow around her neck, and the Pomeranians didn't seem to mind their brightly colored Christmas sweaters. As soon as word had gone out about the spray-paint incident, friends and neighbors, worried about how the skinhead Poms would fare in the extreme cold, had begun showering them with doggie coats and sweaters, most of them handmade by talented local seamstresses or knitters. The dogs now had a larger wardrobe than I did.

And Mother, Cordelia, and Caroline were all dressed to complement the décor. Mother was wearing a tailored dress in a muted deep green wool that looked very well with her improbably blond hair. Cordelia was in a deep red velvet dress. Caroline wore forest-green corduroy slacks and a black sweater with a gold reindeer embroidered on the front. I felt underdressed by comparison and had to remind myself that I had things to do for which jeans and a faded Caerphilly College sweatshirt were the perfect attire.

When Caroline saw me, she jumped up and gave me a hug.

"Meg!" she exclaimed. "You poor thing! Your mother's been telling me all about your visitors. You must be going out of your mind!"

"It's been a little crazy," I said. "Mainly because we had almost no warning before they showed up. But things are getting better. Mother's taken charge of seeing that they're properly fed, and I've come up with a few other ways to keep them happy."

"It really shouldn't be your job to entertain them," Mother said.

"No, but as a good hostess I can at least help them entertain themselves. For example—several of them are bird-watchers. Caroline—if I bring home a few more bird feeders, can you get the boys to help you set them up in the yard this afternoon? I want to make sure every visitor who likes watching birds can do it from his or her bedroom window."

"Of course," she said.

"And can you work with Grandfather to take them on an owling trip? He's willing—"

"But someone needs to organize it and make sure he shows up," she said. "Absolutely."

"By the way, he called just now," I said. "Wanted to know when the hell you were arriving—"

"Direct quote, I assume," Caroline said,

"And told me to tell you he'd be in the Small Mammal Pavilion."

"Hmph," she said. "If he's there, we should rename it the Large Cranky Mammal Pavilion."

For some reason, Cordelia tried to smother her laughter at that. Maybe because she was working hard to keep her side of her unofficial mutual coexistence pact with Grandfather.

"I'll give him a call after lunch," Caroline said.

"He'll be glad to know you're here," I said. "For some reason he was under the impression that you hadn't taken off yet."

"He probably thinks I haven't found the GPS tracker he planted in my purse when I was up here for Thanksgiving," she said.

"He didn't," Cordelia said.

"Oh, yes." Caroline shook her head and laughed. "And I know perfectly well why he did it—he's experimenting with a new, much smaller version, and he wanted to field test it. But he could have asked. I was seriously annoyed when I found it."

"And you left it at the sanctuary to annoy him back." Cordelia nodded her approval.

"Actually I stuck it in a padded envelope yesterday so I could send it to a friend in San Diego," Caroline said. "But I guess the mailman hasn't collected the outgoing mail yet."

"If you like, we could hide you until the mail does go out," I suggested. "And you could watch him getting more and more annoyed as he thinks you're going in the wrong direction."

"Not this time," she said. "But if he does it again, I'll take you up on that."

"By the way, Meg," Cordelia said. "I could also help with the bird feeders."

"I was counting on that," I said. "Can you come with me after lunch? I could use your expert advice on which feeders to buy, and then we'll also set up a bunch of them at Mutant Wizards for the bird-watching Canadians to enjoy there."

"Speaking of lunch." Mother stood up. "I think it's time to evict that . . . person from your dining room so we can get it back in fit shape for a civilized meal." She sailed out of the room.

"Should we help her?" Caroline asked.

"With the cleanup? Sure," I said.

"I think she meant should we help your mother evict your most annoying guest from the dining room," Cordelia said.

"No need," I said. "Mother's got Ian's number."

Sure enough, a minute or so later we saw Ian scurry past the wide archway that gave us a view of the front hall. He flung back the door of the coat closet, stepped inside, and—from the sound of it—knocked down several things while retrieving his coat.

I breathed a sigh of relief when he slammed the door behind him, even though the force of it knocked down something that broke with a sad little tinkling sound.

"I'll go get the broom and dustpan," I said as I stood up.

"And we'll help your mother put the dining room to rights again," Cordelia said. "Can you see what's keeping your dad?"

But by the time I'd swept up the remnants of a tiny glass angel and deposited them in the trash, Dad appeared in the kitchen, inhaling appreciatively all the odors Rose Noire and Cousin Nora were producing.

"What is that I'm smelling?" he asked in a hopeful tone. "And is it for lunch, or are we cooking ahead for dinner?"

"Quiche Lorraine—plus some vegetarian quiche for Rose Noire," Nora said. "And yes, it's for lunch. Go wash up so you don't keep the rest of us waiting."

"Before you do, Dad—could I speak to you for a second?" I asked.

"Sure." He paused just outside the door to the nearby half bath.

"It's a secret," I said. "Let's run down to the library for a minute."

"Make it quick or we'll start without you." Nora had raised six children and didn't put up with much. I could see she was going to be a great help with our current menagerie.

Dad and I trotted down to the library, and I took a quick glance around to make sure there was no one else there. Luckily, the library decorations were limited to the basic evergreen garlands and red ribbons, which didn't offer many hiding places for eavesdroppers.

"Okay," I said. "About that Christmas surprise you're having built in the back pasture—"

"Don't worry," he said. "They put on the finishing touches yesterday. You won't have to worry about any more construction noise."

"I suspected as much," I said. "Given how quiet it's been today. Actually, I wasn't going to complain about the noise. I was going to ask when you plan to unveil it."

"Oh." He blinked, a puzzled expression on his face. "Well, it's a *Christmas* surprise."

"I understand that," I said. "But aren't we well within the Christmas season now?"

"I thought we'd unveil it Christmas morning," he said. "I mean, that's when we usually open gifts. Family tradition and all."

"That's fine," I said.

He turned as if to go.

"Then again, there could be reasons to consider opening it early."

"Such as?" From the stubborn look on his face I suspected he planned to pooh-pooh all my reasons.

"If your whatever is something that would contribute to the happiness or general welfare of our Canadian guests, unveiling it early would not only be a kindness to them, it would make Mother very, very happy. She's being driven to distraction by worrying over them."

"I hadn't thought of that." The stubborn look vanished, replaced by a look of indecision. Few things ranked higher with him than keeping Mother happy.

"Then there's the fact that if your surprise is something that would be easier to enjoy during the present subfreezing weather, the sooner you unveil it the better. Michael happened to mention this morning that they're predicting a warming trend after Christmas."

"You've been peeking, haven't you?" He frowned.

"Only speculating," I lied. "If your surprise is independent of the weather, not a problem—and if it requires warm weather to appreciate, by all means keep it quiet as long as possible. Do you remember the year Rob gave the boys a badminton set for Christmas, and we had that freak snowstorm followed by the cold spell, and it was nearly two months before they could set it up outdoors?"

"They had a lot of fun with it in your basement," Dad pointed out.

"True," I said. "Can your Christmas surprise be easily moved into our basement?"

"No." He sighed. "Good point."

"And if pleasing Mother and taking advantage of the current weather aren't enough to convince you—remember that right now you've got everyone baffled. The longer you wait, the more likely it is that someone will figure out just what your surprise is."

He looked at me with suspicion again.

"Someone who won't be nice enough to keep your secret," I said.

He pondered for a few moments, then nodded.

"I'll do it. I'll announce it tonight at dinner."

"Fabulous," I said.

"I'll go and call Randall," he said. "He'll want to be here for the unveiling."

"Invite him to dinner," I said. "Him and anyone else he needs to have here for the unveiling."

"Right." A sunny smile lit up his face. "This is going to be fun!"

With that he dashed out into the sunroom.

"Where are you going?" I called after him. "Lunch is ready, remember?"

"I just want to make a couple of phone calls first."

"Don't blame me if you end up eating cold quiche," I murmured. And then I headed back to take my place at the dining table.

But Dad showed up only five minutes after me, and lunch was particularly merry. It wasn't just because of the arrival of Caroline, Cordelia, and Cousin Nora the Kitchen Queen, though they certainly contributed. For the first time in several days we didn't have any stray AcerGen employees joining us.

We didn't have to worry about being tactful while briefing newly arrived relatives on why the Canadians were staying with us and how we felt about it. We could indulge in a little mild griping without worrying about hurting their feelings. And we could talk freely without having to explain all the family shorthand for fear the guests would feel left out. And a happy, noisy family lunch was just the distraction I needed from all the unsettling things I'd heard—or overheard—during the course of the morning.

But after lunch I decided to brief Mother and Caroline—both members of the Mutant Wizards board—on what was up.

"I've got a supply of iron poles out in the forge," I said. "Mother, why don't you help me and Caroline pick out the ones to use in our yard."

"I'm sure if you made them they'll all be very lovely," she said.

"Yes, but I have a lot of different designs," I said. "I need your aesthetic vision."

Luckily Mother was paying attention and noticed the phrase "aesthetic vision." Which was our private code for "Don't ask questions—just play along."

Not that it would matter all that much if Cordelia, Rose Noire, or even Cousin Nora learned about the problems with AcerGen. But Dad was still lingering at the table, having thirds on the crème brûlée and discussing future dessert options with Nora, and the best way to ensure that everyone in Caerphilly knew about some bit of news was to share it with Dad.

So Mother, Caroline, and I threw on our coats and trudged across the backyard to the barn. When we got there, I led them to the end where I kept the finished products of my blacksmithing work—just in case anyone was watching before we slid the door shut.

"So what's up?" Mother asked, as she surveyed my supply of long iron poles that arched at the top and ended with hooks suitable for supporting a bird feeder.

"Is there something up?" Caroline asked. "Apart from planning for a lot more bird feeding."

"Top secret Mutant Wizards board business," I said. "Festus wanted me to brief you on something."

Both of them frowned slightly, then listened intently while I told them, as succinctly as possible, about my conversations with Stanley and Festus, and what I'd overheard Ian saying.

"If Festus thinks we need to terminate the contract, I'm not going to argue with him," Caroline said. "And we probably need to keep our eyes open. Make sure Ian's not harassing anyone here."

"I can't say I will be sorry to see the back of that horrible man," Mother said. "But I feel very sorry for all his poor employees."

"So do I," I said. "Which I think makes it more important than ever to do what we can to make them happier—even if it's only in the short term. Getting back to notifying the board—I have an errand that will take me by Mutant Wizards—I'll see if I can get Delaney alone to give her a heads-up. Mother, can you brief Minerva?" Minerva Burke—director of the New Life Baptist choir and wife of Henry Burke, our local police chief—was, like Caroline, a nonfamily board member.

"I can," she said. "And Uncle Tut—he should be arriving at our house today." Uncle Tut—Thomas Underwood Taliaferro Hollingsworth—was an elderly, mostly retired attorney whose legal skills Festus respected—although like most of the board, Uncle Tut had been chosen mainly for sound common sense and the ability to say "no" when Rob came up with what he thought was a brilliant idea. And Rob liked having at least one other man on the board.

Mother and Caroline hurried back to the house. I dragged

half a dozen of my iron poles out of the stack and leaned them against the barn door. As I was struggling with the last one, which had gotten tangled up with its neighbor, I looked up and saw the sleek, black face of Lurk, the smaller and fiercer of our barn cats, who was looking down from the hayloft. Was he staring at me in disapproval because of all the noise I was making with the poles? Of course, he had to put up with a great deal more noise when I was working at the forge. Maybe he actually enjoyed my company and was hoping I was about to settle in for a session of hammering.

Then again, he was probably just hoping for a treat. I reached over to the jar where I kept a supply of Rose Noire's all-natural grain-free cat treats and tossed one up at Lurk, who leaped gracefully and caught it in his mouth. He looked at me briefly before vanishing into the shadows—which was about as much thanks as I could expect from either of our ferals turned barn cats.

I waited a few minutes to see if Skulk would show up. No dice. He'd probably used up his entire week's supply of sociability on Festus.

Then I picked up the half dozen poles I was going to take to Mutant Wizards, rested them on my shoulder, and stepped outside.

The intense cold hit me like a wall of ice and I stopped, just for a second. Then I braced myself, and trudged over to stash the poles in the Twinmobile, as we called the SUV we used for hauling around the boys and their legions of friends and teammates.

Then I went inside to collect Cordelia. And to bundle up a little more warmly before we set out for town.

Chapter 7

"As long as we're heading into town, do we have time to take in all the Christmas decorations?" Cordelia asked. "I never get tired of seeing what Caerphilly looks like in its holiday finery."

"Plenty of time," I said. "And you'll love seeing some of the new things people have come up with this year. Starting over there." I pointed across the road to Seth Early's sheep pasture, which now boasted what we called his partial Nativity scene. Seth hadn't bothered with a manger, wise men, angels, or the holy family. But he'd bought half a dozen secondhand mannequins, dressed them in biblical-era shepherd's costumes, and set them up to abide in his field on a full-time basis. One alert shepherd held his crook like a wizard's staff and gazed out over the pasture with one hand shading his eyes, as if keeping watch over the flock. Two more were lounging companionably against the fence with their backs to the road and their crooks planted in the ground.

The other three were wrapped up in their cloaks and huddled around a very realistic battery-operated fake campfire.

"Ingenious!" Cordelia insisted that I stop the car and pulled out her phone to take a few dozen pictures of the shepherds from various angles.

Our next nearest neighbor, Deacon Washington of the New Life Baptist Church, must have found the same sale on mannequins. He'd set up a celestial choir in his pasture, a dozen white-robed angels with silver tinsel halos, standing in a semicircle holding white hymn books. He'd even repainted their faces with open mouths so it looked, at least from a distance, as if they were singing.

Cordelia documented the choir, too.

"Sorry," she said. "I know you have things to do—"

"And number one on my list of things to do today is to spend some time with my grandmother," I said. "And you can send me copies of your best pictures—I never seem to get around to taking any."

When we reached town, I braved the tourist traffic to take her to see the town square. This year, instead of totally closing off the streets around the town square and turning the whole area into a giant pedestrian mall, we were experimenting with allowing cars controlled access—they could enter at one point only and cruise slowly around appreciating the town Christmas tree, the highly decorated stores, and the strolling musicians in Victorian costume. Stopping long enough to unload your passengers and then continuing on to find parking elsewhere was also permissible, as long as you didn't linger too long before creeping along to the one designated exit. The new system was proving popular with the tourists and a smidgen less annoying to the locals.

We were making our slow circuit, with me focusing on not running into or over any tourists and Cordelia oohing and ahhing. I was already planning the rest of our afternoon's agenda—a stop at the feed store, which carried a good selection of birding supplies. Then on to Mutant Wizards. And then—

"Would you look at that?" Cordelia was pointing toward the life-sized outdoor Nativity scene in the front yard of the Methodist church.

"Look at what."

"That rascal!" she exclaimed. "Can you stop here? Or at least slow down a bit?"

Slow down? I was only going around ten miles an hour. But she'd piqued my curiosity. Since it wasn't safe to take my eyes off my driving, given all the stop-and-go tourist traffic, I pulled to the curb in front of the church, in what was technically a fire hydrant zone. I put on my hazard lights, then looked up.

There was a cat in the manger. A fluffy yellow tabby cat, nestled down in the hay-filled cradle. Mary and Joseph seemed to take this unexpected addition to their family very calmly, but from my angle it looked as if the angel Gabriel was rolling his eyes in exasperation, and the sheep were definitely giving the intruder the side-eye.

"I wonder what he did with Baby Jesus," Cordelia said.

"Their tradition is that they don't put Baby Jesus in the manger until Christmas Eve," I said. "I guess the cat decided to take advantage of the present vacancy."

"Can you stay here while I get a picture of this?" She was already unbuckling her seat belt.

"If the police come by and tell me to move along, I'll go around the back and see if they'll let me into their parking lot," I called after her.

I watched as she pulled her phone out of her pocket and headed up the front walk, stopping every few feet to snap a batch of pictures. When she got within ten feet, the cat stood up and perched nervously on the edge of the manger—nervously and a little awkwardly. I wondered whose cat he was—he was scruffy, but far too fat to be a stray.

Cordelia took another step and the cat ran away. She turned and hurried back to the car.

"You said there was somewhere nearby where you could park?"

"Around back, in the Methodist parking lot," I said as I pulled back out into the slow tourist traffic. "What's wrong?"

"Do you recognize that cat?" she said.

"No," I said. "Which is strange, because he probably belongs to someone. You rarely see strays that fat."

"He's not fat," Cordelia said. "He's a she. And she's pregnant."

"Ah."

"Very pregnant. And from the way she's walking, I wouldn't be surprised if she's giving birth soon."

"Poor thing," I said. "I suspect someone dropped her off here. Someone who didn't want to be saddled with a bunch of kittens."

"Yes," she said. "And it's much too cold to be having kittens outdoors. They might not survive. For that matter, she might not survive. She's a very small cat—quite possibly a first-time mother, and undernourished herself. We need to rescue her."

I nodded, and then focused back on my driving. We reached the town square exit, and once we were back on the open streets it only took two minutes to circle around the block. I pulled up in front of the gate that protected the Methodist parking lot from the swarms of tourists who would otherwise overrun it. I rolled down my window and pressed the button on the intercom.

I was in luck. Instead of Mrs. Dahlgren, the persnickety

Methodist church secretary, I got the mellow Reverend Trask, who didn't even ask why I wanted to park in their lot. Although I explained anyway, just so he'd know when we approached the Nativity scene that I didn't have any sinister Episcopalian designs on his sheep and camels.

Cordelia and I checked the stable, which actually made a reasonably good shelter for a stray cat. It didn't have a real roof—only a few beams and rafters for the Angel Gabriel to perch on—but the solid back wall and the life-sized shepherds and farm animals did a decent job of blocking the wind. But the cat wasn't there. We spent twenty minutes rummaging through the shrubbery, earning a withering glance from Mrs. Dahlgren when she came back from whatever errand she'd been on, but saw no sign of the cat.

"This isn't getting us anywhere," I said. "Let's go back to the car and warm up."

Cordelia didn't propose going inside the church to warm up, which suggested that she'd met Mrs. Dahlgren on one of her previous visits to town.

When we got back to the car, I picked up my phone and called the Caerphilly Veterinary Hospital. Clarence Rutledge, its owner, was a sucker for stray animals of all kinds.

"What's up, Meg?" he asked, when his assistant put me through to him. "One of your critters ailing?" Given that we currently had five llamas, two peacocks, several dozen chickens, two barn cats, five resident dogs, and three or four dogs who were regularly dropped off for what I referred to as our free doggie daycare, we saw a lot of Clarence.

"Last I looked they were all fine," I said. "But we spotted a pregnant stray cat sheltering in the manger at the Methodist church. My grandmother thinks she's probably pretty close to her due date and needs to be rescued. Can we—"

"Stay there," he said. "I'll bring over a couple of humane

traps and you can show me where you saw her and help me set them up."

"Can do," I said.

Cordelia and I waited in my car until we saw Clarence pull up in his battered white van. It took him a lot longer than seemed reasonable to get past Mrs. Dahlgren, but eventually the barrier arm went up and he rattled into the parking lot.

A good thing Cordelia and I had dressed for the outdoors, since we spent half an hour helping Clarence—studying the terrain and figuring out the best places to set the traps. And the four he'd brought were all festooned with shiny gold tinsel garlands, which suggested he was forewarned about the kind of objections Mrs. Dahlgren might raise to their presence on the church grounds.

"We'll probably catch all the local ferals a time or two," Clarence said, when we'd finished baiting the traps with sardines or chunks of cooked chicken, dusted two of them with catnip, and laid a couple of trails of tiny sardine or chicken bits to each trap. "But that's okay. I'm off to West Virginia tomorrow, fetching a load of cats and dogs from a kill shelter—can you drop by and check the traps a time or two? Of course, I could ask Lucas to do it—"

"Lucas will have plenty to do at the clinic if you're going to be gone," I said. "How in the world did you manage before you hired yourself an assistant?"

"I have no idea," Clarence said. "And you're right—I don't want to overburden Lucas, so if you can check the traps a time or two—"

"No problem," I said. "And if we catch her, I'll take her straight over to the clinic. And alert Dad that he's on standby as a substitute feline obstetrician while you're gone."

"Perfect! And you can rebait the traps with this." He handed me a battered paper bag. I peeked in and saw three plastic deli containers—one of chicken, one of sardines, and one of catnip. I made a mental note to label it as cat food when I put it in the fridge, to make sure that Cousin Nora didn't appropriate any of it for tonight's dinner.

We all took a last look at our handiwork, then hurried back to our cars. It wasn't getting any warmer.

At Flugleman's Feed Store we nearly cleaned out their stock of feeders and made a serious dent in their birdseed and suet supply. And I wasn't sure whether to be pleased or dismayed to see that they'd cleared out a space in what was normally their bulb and seed department for a big display of ice skates.

"The skate department is new," I said to the teenage Flugleman who was helping load all our purchases into the Twinmobile. "You really think you're going to sell that many?"

"Well." He looked around as if to make sure no one was eavesdropping. "Mayor Shiffley had us order a pair for him, and when he picked them up he told my dad that according to his granny he'd have plenty of use for them this winter, and if we were smart, we should stock up so we could be the only place in town where you could get them."

"Interesting," I said. "I bet this weather's been helping you sell them."

"So far they haven't exactly been flying off the shelves," he said. "But ever since word got around that Caerphilly Creek's starting to freeze over, people haven't been laughing nearly as much. You might want to get some for your family before the run starts."

The kid had the makings of a good salesman.

"We already have skates," I said. "And I dug around in the attic and found them when I heard about the creek."

"You want to make sure they're nice and sharp," he said. "We can do that, too, same as with garden tools. Just bring them by anytime."

"I'll keep it in mind." Actually, I'd sharpened all our skates myself—it wasn't that much different from sharpening tools, which I did all the time—both my blacksmithing tools and all our various house and garden tools. But I didn't want that to get out, or I'd find myself spending more time sharpening skates than wearing them.

So was Randall Shiffley making sure that at least he'd be able to take advantage of the skating rink? Or had he invented his granny's weather prediction and deliberately fired up Flugleman's to carry ice skates as a way of making sure Dad's surprise didn't fall flat?

Knowing Randall, probably a little of both.

"You think that creek really is likely to freeze over?" Cordelia asked.

"It's been a few years since it did," I said. "But I think our odds of getting in a little skating this year are pretty good."

"I think I'll get a pair, then," she said. "Unless that would interrupt your plan for the afternoon."

"As I said, my plan for the afternoon is to spend time with my grandmother," I replied. "Let's go get you some skates."

As I could have predicted, Cordelia knew exactly what size and style she wanted, so after only a minimal delay we were back on the road, heading for Mutant Wizards.

Chapter 8

If you looked at the rather staid front façade of the Mutant Wizards building, there was no way you could miss the fact that it had started life in the late 1800s as the headquarters of an old-fashioned small-town bank. The original architecture was pretentious rather than distinguished, so not even the most rabid of local preservationists had raised objections when Rob's architect had gutted the interior and expanded the back of the building with a modern extension that seemed made mostly of glass. And not just any old glass but glass so energy efficient that the greatly enlarged building was both more comfortable and cheaper to heat than it had been before the expansion.

I pulled the Twinmobile into a spot at the far end of the parking lot. Cordelia and I grabbed my tools and half a dozen of our new bird feeders and trudged along the side of the building to reach what in summer would have been a lush garden. This time of year—

"A bit on the bare side," Cordelia said. "The bird feeders will help a little."

"The garden's still less than a year old," I said. "Dad has plans for adding what he calls winter interest, but he can't really get started on that for a few months."

"I have some ideas myself," she said. "I'll talk to him. Meanwhile—"

We got started setting up the bird feeders. Luckily I'd had plenty of experience setting up my booth at late fall outdoor craft fairs and knew how difficult it could be to insert anything into frozen ground, so I had brought along the necessary tools—a heavy hammer, and a foot-long iron rod with a pointed end. By hammering the rod into the ground, I could make a hole that would fit the shaft of the wrought iron feeder supports.

"Don't look now," Cordelia said as I was finishing up the first bird feeder. "But we have an audience."

Of course I looked up. Evidently my hammering had attracted the attention of the building's occupants—or maybe our arrival alone had done that. On every floor, the wide expanses of glass revealed dozens of watching faces, and even at this distance, I was sure I could spot a few cell phones, which meant our day's project would be recorded for posterity.

"I hope we're not sabotaging everyone's productivity," I said, as we moved on to the location we'd picked for the second bird feeder.

"It's far more likely that we're enhancing their productivity in the long run," Cordelia said. "I recently read an article about a study that showed dramatic improvements in attention and performance by people who spend even a short break looking at nature."

"That could be useful to bring up if anyone complains that we're a distraction," I said. "Can you remember where you saw it? One of Rose Noire's meditation and yoga magazines, I suppose. Which doesn't mean it isn't valid, of course—"

"The *Harvard Business Review*," she replied.

"Nice," I said. "That should fend off any complaints."

Just then my phone rang. Delaney.

"Is this a Christmas present for the whole staff?" she asked. "If so, thank you. Morale's been a little dodgy around here, but I think this will help pick it up. A couple of people already went home to fetch their binoculars. Is there anything we can do to help?"

"Actually, yes," I said. "Can you send down a couple of strong backs to schlepp the birdseed? I don't want Cordelia trying to do that."

"Why not?" Cordelia muttered. "I do it all the time at home."

"And can you meet me at the Twinmobile?" I asked Delaney. "I have a quick bit of information I'd like to share without any interested ears around."

"I'll head down now."

So Cordelia and I went back to the car. Delaney's recruits not only unloaded half of the birdseed bags from the Twinmobile's cargo area, they volunteered to take the job of installing the remaining five bird feeders off our hands. I handed them the hammer and the pointed iron stake with my blessing. I was doing fine, but between this and our search for the pregnant cat, Cordelia had already been out in the bitter cold for a while, and I didn't want her to overdo it.

"So what's the secret?" Delaney said when the young employees were out of earshot. "Christmas surprise for Rob?"

"Unpleasant surprise for all of us." I gave her a succinct rundown of what I'd learned from Stanley and Festus and from eavesdropping on Ian.

"Damn," she said when I'd finished. "I was hoping I was wrong about Ian."

"You've suspected him of something?"

"Nothing I could prove," she said. "I just never trusted him, but I could never come up with any solid reason why. I guess for the time being, there's nothing we can do but forge ahead. Just damn! Those poor people!"

"The Canadians?" I said. "The Canadians other than Ian, that is."

"He's not really a Canadian," she said. "They're all very quick to correct you if you call him that. So what should we do?"

Luckily I'd already given this some thought.

"Brief Rob," I said. "Pick a time when you're absolutely sure you're alone. And let's plan to have a board meeting tomorrow."

"Okay," she said. "What time?"

"How about if you let us know what time the two of you can sneak away without it looking odd to the AcerGen folks?"

"That works. And in the meantime, I'll keep my ears open for any clues about what Ian's up to."

"And keep Rob from committing to anything that isn't already in the contract," I said. "You know how gung ho he is."

"Yeah." Delaney rolled her eyes and nodded. "I need to go back in. I was on my way to a meeting when you called."

"Sorry," I began.

"No problem," she said over her shoulder. She was already halfway to the front door of the building. "See you."

Delaney ran in. I was tempted to follow—I could pick up the envelope from Kristyn. But I also could do that when I retrieved the tools I'd lent to the volunteers installing the feeders. And if anything else sidetracked me, it would make us even later for dinner. And lately dinners had been pretty spectacular, especially for anyone who liked French food.

So Cordelia and I headed home.

Back at the house we could see more cars parked up and down the road than there had been when we left—a lot more. Most of them probably belonged to relatives who'd come to town for the holiday, although the majority would only be here for dinner. At least a dozen or so who would normally have stayed with us were crowded into Mother and Dad's house or had been farmed out to helpful neighbors, thanks to the Canadian invasion. I also noticed several pickup trucks with Caerphilly County stickers, and a large flatbed truck from Shiffley Construction, so evidently Randall and his crew had arrived for dinner and the ice rink unveiling.

I had a rude shock when I arrived at the driveway. What we called our driveway was a gravel-covered parking area on the town side of the yard, three cars wide and one deep. At the back right side, a dirt lane continued on to the barn, which was helpful for loading and unloading ironwork, llamas, or anything else bulky or heavy we might be hauling around. We normally kept the llama trailer and my ancient Toyota back by the barn, reserving the three spaces along the road for the vintage convertible Michael drove to work in, the Twinmobile, and Mother and Dad's sedan.

The sedan was there in the left-hand space, but another car sprawled crookedly across the other two spaces. It was muffled up in a stretchy light gray car cover, but I recognized the shape of Ian's BMW.

I stopped beside the driveway to glare at it.

"Well, that's annoying," Cordelia said.

"Beyond annoying," I said. "We only lay down two iron-clad rules for our houseguests—no smoking indoors, and no parking in the driveway. We make exceptions for visitors who are elderly or have mobility issues, but neither applies to Ian and this isn't the first time he's done this."

"Drop me off at the front walk," Cordelia suggested. "I'll go in and motivate him to move it."

I had to smile in spite of my irritation.

"I bet you could," I said. "Although since Mother is here—"

"Speak of the devil." Cordelia pointed to where Mother

had just appeared, marching out from our front walk through the opening in the hedge. A group of young men and women hurried after her. Two, four . . . a dozen in all, most of them sturdy young cousins with shelves full of athletic trophies. She waved when she saw me and stopped just outside the opening in the hedge. I pulled up the car beside her and Cordelia rolled down her window.

"I'm sorry, dear," Mother said. "I thought I could get that horrible man's car out of the way before you got home. But if you just wait a minute, we'll have your space clear."

The cousins had arranged themselves on all sides of Ian's car. Some of them squatted down and found places where they could get a good handhold. The rest slid two stout four-by-fours under the BMW and took hold of the ends.

"On three!" one of them shouted. "One! Two! Three!"

They lifted the BMW and began slowly and carefully carrying it out onto the road.

"You sure you don't want to just ask him to move it?" I asked. "Or to give us his key so we can move it?"

"I already did," she said. "And he didn't even look up from his phone. Just said 'first come, first served.' And then he stuck earbuds into his ears so he could pretend he couldn't hear me."

My temper flared. Stealing my parking spot was annoying, but being rude to Mother—

"That's it," I said. "I'm kicking him out."

"I thought there was no room at the Inn," Cordelia said.

"There probably isn't," I said. "He can sleep in his fancy car. Or set up a cot in his temporary office. I don't care."

"Actually, we have a hotel room for him," Mother said. "I sent out one of your cousins to arrange it."

"Where?" I asked. "Every place in town is booked."

"At the Clay County Motor Lodge."

I confess, my jaw dropped. The Clay County Motor Lodge

was a vintage 1930s cabin-style motel located in our unloved neighboring county. In its prime, it might have had a certain rustic charm, but its owners had long since given up any but the most perfunctory maintenance. Caerphillians generally referred to it as either the Roach Motel or Bedbugs and Beyond.

The cousins had carried the BMW out into the middle of the road and rotated it ninety degrees so it was headed back into town. I wasn't sure this was an improvement. I could pull into my parking space, but now the road to and from town was completely blocked. And if they were planning to move it into a more suitable parking space, had they noticed that the road was densely lined with cars on both sides for half a mile in either direction?

Just then I heard the beeping of a truck's backup signal. The Shiffley Construction Company's flatbed truck was slowly backing toward us. It stopped twelve feet from the front of the BMW and, with a whirring noise, lowered a wide metal ramp.

The cousins picked up the BMW again and walked it up onto the truck. Then they all jumped down except for two who tied the BMW safely in place, with the help of the truck's driver—a man whose tall, lanky frame and amiable long-jawed face marked him as one of the Shiffley clan. The truck set off at a crawl, and the cousins all hiked along in its wake.

"Extra crème brûlée rations for all of them," I said to Mother.

"Park your car, dear, while the space is open. But let your grandmother get out first."

Cordelia climbed out of the Twinmobile and strode around to the cargo area. She handed Mother two of the new feeders and took two herself. Then they headed inside.

I parked the Twinmobile in the center space, leaving the right-hand one for Michael. I thought of deploying the cinder blocks we used to guard our spaces when we thought they were likely to be poached—cinder blocks, because the kind of visitor who thought it was okay to take our parking spaces tended to run right over cones. Alas, the cinder blocks weren't where we usually kept them. Ian had probably hidden them somewhere, just for spite. Well, never mind. I collected the remaining two bird feeders and headed for the house.

I met my twin sons, Josh and Jamie, heading outside.

"Gran-gran told us to take the birdseed from your car to the barn," Jamie said.

"Grandma wouldn't let us help carry Mr. Meredith's car." Josh sounded mutinous.

"If we need to have it carried anywhere else, you can help," I said. "I'll tell your grandmother you absolutely have my permission. Now while you're out here, can you figure out where Mr. Meredith hid our cinder blocks?"

My promise improved Josh's mood immediately, and he and Jamie set to work searching the ditches and shrubbery. I hurried inside.

When I stepped into the house, I encountered a medley of cooking smells so heavenly that I stopped in the front hall, closed my eyes, and took several deep breaths. Cordelia, who was still standing by the hall coat rack, laughed at my enthusiasm.

"Lovely, isn't it?" she said.

"Freshly baked bread," I said. "And I don't know what that main dish is, but I'm going to have thirds."

"I think it's the beef bourguignonne your mother was planning," Cordelia said.

"You know, I'm not sure the French cooking is doing all that much to ease the Canadians' homesickness," I said. "I doubt if most of them eat like this at home. Not even the French Canadians."

"Probably not," she said. "But let's not tell your mother just now."

"I have no intention of disillusioning her," I said. "Especially now that Cousin Nora is here and will probably kick me out of the kitchen if I even volunteer to help. I'm going to work on finding out what each of our guests would really like to eat. If it turns out most of them are like a lot of Rob's employees and actually like living on pizza and ramen, we'll serve them that. But in the meantime, I intend to enjoy all of this."

"Amen."

Dinner was buffet style, since our dining table was barely big enough to hold all the food, much less individual place settings for everyone.

I spotted Ian collecting his laptop and his hand exercisers from a chair in the corner of the dining room, where someone had moved them to make room for the food. He made a big show of checking the laptop to make sure it hadn't been damaged, all the while muttering about the nerve of people, touching someone else's property. Not only was he casting a pall over the evening, he was keeping people from coming in and joining the buffet line.

I started working my way through the crowd toward the dining room door, but my nephew Kevin—who was standing right behind Ian, plate in hand—beat me to it.

"There better not be any damage," Ian was saying. "Or—"

"I'm the one who moved it," Kevin said. "So if you have any problems, come see me. And meanwhile, either grab a plate and feed yourself or stand aside and let the rest of us get started."

Ian opened his mouth as if to argue, then thought better of it. Kevin was a tech expert whose skills were so impressive that from what I could see most hardware and software problems seemed to fix themselves as soon as he frowned at them.

He knew how to move a laptop properly. But more important, from Ian's point of view, Kevin was a department head at Mutant Wizards, and if Delaney was Rob's right hand, Kevin was most certainly his left. Ian shot a surly glance at the crowd, then picked up his laptop and slouched out, making no particular effort to avoid jostling people on the way.

Kevin's eyes followed him out. I wondered if they had clashed down at the office, or if his visible dislike of Ian stemmed solely from observing his cloddish behavior here at the house. While we joked that Kevin hardly ever emerged from the basement, where he lived amidst a Luddite's nightmare of computer equipment, I'd generally found him fairly knowledgeable about what went on over his head.

And was this just Ian's normal rudeness? Or was he especially cranky because Mother had already put him on notice that he was being evicted?

I decided to confront him and find out.

Chapter 9

Ian was heading toward the hall that led to the library. Two of the Pomeranians were in his path, tussling happily over the tattered remnants of a dog toy. I felt a sudden surge of protective panic. What if Ian didn't see them, and kicked or stepped on them? Or saw them and didn't care if he ran into them? Or—

But the Pomeranians spotted Ian and fled, disappearing down the hallway, uttering small anxious yips. Strange. The Poms usually loved everyone. I decided to check out what was happening.

Ian barged ahead, entering the hallway and disappearing to the left. Suddenly I heard a loud yell and a sharp bark. I quickened my steps.

I found Ian and Spike in a standoff. The Small Evil One, resplendent in a red-and-green Christmas sweater, was glaring up at Ian, teeth bared. Ian was holding up his laptop as if about to bash Spike with it.

"I'm calling the cops," Ian said. "Your vicious dog tried to bite me."

"Call away," I said. "And while they're here, we'll see if any of the small dogs have fresh bruises. Because yeah, Spike's about as cuddly as a piranha, but I've never seen the Pomeranians behave like that unless someone was mistreating them. And even Spike doesn't usually attack for no reason. Why don't you put that thing down and back away?"

Ian lowered the laptop and took a couple of steps back. Spike didn't move a muscle, but at least now Ian was out of lunging range.

"I'm going up to my room," Ian said. "This place isn't safe."

Which would probably have been a good time for me to find out if Mother had already broken the news that it wouldn't be his room much longer. But I wanted to check on the dogs. Ian hurried out, passing Josh and Jamie, who had arrived at the far end of the hall and were watching anxiously.

"He's a liar," Josh said. "Spike wouldn't bite him."

"Well, he might if Mr. Meredith did something to him," Jamie said. "But if Spike got his teeth into him he wouldn't have let go."

"Good point," Josh admitted. "Yeah, he'd still be hanging off the Sasquatch's ankle."

"Or his nose." Jamie laughed, a little nervously. They loved Spike, in spite of his bad temperament.

"He only said Spike *tried* to bite him," I said. "If he ups the ante later on and claims an actual bite, I'll deal with him. But let's try to keep Spike out of his way as long as Mr. Meredith is still here."

"Whoa, look at that," Josh said.

I turned, a little anxiously. Spike was now sitting down in the middle of the hall, looking triumphant, as if he'd won a battle. The Pomeranians scampered down the hall, yipping happily, fluffy little tails wagging. They ran up to Spike and gamboled about him. One of them even tried to lick Spike's ear, but a small growl made him think better of it. Spike, who usually seemed to find the Poms annoying, now appeared happy to accept their effusive attentions, as long as they kept their distance.

"They're thanking Spike," Jamie said.

"I think you're right," I said. "Why don't you take him back to the living room and give him a really nice treat?"

Jamie picked up Spike—something the Small Evil One tolerated only from the twins—and he and Josh hurried off. I checked over the Poms. They seemed back to their normal rambunctious selves, with no bruises, wounds, or tender spots. One of them was Widget, Kevin's dog. I wondered if I should warn Kevin to keep Widget out of Ian's way. And the other was Winter Solstice, aka Winnie, Rose Noire's pup. I wasn't sure how well my cousin would stick to her strict non-violent principles if she found out someone was mistreating a small animal.

I'd worry about that later. Meanwhile, I gave them both a good head scratching and led them back to the living room.

The buffet line had begun. After filling my plate, I strolled around with it for a while, making sure Ian had really gone up to his room and checking to see that everything was going well. Two of the Canadians took their heavily loaded plates and vanished upstairs, but most of them settled in the living room or headed down to the library. And most of them seemed to be deep in conversation with one or more Hollingsworth family members.

I was drawn into one conversation myself with the two genealogists in the Canadian party. Even with Kristyn's cheat sheet I was still working to attach names to the eight twenty-something programmers—two female and six male. But I'd managed to sort out Angela and Maeve. Angela was in her forties, short and round, and often seen knitting when she had a free moment. Maeve was in her fifties with a tall, athletic frame, and even in the brief time she'd been here I'd gotten used to seeing her striding off into the distance with her binoculars hanging around her neck.

"Meg, just how many brothers and sisters do each of your parents have?" Maeve asked. "I think we've met seventeen of your aunts and uncles tonight alone, and I've lost count of the cousins."

"It's not that we're nosy," Angela put in. "We were thinking of doing an illustrated family tree—as a sort of thank-you for everything you and your family are doing for us."

"Which was going to be a surprise." Maeve frowned slightly at Angela.

"Well, we can't very well surprise them if we can't sort it all out, now can we?" Angela countered.

"Dad doesn't have any siblings that we know of," I said. "The aunts and uncles are all on Mother's side, and technically speaking a lot of them aren't actually aunts and uncles."

"Then why do they say they are?" Maeve asked.

"As genealogists, I'm sure you'll be horrified," I said. "But we just call anyone about our own age 'cousin' and anyone in our parents' generation or above 'aunt' or 'uncle'—it makes things a lot easier."

"But that's so . . . imprecise," Angela murmured.

"Actually, most of us can parse out the precise relationships if we need to," I said. "Take Rose Noire, for example." I pointed to where she was handing out small organic dog treats to a circle of eager Pomeranians. "She's my second cousin once removed, on Mother's father's side of the family."

"This is going to make our project very difficult," Maeve said.

"Not at all," I said. "Talk to Aunt Ida—over there in the orange sweater—who is actually my great-aunt and Mother's maternal aunt, if it matters. What she doesn't know about the family history probably isn't recorded anywhere. Just don't get her started if you don't have an hour or two."

"Perfect!" Angela exclaimed.

"One more thing," Maeve said. "We don't want to step on any land mines, but . . . well . . . I gather your grandparents are divorced, and that it wasn't amicable."

"Grandfather and Cordelia? They never married," I said. "Which was probably a good thing, because if they had, one of them would have murdered the other by now. Get Dad to tell you the dramatic story of how the Ecuadorian postal service parted them, how he was left as an infant in the mystery section of a Charlottesville library, and how he was reunited with his parents not that long ago, thanks to a combination of DNA and my uncanny resemblance to Cordelia when she was my age."

"My goodness," Angela exclaimed. "We will."

"But what was their quarrel about?" Maeve asked.

"If they ever actually quarreled, I don't know the reason," I admitted. "As far as I know, they're just two stubborn, strong-minded, outspoken people who almost never see eye to eye about anything and kind of enjoy sniping at each other. But Mother finally read them the riot act about not setting a bad example for their grandchildren and great-grandchildren, and these days they mostly behave."

They looked disappointed. I suspected they'd had some romantic notion about a lovers' quarrel that could be mended to bring about a fairy-tale happy ending. They wouldn't be the first. And I wasn't holding my breath. Call me unromantic, but I suspected Grandfather and Cordelia were both perfectly happy with things as they were.

I wandered on, and before I'd gone very far, I saw the two genealogists making a beeline for Aunt Ida.

Most of the guests seemed reasonably happy—I was keeping an eye out for discontented relatives as well as morose

Canadians. By the living room fireplace, two of my college-age cousins were recruiting a tall, lanky Canadian for some pickup basketball. Bridge had broken out. I hoped the two Canadians who were playing actually wanted to. The bridge players in my family were so keen on the game that the only way to avoid playing was to disavow any knowledge of the rules. The Canadians appeared to be coping. In the front hall, several more cousins were talking another Canadian into joining them for some caroling expeditions. In the library, Kevin was explaining some kind of role-playing game he'd be running after dinner to an interested audience of three young Canadians.

Okay, make that an interested audience of two young Canadians. I soon realized that Claudine, the AcerGen project manager, was only feigning interest in whatever Kevin was saying. When her phone trilled, she hurriedly grabbed it out of her pocket. She glanced at the screen, and whatever she saw made her frown. She muttered a distracted "*pardon*" to the others and strode to the far end of the library as she answered the call and stood there, almost leaning against the bookshelves, talking.

When I noticed where she was standing, I didn't even try to resist temptation. I nodded to Kevin, left the library, and went next door to Michael's office.

The large, double-height room we used as a library had been built as a ballroom by some previous owners with serious social aspirations. The small room where Michael had his home office had served as a sort of staging area where the waitstaff arranged their trays of food and beverages before heading out to circulate on the fringes of the dance floor. It had originally had a pass-through to the ballroom. When we'd converted the rooms, we'd had the pass-through boarded over and it was now invisible behind the bookshelves. But noise still carried from one room to the other. One of these days, I'd arrange for Shiffley Construction to install some more insulation where the pass-through had been. In the meantime, Michael had a little white noise machine he could turn on if he was having a conversation that needed to be private—or if he was trying to concentrate while something lively was happening in the library. And we tried to avoid discussing secrets while standing in a particular spot in the library.

The precise spot where Claudine was now standing.

I let myself into Michael's office and tiptoed over to the wall. On this side, we'd turned the former pass-through into a useful storage area by installing shelves behind a curtain that helped to damp the sound leakage. I could hear Claudine's voice already. When I drew the curtain aside, I could hear it quite clearly.

Unfortunately, she was speaking in French. I'd long ago forgotten most of the French I'd learned in high school, and for that matter, even fluent French speakers like Mother and Cordelia admitted that Québécois, the dialect our three French Canadians spoke, was a challenge.

But they were getting better at it. So since it had worked so well when I was eavesdropping on Ian, I whipped out my phone again, turned on the voice recorder, and pressed it against the intervening wall.

I kept listening. After all, Claudine was completely fluent in both languages, often switching from one to the other in mid-sentence, depending on who she was talking to or what language was better suited to the topic of the conversation. I could always hope she'd switch to her quick, lightly accented English instead of machine-gun French.

No such luck. I heard the occasional recognizable word, like *génétique, généalogie,* and especially *Ian.* But after a couple of minutes she said "*Salut,*" which seemed to be how she and the other French Canadians ended their phone conversations. And then I heard her voice, slightly farther off.

"I'll see you later," she said, presumably to Kevin and her colleagues.

I shut off my phone's voice recorder, stuck it in my pocket, and returned to the party—keeping a weather eye out for someone who might serve as a translator.

Back in the living room, the two Canadian bridge players were teaching a posse of my relatives a new bidding system they'd invented. So much for worrying about whether they wanted to play. Aunt Ida and the two genealogists had taken over the dining room table and were busily drawing the sort of sprawling family trees you needed to document the Hollingsworth family. A mixed group of relatives and Canadians had gathered around the piano and were rehearsing "Un Fambeau, Jeannette, Isabelle."

And while none of this was out of character for my family, normally a friendly and welcoming group of souls, I had my suspicions about whether all of it was entirely spontaneous. My suspicions were confirmed when I ducked into the kitchen while looking for Dad and found Mother sitting at the kitchen table with a small notebook in front of her, receiving a report from one of my elderly aunts. Who was technically a second cousin once removed, but I'd been calling her aunt for most of my life, so I wasn't going to change now. I parked myself by the stove, the better to enjoy the pine, cinnamon, and clove fragrance of the stove-top holiday potpourri that was bubbling merrily on a back burner.

"She said the flower-arranging class sounded interesting," the aunt was saying. "But I'm not sure she was really all that enthusiastic."

"Maybe she uses 'interesting' the way Mother does," I suggested. "When you can't think of anything else polite to say."

"Also possible," the aunt said. "In fact, highly probable."

"Still very useful information," Mother said. "That was Emily?"

"Yes." The aunt nodded. "And I'm not getting much interest in the classical music concert from any of them."

"They're mostly in their twenties," I said. "We should try them with a concert by a more contemporary artist."

The aunt looked baffled.

"Like the Beatles?" she asked.

"They're not giving that many concerts these days," I said. "How about Rancid Dread? That's our local heavy metal group. Pretend you're trying to figure out a polite way to decline an invitation to one of their rehearsals."

"It's worth a try," Mother said. "And we should definitely find out if they want to attend the New Life Baptist Christmas concert."

"Rancid Dread. Heavy metal. New Life Christmas concert. Check." The aunt dashed out of the kitchen.

"Thank you, dear," Mother said. "Very helpful suggestions."

Just then the back door opened and Dad entered, bringing in a blast of cold air.

"We're all ready to go!" he exclaimed as he began to struggle out of his wraps.

"All ready to go where?" Mother asked.

"He's going to unveil his surprise," I explained, as I tried to untangle Dad from an overlong knitted scarf.

"In the dark?" Mother asked.

"I had Randall bring over some of those big lights they use when they have to do a nighttime construction job," Dad said. "Should have thought of that to begin with—we've got some permanent ones on order now. But Meg was right—time to let everyone see it."

Mother smiled and gave me an approving nod.

"You want me to gather everyone in the living room for your announcement?" I asked.

"Perhaps the library," Mother said. "I'm not sure everyone will fit in the living room."

"No—I'm going to lead them all out there." Dad dashed off.

Mother gave a small sigh. Then she looked at me.

"Am I going to approve of this surprise?" she asked.

"I think so," I said. "I think it will make some of the Canadians happier. And Cordelia. And Josh and Jamie are definitely going to love it."

"And it seems to be giving your father a great deal of enjoyment." She didn't come right out and say it, but her tone suggested that Dad just might be forgiven, at least provisionally, for having baffled her. "Let's go hear his announcement."

Chapter 10

I went out into the living room. Dad was off in a corner, conferring with Randall Shiffley. I found a place along one wall with a good view of the room. To my right was a cousin who seemed to be recruiting one of the Canadians to a book group.

"Every month we read a book that has been banned somewhere in the world," she said. "Last month we did *A Separate Peace,* and this month it's Toni Morrison's *Beloved,* followed by *Catcher in the Rye* in January and *Midnight in the Garden of Good and Evil* in February. . . ."

I made a mental note to find out when the group was meeting—it sounded like my kind of crowd.

"Attention, everyone! I've got an announcement!" Dad called out. He was standing on the hearth, which made him a little more visible to the crowd. Between the buzz of conversation and the clink of cutlery on plates, very few people heard him—but those of us who did began tapping our forks on our glasses to call for silence. It took a while, but eventually everyone who'd been anywhere downstairs was crowded into the living room or peering in from the front hall.

"I know some of you have been wondering about my top secret project in the backyard," Dad began.

"Are you finally going to tell us what it is?" Josh's tone was impatient.

"Hurray!" the more laid-back Jamie cheered.

"No," Dad said. "I'm going to show you. Everybody! Wrap up warmly—it's around twenty-five degrees Fahrenheit—that's minus four Celsius for our friends from the Great White North. And meet me in the back pasture!"

Dad hopped off the hearth and bounced through the crowd, fending off curious questions with a "You'll see" or just a chuckle.

"The line for the coat racks starts here!" Mother called, warding off what could have been a mad scramble. Evidently queueing came just as naturally to Canadians as it did to members of the Hollingsworth clan. In seconds, an orderly line was moving people into and out of the front hall faster than I could have imagined.

The few of us who kept wraps handy by the back door managed to be the first ones out into the backyard. We found about a dozen Shiffley Construction workers—most of them also Shiffley family members—holding up bright LED camping lanterns at regular intervals to illuminate the path from our back door to the back pasture. They were all grinning as if looking forward to the grand reveal.

The last two Shiffleys stood in front of the privacy fence, on either side of a wide space where the fence was covered with what appeared to be dark red fabric. No, the fabric wasn't covering the fence—it had replaced it, and I recognized the heavy faux velvet curtain that we used in the summer, when the town square was the site of Randall's latest tourist idea, a series of outdoor performances of plays. I assumed he'd also installed the portable framework they used to hold up and draw the curtain, though in the dark it was impossible to tell.

I took a place near where Dad and Randall were standing, looking very pleased with themselves. Josh and Jamie were almost the next arrivals. I hoped Mother managed to keep the coat rack line moving—it was beyond cold out in the pasture.

When he had everyone assembled—or at least everyone willing to venture outside in the cold and dark—Dad climbed partway up a stepladder that stood at the right side of the curtain. Several Shiffleys hurried over, probably because they knew Dad well enough to realize that he and ladders made a potentially disastrous combination. One grabbed the ladder to steady it while the other took a position that would give him a good chance of breaking Dad's fall if he lost his grip and fell off the ladder.

"Ladies and gentlemen!" Dad began. "Family and friends! I'd like to present something I hope will add a little more fun to our lives in this cold dark season. Randall?"

Randall nodded, and two of his workers pulled the ropes to open the curtain, while somewhere out of sight someone hit a switch and several banks of lights flashed on to reveal—

"Oooh!" "Lovely!" "Wonderful!"

"Merry Christmas, everyone!" Dad shouted.

The skating rink was revealed in all its glory. It was much bigger than I'd expected—at least twenty feet wide and fifty long. The smooth surface of the ice glittered under the banks of lights. My interest in the ice rink had been fairly practical, even theoretical. The boys and their friends would love it. As would Michael. And many of the visiting relatives. With luck it would raise the morale of at least some of the Canadians. We'd probably see a lot more of our friends, but I could set up a schedule. People could reserve times to skate. We'd manage.

But gazing out at that beautiful, glossy blue-white surface I felt a sudden longing to glide across it.

And then my practical side returned. I was reassured to see that although the framework enclosing the ice surface looked quite sturdy, it was painted a soft grayish beige that blended in nicely with the dormant grass in the surrounding pasture. I noted, with approval, that along the right side of the rink was a huge canvas tent. Shelter from the wind, and if Dad hadn't thought to provide a few space heaters inside, I could take care of that tomorrow. And all around the outside of the rink were benches where skaters could sit to change into their skates and observers would watch in comfort—well, when the air got a little warmer.

We all just stared for a minute or two. Josh was the first to break the spell.

"Mom!" he said. "Do you know where our skates are?"

"Can we go get them?" Jamie asked.

"In the sports closet," I said. "And of course."

They dashed away.

"I'll go fetch ours," Michael said.

"I didn't bring my skates," one of my teenage cousins said in a mournful tone.

"Mine are back home in Toronto," one of the young Canadians murmured.

Everyone's initial excitement seemed to be rapidly fading as everyone realized that only those with skates would be able to enjoy Dad's surprise.

Evidently Dad had anticipated this. Dad—or more likely Randall.

"Never fear, ladies and gentlemen," Randall said. "The equipment rental pavilion is now open for business."

The two Shiffleys who had tugged open the curtain jogged over to the tent, lifted its door flaps, and ducked inside. A few seconds later, they each emerged pushing a four-foot long folding table. One table had a sign attached to the front that said CHILDREN'S SKATES while the other was marked ADULT SKATES.

A cheer went up, and about a third of the crowd surged forward and began hiking around the outside of the rink to reach the tent. The remaining crowd was about equally divided between people who seemed eager to stay and watch and people who headed back to the house, many of them murmuring comments about coming back to test the ice tomorrow, when it would be daylight and maybe a little warmer.

I had to laugh when I realized that all the skates available at the tent were in really gaudy fluorescent colors—lime green, hot pink, and blaze orange. Had Randall found a deal on surplus skates in colors so garish no one would buy them? Or had he deliberately sought out skates that would be fairly easy to spot around town if some light-fingered person decided to steal them?

I was also relieved to see that the rental cost, according to a sign posted on each table, was one cheerful holiday greeting. Cries of "Merry Christmas!" and "Happy Holidays!" rang out, with an occasional "*Joyeux Noël!*" "*Heri za Kwanzaa!*" or "Happy Solstice!"

Just then Michael arrived with both his skates and mine, and we sat on one of the benches to change into them. The boys had already scrambled into theirs and were taking their first few turns around the unmarred surface of the ice. Most of the people taking to the ice now were children and teenagers, as if the grownups had decided to let the younger set have the first chance. Or maybe it was mostly the kids who were excited enough to go out skating in the subfreezing nighttime temperatures.

Maybe I should have stood back and let others enjoy the rink first, but I'd been enduring the construction noises— and Mother's constant fretting about them—for several days

now. I deserved some time on the ice as a reward for that—
and for managing to keep Dad's secret over the past few
days. But if anyone gave me a hard time for not standing back
and letting my guests have first crack at the rink, I could
explain, with great seriousness, that I needed to check out
the whole thing for safety. Were there uneven places where
people could trip and fall? Protruding bolts or splinters in
the wooden perimeter wall that could injure passing skaters?
Pure nonsense, of course, since the whole thing had passed
Randall's safety inspection, but if anyone gave me grief, that
would be my explanation. And I'd armed Michael with the
same excuse.

The rink was certainly a big hit with the several dozen
family and friends using it on its inaugural night. The cold
tended to keep the crowd on the ice down to a manageable
level. At any given moment, at least half the people here at
the rink would be in the tent, warming up around one of the
space heaters that Randall had provided.

Randall had also set up half a dozen wireless speakers
around the perimeter of the rink, and we took turns feeding
our playlists into it. For a while, we had a musical tug of war
as the adults annoyed the kids with our golden oldies, only
to be annoyed in our turn when the kids took control of the
speakers. But after a while we settled for one of the holiday
playlists Mother used for the little speakers in the house, and
if anyone didn't like it they refrained from saying so and being called a grinch.

All in all, the rink was pretty near perfect as far as I could
see—but apparently Mother saw a shortcoming. Shortly after
the unveiling she disappeared and then returned at the head
of a small column of cousins carrying stepladders and evergreen garlands. So while the skaters whirled and glided—or
stumbled and thudded, depending on their skill level—Mother

and her posse hung garlands on the inside of the privacy fence, with a few more inside the tent and around its opening flaps.

"We'll save installing the holiday lights until tomorrow," I overhead her say.

The evening raced on. I skated a bit. I spent even more time along the side of the rink, taking photos and little bits of video: Dad, flailing along, looking as if he would slip and fall any second, and yet never quite doing so. Grandfather, skating with characteristic drive and intensity, as if on his way to rescue something. Mother and Cordelia, skating elegantly around the perimeter, arm-in-arm. Josh, trying repeatedly and finally mastering a jump—the Salchow, as he informed me. Jamie, patiently teaching the basics of skating to several of the younger cousins. A young Canadian programmer we'd all nicknamed Eeyore, gliding and jumping across the ice wearing the first smile we'd ever seen on his face.

By ten o'clock I'd had my fill of skating for the day, and was mostly sitting in the warm tent, talking to others who were also skated out but not yet in the mood to call it a day and go to bed. Although people were gradually giving in to the late hour and taking their leave.

"I have to hand it to your father," Grandfather said as I was helping him into his wraps. "He did manage to surprise us, after all."

"Were you trying to figure out the surprise?" I asked.

"Of course," he said.

Should I feel guilty that Grandfather didn't resort, as I had, to sneaking out and peeking over the privacy fence?

"I even hid one of my little tracking devices in the lining of his coat," he went on. "Figured maybe I could guess what the surprise was by tracking his movements, but he didn't seem to go anyplace out of the ordinary."

Okay, not feeling the least bit guilty.

"You really should stop doing that, you know," I said. "Planting those things on people, I mean. It might be illegal, and it's certainly upsetting to most people."

"How am I supposed to test my devices, then?"

"You can't just test it on animals?"

"The animals at my zoo just don't have the kind of range I need for the tests," he said. "And if I put a device on a wild animal, I might never get it back. I can always ask a human to retrieve it and bring it to me when I've finished tracking them."

"Then why don't you try asking people if they'd be willing to help you test the devices?" I said. "I'm sure a lot of us would be perfectly willing to carry one around as long as you asked us nicely. And we could even help you out—if we suddenly became invisible to your tracking device, for example, you could call and ask what happened. It would help, wouldn't it, to know that we'd just gone into a cave or a basement and it wasn't your device malfunctioning,"

"That might work," he said. "I'll think about it. And I could have sworn I told Caroline that I'd put one of my devices in her purse. She probably just forgot."

I was about to suggest that maybe it wasn't Caroline who'd forgotten, but just then he spotted Mother and Dad, who were waiting to give him a ride back to their farmhouse, so he nodded and strode off.

I decided it was time for me to call it a night as well. I was circulating around to say good night to a few people when suddenly we heard shrieks and shouts coming from the rink. I raced for the tent door—as did every other parent still there in the tent.

Chapter 11

"What's the problem?" I shouted as I flew out of the tent.

I found Michael and the twins just outside the rink, comforting one of their younger cousins, a tall, skinny ten-year-old girl whose hot-pink down jacket perfectly matched her borrowed skates. Her mother, a cousin about my age, was hurrying over to her. I followed.

"She's not hurt," Michael said as the anxious mother enveloped her child in a bear hug. "Just startled."

"But it's only luck she wasn't hurt," Josh said, patting the girl on the shoulder.

"Mr. Meredith was not skating very carefully," Jamie said. "He almost knocked Emma down."

"He was skating like a lunatic," Josh said. "And ignored us when we told him to slow down."

"And then he deliberately skated really close to Emma and startled her," Jamie said. "I think you should ask him to leave."

"Better yet, kick him out of the rink," Josh countered. "For good. I'll do it if you want."

I looked out on the ice. It was empty at the moment, except for Ian. He was skating full speed toward us, nudging a hockey puck ahead of him with what I recognized as Josh's hockey stick. No, actually Ian didn't have a hockey puck—he had substituted a round, flat can of water chestnuts, which I supposed was about the right size and shape. As we watched, he swung his stick and sent the can shooting toward the near end of the rink. It bounced off with a hard thud that made many onlookers flinch. He uttered a cheer—actually, more like a bestial howl—and skated more slowly in a wide circle, holding the hockey stick over his head with both hands and shaking it.

"Mr. Meredith will be leaving," I said.

"You're kicking him out of the rink?" Jamie asked.

"Good!" Josh said.

"We're kicking him out of the house," I said. "Your grandmother has found a more suitable place for him."

"The county jail?" Josh asked.

"The Clay County Motor Lodge."

"Wow," Jamie said. "Pretty harsh. But yeah, he deserves it."

"Shall I inform him that he's no longer welcome?" Michael asked.

"Let's do it together," I said.

So Michael and I skated out onto the ice and approached Ian.

"Hey, get whoever built this to rig up some goals." Ian began skating in a wide circle around us. "And we can get up a game."

"Mr. Meredith," I said. "You are no longer welcome here."

"You're kicking me off the ice?" He snickered. "Too bad—there's no penalty box. Guess you're out of luck."

"Off the ice and out of our house," Michael said. "Please

pack your things. Meg's mother has found a room for you at a local motel."

"You can't do that!" Ian snarled. "It's not fair."

"You have been rude and surly to multiple members of our family," I said. "I suspect you have been mistreating our family pets. And just now you terrified and could have injured a child. You are no longer welcome here as our guest."

"Evening, folks." I glanced over my shoulder to see Randall's cousin Vern Shiffley walking carefully across the ice toward us. He was wearing a bulky down jacket, but his deputy's badge was pinned to it, and his hat, khaki trousers, and gun belt were completely visible.

"Evening, Vern," Michael said.

"Miz Langslow asked if I'd make sure Mr. Meredith here knows how to find his new lodgings," Vern said. "It being so dark and all, and with him probably not having spent all that much time over in Clay County."

Even Ian probably wasn't stupid enough to mistake Vern's Cheshire Cat smile for a sign of friendliness. Ian shot Michael and me a surly look, then skated to one of the breaks in the rink wall and left the ice. He stomped over to where he'd left his shoes and began pulling off his fluorescent orange skates.

"Of course, I can't force him to go over to Clay County," Vern said in an undertone. "But your mama said you wanted him off your property. I can make sure that happens."

"Always possible he'll go and sleep in his guest office at Mutant Wizards," I said. "Which isn't a problem, as long as he doesn't take out his temper there. I'll give the night guard a heads-up."

Vern nodded. I pulled out my phone and texted my warning to the guard.

Ian's arrival had put a damper on skating for the evening—or maybe just reminded everyone that it was getting late and tomorrow was a weekday. The remaining skaters were changing back into their shoes and heading up to the house.

"Have you eaten?" I asked Vern.

"Not recently," he said.

"There's plenty of leftover beef bourguignonne in the kitchen," I said.

"Is that something you think I'd like?" he asked.

"It's French for beef stew with red wine in it," I said.

"Sounds good," Vern said. "I'd greatly appreciate it."

Ian set off for the house, still muttering—which was useful, since it gave everyone in his path enough warning to step aside and avoid being jostled.

"I'm going to help close up the rink for the night," Michael said. "Call me if you need any help with Ian."

"Not to worry," Vern said. "I should have him on the road by the time you get back to the house."

In the kitchen Rose Noire, Mother, and Cordelia were clustered together, frowning and shaking their heads, and glancing at the doorway that led to the hall.

"I gather Ian went thataway," I said.

Mother brightened at the sight of Vern and me.

"Yes, dear," she said. "He went upstairs to pack. Thank you for dropping by, Vern. I'm hoping that rude young man will go quietly."

"But if he doesn't, I'll deal with him, ma'am."

"And while Vern's waiting we're going to feed him some leftovers from supper," I said.

"Planned-overs, dear," Mother corrected.

Rose Noire rushed to microwave a bowl of the beef bourguignonne. The rich, savory odors filled the kitchen again, and any doubts Vern might have had about it vanished by the time the timer dinged.

Dad and Michael appeared while he was still eating.

"Randall's going to lend us a couple of his people tomorrow," Dad said. "Just until we learn all the ins and outs of maintaining the rink."

Maintaining the rink? If very much maintenance was going to be required, I'd speak to Dad about hiring someone to take care of it. A great part-time job for one of the college students.

"Only one pair of skates went missing," Michael said. "Men's size ten, color orange."

"Probably Ian's," I said.

"Want me to retrieve them?" Vern asked, through a mouthful of buttered French bread.

"Let's just get him out of here tonight," I said. "And deal with the skates tomorrow. The skates and any other possessions of ours that happen to go AWOL. It's late."

Vern nodded.

"I'm heading up to bed," Michael said. "My first class isn't till noon, so I'm going to take the early shift wrangling skaters down at the rink tomorrow."

"And I'll be over long before you have to leave," Dad said. "So, didn't that turn out to be a rather nice Christmas surprise?"

We all enthused over the skating rink for a few minutes. Then Mother and Dad rounded up Grandfather and headed home. Cordelia and Rose Noire slipped upstairs. Michael gave me a quick kiss and followed them.

I sat down at the kitchen table with Vern and nibbled a bit of French bread while he tackled seconds on the beef bourguignonne. We didn't talk much—both of us were listening for signs that Ian was complying with our eviction order.

"Maybe I should go up and see how he's doing." Vern mopped up the last bits of the bourguignonne sauce with a crust of bread and sighed with satisfaction.

But just then we heard footsteps on the stairs. One set stomping heavily, and several others who seemed to be making an effort at not waking up their fellow guests.

Vern and I headed out into the hall and watched as Ian stormed into the front hall, donned his wraps, and stomped out the front door, leaving it open behind him. He was followed by three of the young Canadian programmers, each carrying several suitcases or boxes. They all glanced apologetically at me before following Ian. The last in line shut the door.

Vern and I followed them as far as the front porch. We could see Ian striding down the middle of the road at a near run. His baggage train followed at a more sedate pace.

"Poor souls," Vern said. "I hope he's not making them go with him."

"I'm just glad I wasn't around when he figured out his car had been moved. I bet there were fireworks." I was suddenly very tired, but I wanted to lock up, which meant waiting for the probable return of the Canadians.

Vern suddenly focused on the street. A car went past, heading toward town. Which was slightly unusual, since there weren't all that many places to go beyond our house. After passing a few farms, the road dead-ended at Caerphilly Creek. There you'd find the Spare Attic—an old textile factory converted into an off-site storage facility—and the Haven, a former budget motel that Rob had bought and fixed up to provide affordable rental units to some of his employees.

"That silver Corolla," Vern said. "Recognize it?"

"No," I said. "But that doesn't really mean anything. I have enough trouble recognizing my own car in a parking lot. I couldn't even have told you for sure that it was a Corolla. It might belong to someone who lives at the Haven."

"It might," Vern said. "It's a rental car. And one of them could be driving a rental car. That's what I figured when I saw it go past about half an hour ago. But now it's coming back. Could be someone visiting the Haven, but then where are they going this time of night? I hate to admit it, but when the tourists complain that Caerphilly rolls up the sidewalks at midnight they're not far wrong."

"Should I worry about it?" I asked.

"No, you've got me for that," he said, with a laugh. "That's what they pay me for. Having a naturally suspicious mind and worrying about stuff that probably doesn't amount to anything."

"As far as I know, everyone who's staying with us is here, and most of them are probably in bed already," I said. "But we don't check them in and out. And last I heard, only two of them had rental cars, and neither one's a Corolla. We arranged a mini-bus to take them to and from the office and most of them just use that."

"I've got the license number," he said. "So if whoever's driving the Corolla gets up to anything we'll know who they are. But it's probably nothing. Maybe another bunch of tourists who think there must be some bed-and-breakfasts out this way that aren't listed in the town brochure. You were there, weren't you, when the Reverend Robyn was having that big shindig for her congregation—"

"And that carload of tourists marched in and demanded a room." I laughed at the memory. "I think Robyn would have taken them in with no charge if they'd been even halfway polite."

"Yup." Vern smiled. "Could be something like that. Someone seeing all the cars up and down the road and thinking your place must be a bed-and-breakfast. I'll keep my eyes open."

And I suspected he'd also pass along the word to the other deputies on duty overnight.

By this time, the three young Canadians were returning, rosy-cheeked from the biting cold outside. Vern and I stood aside to let them enter. They all nodded and murmured thanks, their faces a curious mixture of embarrassment and relief.

"Time I hit the road," Vern said. "I'll see you later. And

my compliments to the cooks on that fancy beef stew. Mighty good eating."

"Drop by at dinner tomorrow," I said. "I think they've having coq au vin. Chicken cooked in wine."

"The French surely do have a nice way with the wine." He was heading down the front steps. "If that's a real invitation, I'll definitely take you up on it."

"You're on," I said. "Good night."

I shut the door behind Vern and made my rounds, checking doors and windows, turning off stray lights, and making sure nothing else was amiss. No humans in the living room, only a tangle of dogs by the fireplace—Tinkerbell plus at least two Pomeranians. No, three, which probably meant Horace was on duty and had left Watson, his Pom, here where several of his siblings could keep him company. The dining room was ready for tomorrow's buffet breakfast. The kitchen was spotless. Even the library was empty—tomorrow being a work day, Kevin had probably shut down the role-playing and strategy games early.

I trudged upstairs. Michael was already asleep, which was a good thing if he was getting up at dawn to supervise the rink. I got ready for bed as quietly as I could. And needn't have worried about making noise. Michael was out like the proverbial light. Probably the exercise. With luck, it would help me sleep, too. And I was pleased that at least so far, I felt only a slight soreness from my evening's exertions. Always possible that I'd wake up with a few aches and pains—although I tried to stay active and fit, skating was bound to use a few muscles in an unfamiliar way.

As I settled down to sleep I cast my mind back over my day. I'd gotten into the habit of doing this, savoring the things that had gone well and letting go of the ones that hadn't. And if I had any trouble letting go of something bad or unfinished, I'd grab my notebook and my tiny book light and jot down whatever task I could do tomorrow to fix things. Strange how well the act of writing something down to be handled in the morning helped me clear my mind and fall asleep.

And something unfinished did pop up. I reached for my notebook and then changed my mind and picked up my phone instead. Why write down what would only take a couple of minutes to just get done? And all I had to do was send an email to get this worry off my own plate. I preferred my laptop for emails of any length, but it was out in my office in the barn, and this email could be short. I addressed it to Festus and Mother.

"Let's have a board meeting tomorrow to terminate Acer-Gen," it said. "I can be free any time."

I felt better as soon as I'd sent it. Mother was chair of the Mutant Wizards board, and Festus the general counsel. They'd make it happen.

With that happy thought I drifted off to sleep.

Chapter 12

I came awake suddenly and wasn't sure why. I glanced at the clock: two a.m. I hoped I wasn't in for a bout of insomnia. Curiously, I didn't remember having much trouble with insomnia until Dad took a sudden, intense interest in the science of sleep and began interrogating everyone about their sleep habits. And I found that the more I thought about whether I was sleeping properly, the less I slept. For a while, I did have rather bad insomnia, and none of the medical or New Age remedies Dad and Rose Noire recommended worked at all. Breathing exercises, lavender, magnesium, meditation, melatonin, yoga, mantras, counting sheep—all useless. But as soon as I found my own solution, my sleep habits went back to normal. If I woke in the night, I'd turn on my tiny book light and commune with my notebook. Sometimes, if I could figure out what was bothering me and break it down into lists and tasks, I could go back to sleep. Rarely, if my beloved notebook didn't help, I'd get up and get things done—quiet things—until my eyelids finally started drooping.

And I could think of one thing that needed doing right now. I could turn off the Christmas carols. It was a relief to realize that a real, external noise had awakened me. And I was so used to hearing carols in the background for the last several weeks that I hadn't immediately realized I shouldn't be hearing them now. We turned them off at bedtime. The house had been silent when I came upstairs—not a creature stirring, and the little speakers hidden all through the house—downstairs, anyway—were quiet. But now I could hear carols. Specifically, a lyrical hammer dulcimer version of "The Holly and the Ivy." And it was playing at more decibels than we usually permitted indoors.

A good thing no one was sleeping downstairs—well, apart from the dogs. But I needed to deal with the rogue carols quickly. By now, I had most of Mother's Christmas playlists memorized. The next selection, a solo violin version of "What Child Is This?" probably wouldn't cause too much commotion, but after that would be Mannheim Steamroller's enthusiastic rendition of "Carol of the Bells," which was much more likely to rouse our sleeping guests.

I slid out of bed, shoved my feet into my slippers, and hurried out of the room. But to my surprise, the music didn't get louder when I stepped out into the hall. It wasn't coming from downstairs.

I slipped back into the bedroom. The music was slightly louder there. And even louder when I got close to one of the back windows.

The music was coming from the backyard. No—from the back pasture. The skating rink. And all the outdoor lights around the rink were on.

My first impulse was to run downstairs, throw on my coat,

and race out to the rink. Accost whoever was out there. But I knew very well that this wasn't the smartest idea. In fact, whenever the heroine of a book Dad was reading did things like that, he would shake his head sadly, and murmur, "Alas! The all-too-familiar Too Stupid to Live Syndrome."

So I woke up Michael.

"Someone's out there skating on the rink," I said.

He blinked, and glanced at the bedside clock.

"At two in the morning?"

"Probably Ian."

"Damn the man." He sounded more awake. "Let's go out and evict him, then."

"Let's also call for backup,"

Michael nodded, and began quickly throwing on clothes. I dialed 911, and then started dressing myself.

"Nine-one-one," Debbie Ann, the dispatcher said. "What's your emergency, Meg?"

"We may have a trespasser," I said. "Or a prankster. Back at the ice rink. Michael and I are going out to check."

"I'll send someone over," she said. "Vern's only a few minutes away. I don't suppose I can talk you into staying inside until he arrives."

Just then the Mannheim Steamroller track started.

"We'll be careful." Michael and I were heading downstairs. "I suspect it's only Ian Meredith."

"Vern said you ordered him off the premises last night."

"We did," I said. "And Vern made sure he left. I'd just let Vern deal with him now, except that I need to turn off the music at the rink before it wakes up the whole household."

"Stay on the line with me, then," she said. "I'll tell Vern to go directly to the rink."

By this time Michael and I had thrown on our coats. We stepped outside, paused briefly to register how miserably cold it was, and then strode toward the back pasture.

As we got closer, I could see that the ice was empty. No solitary figure in fluorescent orange skates whacking the can of water chestnuts up and down the ice. No primeval bellows of triumph. It wasn't like Ian to be unobtrusive.

Maybe I was blaming him for some kind of technical glitch. This far out of town power supply interruptions and fluctuations were common—so common that we kept any piece of equipment we cared about on a surge suppressor or, better yet, a universal power supply. But all the equipment out at the skating rink was powered by a cable from the barn, and I doubted that they'd thought of surge suppressors when they set it up. So could a sudden blip in the power have turned the lights and speakers on? It didn't seem very likely.

"So far we're not seeing anyone," I said to Debbie Ann as we drew near the rink.

"Vern's almost there," she said. "Be careful."

"I'll stop the music," Michael said. "We were running it out of the tent." He began jogging around the perimeter of the rink.

I was heading in the other direction, toward the nearest bank of lights. But then something caught my eye. A splash of red to my left, on the blue-white surface of the ice. And then a flicker of movement to my right, in my peripheral vision. I whirled toward the motion.

"Who's there?" I called. "I know there's someone out there. Who's there?"

No answer. I held up my phone as if taking a picture.

"I can see you, you know," I shouted. "And the police are on their way."

I wasn't even sure I could be heard over the music. For that matter, I wasn't sure there was anyone there to hear me.

"Who was it?" Debbie Ann asked.

"No idea," I said. "I was only bluffing. I thought I saw motion, but it could have been a fox, or an owl, or just a leaf caught in a gust of wind."

Just then the music stopped, leaving behind what suddenly seemed like an eerie silence.

I turned back to the rink and drew closer so I could look over the edge of the surrounding wooden supports. Ian was sprawled on the ice. His legs were splayed, and the bright orange skates on his feet would have made the only spot of color if not for the small pool of blood still slowly spreading out from his head.

Chapter 13

"Michael!" I called. "Over here!" And then, into the phone. "It's Ian Meredith. He's injured. His head is bleeding. I'm going to check his pulse."

"Sending the ambulance," Debbie Ann said.

As I walked toward Ian, I turned on my phone's camera and took a few seconds of video. Then I reached his side, knelt down, and reached for his wrist.

"He's got a pulse," I said into the phone. "But it's very weak."

Michael arrived at my side.

"Your dad's on the way, too," Debbie Ann said.

I started to ask why she'd called Dad at this hour, but then realized that maybe he'd been having insomnia lately. It would explain his sudden fascination with the science of sleep. And of course he would while away any sleepless hours listening to his beloved police radio. He'd probably called her instead of the other way around.

"Since Dad's awake, can you ask him something?" I said.

"Should we move Ian into the tent, where we can keep him warmer till the ambulance gets here? Or does the head wound make it more important to keep him immobile till the experts arrive? And should we try to stop the bleeding or keep our hands off his head? He's not exactly bleeding heavily but it's a bit more than a trickle."

"Asking."

"I'll get something we can move him on if your dad says to." Michael ran back toward the tent.

"I'll text Dad some pictures," I said.

Ian's head wound looked pretty grisly. I took a couple of pictures and deliberately didn't look too closely at them before I sent them.

"Your dad says don't move him for now," Debbie Ann reported. "The blow to the head could also have caused an injury to the spine, and besides, he and the ambulance should both be there within fifteen minutes. If you have a blanket handy, throw that over him. And probably better not to touch the wound or wounds."

I nodded, and then realized she couldn't see me.

"Right." I was just as happy to be given hands-off orders.

Michael returned with one of the folding tables we'd used for the skate shop.

"In case they want him off the ice," he said.

"We hold off on that for now," I said. "But let's get something to throw over him."

"Already thought of that."

He set down the folded table nearby. I sat down on its flat surface—better than sitting on the ice, and my knees were a little shaky. He went over and draped a blanket over Ian's body, gently tucking it in just under his chin.

I tried to keep my breathing steady and focus on the practical.

"Do you suppose he fell and hit his head on the ice?" I

asked. "His wound looks more like what you'd get from running headlong into something, but there's nothing anywhere near him."

"I don't think he fell and hit his head," Michael pointed to a far corner of the rink. "Look over there."

A hockey stick was lying on the ice, near one edge of the rink. Josh's hockey stick, the one Ian had been using. And was that a small splash of red on the ice near the stick?

"Let's leave it where it is," I said. Not that Michael looked ready to walk over and pick it up. Like me, he didn't inhale mystery books by the hundred the way Dad did, but he'd read enough to know not to pick up evidence at what could be a crime scene.

Only an assault-and-battery scene so far. And I was very much hoping it stayed that way.

"Your dad was telling me recently that they're using hypothermia a lot these days to reduce brain damage in the case of traumatic head injuries," Michael said.

"Let's hope it helps Ian," I said. I lifted up my phone and spoke into it again.

"You might want to send Horace," I said. "And notify the chief. We think someone hit Ian over the head with a hockey stick."

"Copy," Debbie Ann said.

Dad and the ambulance arrived together. The ambulance drove up the rough dirt track through the woods to the edge of the rink, and evidently the EMTs had picked up Dad on their way from the road, because he hopped out of the back of the ambulance before it had come to a complete stop. Michael and I retreated to the tent and turned on one of the space heaters. Which would have done a better job of keeping us warm if we'd closed the tent flap, but neither of us could tear ourselves away from watching Dad and the EMTs. Although they didn't wait very long before hauling Ian away.

Vern had arrived by then.

"They don't look too cheerful," he said, nodding at the departing EMTs.

"Ian doesn't look too healthy," I said. "Maybe we shouldn't have kicked him out."

"Don't be thinking that way," he said. "You wanted him out for good reason. I saw him safely off your property. Sneaking back here in the middle of the night—that's on him."

"Maybe one of us should go back to the house," Michael said. "Send the arriving troops back here if they come to the door. Start some coffee. Keep the rest of the civilians from coming out here to rubberneck."

"You go," I said. "Unless you'd rather stay here."

"I'd rather be inside where it's warm," he said. "Wouldn't you?"

"No," I said. "You go. I'd rather stay out here for a while longer. I'll follow as soon as I'm sure there's nothing helpful I can do here."

He nodded, and headed back toward the house. The ambulance was pulling away. The driver thoughtfully waited until they were almost out of sight before starting his siren, but it still sounded loud in the quiet of the night.

Vern reached inside his jacket and took out a small notebook and a pen.

"While we're waiting for the chief, why don't you start telling me what happened?" he said.

So as we huddled around the space heater I filled him in on waking up, hearing the music, and coming back here with Michael to shut off both lights and music.

"You think that's what woke you up?" he said. "The music starting?"

"Could be," I said. "But not necessarily. Let's hope we have at least one insomniac who can tell us exactly when it started."

"Wonder who turned it on," Vern said. "Was Mr. Meredith familiar with the controls?"

"No, but anyone who went into the tent would probably see the little control box," I said. "Randall even made sure all the controls were carefully labeled—probably out of self-defense, so we wouldn't be calling him every five minutes to ask questions."

"He's thorough that way," Vern said. "So anyone could have turned it on."

"Yes," I said. "Ian could have turned it on to annoy us. Or whoever attacked Ian could have used it to cover up any noise he made."

"I don't think Ian ever made it over to Clay County." Vern was probably trying to distract me from those uncomfortable thoughts about why the speakers were on. "He drove over to the Mutant Wizards building and stayed there in the parking lot. Saw him a time or two while making my rounds. Last time I went by his car was gone. I thought he'd finally cooled off and headed over to the motor lodge, but the last time I saw him was only about forty-five minutes ago. There wouldn't have been time for him to go to Clay County and back again."

"He probably waited in the parking lot until he thought we'd all be asleep," I said. "And then came over to use the rink."

"That's what I figure."

We fell silent. Although I could tell Vern wasn't just killing time waiting for the chief's arrival. His eyes were darting around as if studying every inch of our surroundings.

It was about fifteen minutes later when we spotted two figures trudging out toward us.

"Horace and the chief," Vern said. "I'll go fill them in."

I pulled one of the folding chairs closer to the space heater and sat down.

I imagined, just for a moment, how this middle-of-the night event should have gone. Michael and I would have walked out and given Ian his marching orders. He'd have left, either under his own steam or escorted by one of the night shift deputies. And Michael and I would already be back asleep in our warm bed. Better yet, Ian could have accepted his exile and bedded down at the motor lodge or in his temporary office. Michael and I would both have gotten a good night's sleep and Ian wouldn't be lying unconscious on the ice. And then, in the morning, the Mutant Wizards board would have voted to terminate the contract with AcerGen and Ian would have been on his way back to Toronto and out of our lives for good.

Maybe I should go inside, now that the chief was here. Going back to bed wasn't in the cards for a while—the chief would want to interview me. And I wouldn't be able to sleep until I heard from Dad about how Ian was doing. But at least I could stay warm.

I turned off the space heater and hiked around the edge of the rink. The chief saw me coming and met me at the point where the traffic to and from the skating rink was already wearing a path.

"Horace is going to work the scene," he said. "With Vern to watch his back. Let's get you inside."

And you, I almost said. He looked as if his teeth were about to start chattering.

"Can you describe how Mr. Meredith was lying when you found him?" he asked as we strode along. From his pace, I assumed he was as eager as I was to get inside.

"I can do better than that," I said. "I took video." I pulled out my phone, called up the video, and handed the phone to him.

He watched it. Several times before finally handing my phone back.

"These modern times," he said. "Email that to me, please. Looks like you've got lights on in the kitchen. Did you and Michael leave them on when you came out?"

"Not that many."

We found Rose Noire and Cousin Nora in the kitchen. I heard Michael out in the front hall talking to someone.

"They're all back at the skating rink," he said, so I assumed he was talking to a newly arrived deputy.

Rose Noire was making coffee. Nora was making bread. Had she planned to get up at—yikes, not quite three in the morning—to start her baking? Or was she making the best of being awakened in the middle of the night? I'd ask later, when she didn't look quite so busy. Rose Noire helped us take our wraps off and then hurried over to the counter.

"Coffee?" She held out a steaming mug.

"I won't say no." The chief took the mug, wrapping both hands around it.

"I've got hot chocolate for you, Meg." Rose Noire dashed over to the microwave and handed me my own steaming mug. "Since I know you don't like coffee."

"Meg, I'd like to start by interviewing you," the chief said.

"Of course." I was actually looking forward to talking to him.

"Let's go into your dining room," he said. "Where we won't be interrupting the ladies."

He smiled and nodded at Rose Noire and Cousin Nora. Rose Noire smiled back. Cousin Nora was so busy kneading a batch of dough that she didn't even appear to notice we were leaving. I was momentarily envious—the kneading looked like an excellent way to work out stress or anxiety. Even better than the mindful breathing Rose Noire was always recommending, and almost as good as hammering a glowing bit of iron. Maybe I'd offer to help her later.

But for now I followed the chief out of the kitchen.

Chapter 14

"Since when do you not like coffee?" the chief asked as we walked down the hall. "I've certainly seen you gulp it down often enough."

"Not lately, though."

"No, but giving it up is different from not liking it."

"I used to assume that I liked coffee," I said. "I mean, in our society, who doesn't? I definitely liked the caffeine. Not just liked, but craved it. And sometimes the warmth was comforting, and I really liked all the rituals society has built around it—the social aspects. But one morning when I was about to pour myself a cup, I suddenly realized that I was dreading the actual taste. That I had never really liked the taste. So I put down the cup, swigged a cold, caffeinated soda instead, and that was the end of my coffee drinking."

He pondered that as we went into the dining room. I turned on the lights while he shut the door, and we settled in two chairs at the closest end of the table.

"Makes sense," he said finally. "Of course, now you've got me wondering if I really like the taste or if I only like it because I associate it with that whole burst of energy. Maybe I should give the stuff up myself."

"Only if you want to," I said. "About the time I gave up drinking it I started seeing articles saying that in moderation it's actually good for you."

"Ironic." He shook his head. "Well, back to business. Although—before we get started . . ." He pulled out his phone. "Excuse me a second—I need to send Minerva a message about the rink being closed for the time being—Jamie and Josh invited Adam to come over at dawn and get in a little skating with them before school, but obviously that's not happening. We'll let you have the rink back once Horace has finished with it, but that will take time."

"Understood," I said.

He nodded, typed on his phone for a few seconds, then put it down on the table.

"Vern tells me your Mother called him last night to ask for help evicting Mr. Meredith," he said. "And that he ended up escorting him off your property at eleven fifteen."

"I can't vouch for the exact time," I said. "But that sounds about right."

"And you didn't see him again?"

"Not until we found him lying out there on the ice."

"I gather he hasn't exactly endeared himself to anyone," the chief said. "Either here at your house or down at your brother's company. But do you know of anyone who might have hated him enough to attack him like that?"

"I can think of several possibilities."

He looked up from his notebook at that, a little startled.

"Let me bring you up to speed," I said, "on everything I've learned about Ian and his company in the last twenty-four hours."

I filled him in on my discussions with Festus and Stanley, and what I'd overheard while eavesdropping on Ian in the dining room—although I didn't mention that I'd been eavesdropping from the dumbwaiter. No sense in giving away all my secrets. The chief scribbled a satisfyingly large number of notes. I even filled him in on Ian's sins against Emma and the Pomeranians.

"Nothing but pure meanness, treating a little girl that way," he said. "Or a little dog. I know the Pomeranians can be exasperating sometimes, but . . ."

His voice trailed off and he shook his head. The chief was well aware of how exasperating the Poms were, since his grandson Adam had also adopted one of the litter. And while I knew the little furball they'd named Willie Mays had turned the Burke household upside down, I had also seen the chief with him often enough to know how fond he was of the pup. Luckily for their continued survival, the Poms were as endearing as they were mischievous.

"Anything else?" he asked. "Not that you didn't just give me an impressive amount of information."

"Want me to forward the audio recordings I made when I was eavesdropping on Ian?"

He blinked, then smiled.

"That would be very helpful."

I pulled out my phone and was forwarding all of yesterday's audio files when he asked another question.

"Did the name Katherine Anne Koenigslutter come up in any of your conversations with or about Ian?" the chief asked.

"No," I said. "Never heard of her. Who is she?"

"Woman from Wisconsin who rented the silver Toyota Corolla Vern saw cruising by your house a time or two last night," the chief said.

"You can't possibly have found that out already from the rental company," I said.

"No." He chuckled. "Vern thought she was behaving a mite suspiciously, so he put out the word, and Aida caught her blowing through the stop sign at the corner of Bland and West. Only gave her a warning, but that let her see the woman's driver's license. So now we'll be trying to locate Ms. Koenigslutter to see if she has any connection with Mr. Meredith."

"Never heard of her before," I said. "But I'll let you know if I do. Or if I see the silver Corolla again."

"Can you pull together a list of everyone who was here last night?" he asked.

"Staying here?" I asked. "Or do you want me to include the ones who were just here for dinner?"

"All of them." The chief closed his eyes for a second, as if bracing himself for the totals. "And—" His phone rang, and he glanced down at it. "I should get this."

"I can leave if—"

"No need. Yes, Debbie Ann?" He frowned slightly, and then set his jaw. "Thank you."

He hung up without another word.

"Bad news?" I asked.

"Mr. Meredith didn't make it."

We both sat in silence for a minute or so. I wasn't sure what to think. I'd been angry at Ian. I was still angry at him, or at least resentful, maybe a little irrationally. It was his fault that the innocent joy of Dad's Christmas surprise had been tainted by violence. If Ian hadn't come sneaking back onto our property, he wouldn't have been attacked here—maybe wouldn't have been attacked at all, in which case he might still be alive.

Probably more logical to direct my anger at whoever had killed him.

And was it cold-blooded murder? Or had someone simply lost their temper and lashed out at him?

The chief pulled out his phone and called someone.

"Just thought I'd let you know," he said into the phone. "It's homicide now. . . . Right."

He ended the call and put the phone in his pocket.

"I thought Horace would like to know," he said. "Would you mind if I used your dining room for interviewing the rest of the witnesses? Since I know I won't be overheard here. Unless you need it for feeding everyone."

"No problem," I said. "We'll set up a breakfast buffet in the kitchen. And I'll go get you that list of people who were here."

"And maybe you could send in the first of the people I need to interview," he said.

"Anyone in particular?"

"Anyone who's awake. How about Michael, since he's the other person who found the body?"

I nodded and went out.

And something occurred to me. The chief had said "Since I know I won't be overheard here."

"Won't." Not "can't." He knew about the dumbwaiter's existence. Did he also know that I had, on occasion, used it to eavesdrop on people having conversations in the dining room? Including him—though not recently. Over the years since then we'd become friends, in a large part—though not entirely—through Josh and Jamie's friendship with Adam, the youngest of the three grandsons he and Minerva were raising. He'd seen the boys fooling around with the dumbwaiter often enough. By saying "won't" rather than "can't," was he saying that he trusted me enough to use the dining room in spite of the dumbwaiter?

Or maybe I was overanalyzing. Still. Eavesdropping on Ian was one thing. I wouldn't be spying on the chief.

I went back to the kitchen. After producing several large baskets of croissants, Nora had moved on to cinnamon rolls and had just taken the first batch out of the oven. Michael was sitting at the kitchen table, blowing on one and tossing it from hand to hand.

"Nora, those smell wonderful," I exclaimed. She nodded absently, and I turned to Michael. "The chief's interviewing his witnesses in the dining room, starting with us body finders. Why don't you take him a cinnamon roll when you go?"

"And sweeten his temper before he starts interrogating me?" He stood up, grabbed a plate, put his roll and another on it, and headed for the dining room.

"Interrogate him?" Nora was frowning. "If your chief of police suspects Michael—"

"He was kidding," I said. "Chief Burke's a family friend."

She nodded and went back to her baking.

I sat down, sipped the last of my now-lukewarm chocolate, and grabbed another croissant. Probably a good idea if I found someone other than Cousin Nora for the chief to interview when he finished with Michael. She'd probably want to wait until she got her baking done.

Of course at—good grief—four in the morning, very few of the people he'd want to talk to would be up. Even Rose Noire seemed to have disappeared. So I pulled out my phone and sent an email to Rob and Delaney, telling them that someone had killed Ian and the chief would probably want to interview them as soon as possible. And another email to Festus and Stanley to share the news about the murder. Should I notify Mother? Dad had probably already told her. If he hadn't, maybe I should let her sleep a while longer.

The chief would definitely want to talk to Kevin, who saw more of Ian than most of us, since he was one of the key Mutant Wizards staffers working on the AcerGen project. I sent him a text: "Let me know as soon as you're up." I was about to pocket my phone and go in search of any other witnesses who happened to be awake—but then a reply appeared.

"Up. What's up?"

"Will come down and tell you."

I grabbed a couple of Nora's still-warm croissants and took the stairs down into the basement.

Kevin kept his part of the basement somewhat dimly lit, with only strategic task lights for places where he occasionally had to see things in person rather than on a monitor. This morning, as so much of the time, it was lit only by the half dozen monitors lined up on a wide, built-in desk counter that stretched across one entire wall. All the tiny lights that either blinked or glowed steadily to show that various bits of equipment were alive and doing their thing added a bit of incidental light but the overall effect was mysterious and curiously restful.

But it could also be a bit unnerving to walk in and have no idea where Kevin was.

"You here?" I asked, scanning the darkness before me.

A light came on at my ten o'clock, revealing Kevin sitting in his battered, ancient armchair, with Widget, his Pomeranian, in his lap.

"Why are we both awake in the middle of the night?" he asked.

"You're the one who stays up all night half the time." I tossed him a croissant and took a bite of mine. "I'm the one who's usually asleep right about now."

"I try to keep mundane hours when I have to show up for work with normal people." Strange how he made "normal" sound like a deadly insult. "Some jerk upstairs turned on the music and woke me up, and before I could get back to sleep I heard a siren." His tone was almost casual, but I could detect a slight, well-concealed note of worry. "Someone get hauled off to the hospital?"

"Ian."

"I thought you kicked him out."

"We did," I said. "He snuck back and was skating on the rink. Then—"

"We shouldn't just kick him out." Kevin fed Widget a scrap of croissant. "We should kick the whole AcerGen project to the curb."

"Really? Why?"

"Because they're phonies. Incompetent. They don't really know anything about DNA and they don't even care. Correction: Ian doesn't even care. He came up with this project to make money and save his company. They don't even do their own in-house lab work—they send it out, and to the cheapest vendor they can find. They used to be a fairly decent genealogy site—they should have stuck to that. But the way Ian is running their DNA angle, it's going to blow up in their faces, and Mutant Wizards should cut all ties with them before they ruin our reputation along with theirs."

"Wow," I said. "I'd have been happy with 'I can't stand Ian.'"

"I can't, but that's not the point. Look, I know a little something about the forensic use of DNA, you know."

I nodded. Kevin and his friend Casey ran *Virginia Crime Time,* a successful true-crime podcast. One of the show's greatest strengths was their very different but complementary areas of expertise. Casey was a graduate history student whose research and analysis skills were off the charts. Kevin, in addition to being able to find anything that was hidden anywhere in cyberspace, could make data sit up and do tricks. And since DNA had become such an important factor in crime solving, lately both of them had been learning everything they could about the subject. Kevin could probably have earned a PhD in genetics, microbiology, molecular biology, or any of half a dozen related subjects if he'd been working through an academic program instead of on his own, in what free time he had left over from managing a department at Mutant Wizards.

"There are companies out there doing incredible work with DNA," he said. "They can work with old, degraded DNA, contaminated DNA, DNA in such small quantities that it would have been useless with the old methods. These companies are revolutionizing forensic genomics. And then you have AcerGen, coming along and saying 'Hey! I had a chemistry set when I was a kid! I can do this DNA stuff!' They're just hopping on a bandwagon and trying to exploit the situation. I don't care how much money we lose, we should break our contract with those clowns before it's too late."

"We're not going to break our contract," I began.

Kevin rolled his eyes.

"The proper word is *terminate*," I went on. "And Festus thinks we can probably do it without any particular difficulty, thanks to our having had the wisdom to let him negotiate the contract."

"Seriously?" Kevin sat up straight, almost dislodging Widget. "Festus thinks we should dump them? Hallelujah!"

"We may need you to help us convince Rob," I said. "Since the whole project was his baby. He might put up a fight."

"Yeah," Kevin said. "The trick is going to be making Rob see through Ian's bull—uh, nonsense. I mean, he's figured out that Ian is annoying, but he still buys the jerk's business model."

"That shouldn't be a problem now." Probably time I broke the news. "That ambulance you heard was taking Ian to the hospital. And he didn't make it."

Chapter 15

"Damn," Kevin said. "You're not going to make me feel guilty about speaking ill of the dead, are you? Because no matter how much of a jerk he is, I didn't want him dead—just elsewhere. What happened to him, anyway?"

"Someone bludgeoned him with Josh's hockey stick."

His mouth fell open, and he stared at me for a few seconds until Widget nudged his hand, begging for more of the croissant.

"That's not good," he said as he handed over a bit of croissant. "It's going to be a big headache for Chief Burke, given how many enemies Ian must have had."

"Maybe we can help him," I said. "And by 'we,' I actually mean you. Could you do a little research on some of Ian's enemies?"

I was getting good at explaining all the dirt on AcerGen that Festus and Stanley had uncovered. And I hardly had to look at my phone anymore to forward my audio files of

Ian's phone calls. When I finished, Kevin nodded and looked thoughtful.

"The Cyrus Runk case," he said finally. "Guess I should tell Casey we won't be covering that one on the podcast for a while, no matter how much our fans want us to. Not until Mutant Wizards is free and clear of AcerGen."

"Was it a case you were planning on covering?"

"Maybe," he said. "Wasn't that interesting at first—just a nasty, brutal murder."

"In Virginia," I pointed out. "Your turf."

"Yeah," he said. "In Buchanan County down in southwest Virginia, the part that could just as easily have ended up as Kentucky or West Virginia. Inconveniently far away if we needed to do boots-on-the-ground research, and besides, there was nothing really special about the original crime. We don't cover cases just for the gore. We only heard anything about it because they found the killer through DNA, but even that's not really big news anymore. But when Runk's conviction got overturned, Casey thought would be a good hook for an episode about false confessions. Guess I'll tell him to put that one on ice for the time being."

"Or use some other case as a hook," I said. "Plenty of people out there in prison on false confessions."

"Tell me about it."

"Is it just me, or is it weird that AcerGen would have helped the police with the DNA match," I asked.

"Very weird," Kevin said. "And part of the reason we should cut ties with them, the fact that they keep doing stuff like that. Most places doing consumer DNA have strict privacy rules. Law enforcement is pretty much limited to searching CODIS and a couple of databases where you opt in by uploading your own DNA profile."

"Well, maybe Cyrus Runk has got it wrong," I said. "Maybe the police found him some other way."

"Or maybe he's got it right and Ian ignored his own company's policy. Sounds like his kind of stunt."

"Let Festus know what you find out," I said. "More fodder for terminating the AcerGen contract."

"And maybe a motive for Runk to terminate Ian."

"Yeah." Not a pleasant idea. "I noticed you said 'they keep on doing stuff like that.' Does that mean you know of other times AcerGen has played fast and loose with their customers' privacy?"

"That's the only case I know of for sure," Kevin said. "But I've overheard occasional bits of conversation between the Canadians that are making me wonder, so I'm going to do some snooping. I mean, if Ian's managed to tick off multiple convicted murderers I bet the chief would like to know about it."

I nodded.

"I did overhear something yesterday," he said. "A couple of the Canadians were talking about some woman who was hopping mad that AcerGen found a half brother she never knew she had. A brother who was only about six months older than her. And it wasn't so much finding out that her late father wasn't a model of marital fidelity that upset her—supposedly the half brother is bad news."

"Maybe she should blame her father instead of AcerGen," I suggested.

"Right," he said. "And maybe herself for getting in touch with the guy."

"Maybe he got in touch with her."

"Doesn't work that way," he said. "Both parties have to be willing to talk to each other for them to release contact information."

"That's probably the way it's supposed to work," I said. "But what if AcerGen broke that rule, too?"

"Yeah," he said. "That would be a big problem. And given

how much of an idiot Ian is, it's possible. I'll see what I can find out."

"One more thing," I said. "Can you see what you can find out about a woman named Katherine Anne Koenigslutter?"

"Can you spell that?"

"I can try," I said. "But I couldn't guarantee that I had it right. She set off Vern's spidey sense last night by driving past our house a couple of times in her rental car. Aida got her name from a traffic stop, and the chief asked if we knew anything about her. I don't."

"I'll find her," he said.

"But before you start, go up and talk to the chief," I said. "He should be finished with Michael pretty soon. You can tell the chief more than we ever can about Ian's interactions with people at work."

"And finger any Mutant Wizard employees who might have it in for him? Great."

"Having it in for him is one thing," I began.

"And killing him's another. I get it."

"By the way," I said. "Whoever Ian was talking to said something about their lab having quality control issues. Have you heard about that?"

"No," he said. "But I'll see what I can find out."

"What kind of problems could that be?"

"Well, you could ask Great for more information," he said, using the boys' nickname for their great-grandfather. "His DNA lab's doing some pretty cutting edge things these days, and he likes to stay well informed about what they're up to."

"I want a short, practical answer, not an hour-long lecture," I said.

"Good point." He chuckled. "Okay, possible quality control issues. The one that seems most likely to me is that if the lab didn't have good procedures they might have problems with cross contamination, either between two samples or between a sample and a staff member. Then again, if they're really incompetent, it might be as basic as mixing up the labels, so they're giving the right results to the wrong person."

"What if that happened in Cyrus Runk's case?" I asked.

He frowned for a few seconds, then shook his head.

"Unlikely," he said. "Because AcerGen didn't give the police Runk's DNA—they didn't have it to give. They handed over his cousin's DNA profile, and the police checked the cousin's male relatives until they found Runk. Then they did their own test on Runk, and it turned up a complete match. And the cops would have had their testing done by the state crime lab, which is pretty well regarded."

"So we don't have to worry that AcerGen might have accidentally framed an innocent man."

"No way. Besides—"

He looked down at his phone and winced.

"Dammit."

"What's wrong?"

"Just another message from our stalker."

"What do you mean, 'our stalker'? Who's being stalked?"

"*Virginia Crime Time.*" He rolled his eyes. "Some woman who's decided Casey is her soulmate."

"Then why is she messaging you?"

"She's not messaging me—she's messaging the podcast's Facebook account," he said. "And Casey's kind of freaked by the whole thing, so until we figure out how to shake her off, I'm handling our social media. Major pain in the you-know-what."

"I can imagine," I said. "And maybe a little worrisome."

"A little." He looked—at least for Kevin—curiously thoughtful. "But you know something? Hearing the news about Ian kind of puts it all in perspective. If the worst thing happening to us is some chick getting a crush on Casey sight unseen—well, it sure beats Ian's week."

"Sight unseen? You guys don't have photos to let your fans know what you look like?"

"Not yet." He looked uncomfortable. "I suppose eventually, if our audience keeps growing, we'll do stuff like starting a YouTube channel, or making an appearance at places like CrimeCon. At least I might. I think Casey would rather stay out of the limelight indefinitely. But right now, even I kind of like just being mysterious and anonymous."

I nodded. I could understand. I didn't miss the days when fans stalked Michael, thanks to his acting appearances on a syndicated sword-and-sorcery TV show that had become a surprise cult favorite. He still attracted a certain amount of attention because of his good looks, but the show had been off the air long enough that only the occasional die-hard fan would still gasp and exclaim "The wizard Mephisto!" when she saw him.

"Katherine Anne Koenigslutter," Kevin muttered. "What if she's Cat Lady?" He glanced up and saw my puzzled face. "That's the screen name our stalker uses. CatLady517. Cat's a nickname for Katherine, right? Online she mostly just goes by Cat Lady. She keeps saying she's going to come and see us—see Casey, actually. I just figured that was wishful thinking. But what if she has actually figured out where we are?"

"Let the chief know," I said. "They're already on the lookout for Ms. Koenigslutter. If she's dangerous, they can deal with her. Or any other suspicious strangers who show up at our door."

"Yeah." He closed his eyes for a few seconds and took a few slow, deep breaths. Was he actually listening to Rose Noire and taking yoga breaths to calm himself?

Then he opened his eyes, set Widget down, and stood up.

"Let's get this over with," he said.

Widget and I followed him upstairs.

Kevin and I loitered in the front hall until Michael emerged from the dining room. Kevin marched in with Widget on his heels and shut the door.

"You look done in," Michael said.

"Said the pot to the kettle," I replied. "Why don't you get some sleep? You have classes."

"Not till noon."

"Noon, and two, and three, right?" I asked. "Not much time for a nap. Get some sleep, if you can."

"And leave you to deal with whatever the chief needs for his investigation?"

"Only until a few more larks get up," I said. "Then I'll draft someone to replace me and take a nap myself. Correction—I think what I plan to do counts as going back to bed."

He smiled slightly, nodded, and trudged upstairs.

Things were slow for a while. Kevin was in the dining room with the chief for so long that I began to get genuinely curious about what he could possibly be saying.

But then Kevin could give the chief chapter and verse about Ian's and AcerGen's relationship with Mutant Wizards. Given the long hours they were working, he'd probably gotten to know the Canadians much better than I had. And as long as he was in with the chief, I didn't have to worry about finding the next possible witness.

After a while, Caroline came downstairs.

"What's going on out at the ice rink?" she asked.

"I'm sorry," I said. "Did the siren wake you up?"

"No, my bladder did," she said. "If there were sirens I slept through them. But on my way back from the bathroom I glanced out the window and saw that all the lights around the rink are on and Horace is crawling around the ice with his camera. Police or ambulance?"

"Both," I said. "Someone did Ian in with a hockey stick. Are you planning to go back to bed?"

"Not sure I can after hearing that news. Do you need me to do anything?"

"I've only had two hours of sleep," I said. "Can you take over my job? Which is to grab everyone as they wake up and send them in for the chief to interview."

"Of course," she said. "Shoo."

I trudged upstairs. Michael was fast asleep and not quite snoring. I kicked off my shoes and then fell into bed fully dressed. The warmth of the electric mattress pad was comforting and I just didn't want to deal with taking off my clothes, which had warmed to body temperature, and putting on chilled pajamas. Besides, it would save time when I woke. And I'd be ready if any fresh crises happened before I'd slept my fill. For a few minutes I worried that my busy brain would keep me awake in spite of my exhaustion. I kept wondering what the chief was doing . . . what Horace was finding . . . whether they'd located Katherine Anne Koenigslutter . . . whether Cyrus Runk was in jail . . . should I text Festus and ask him to find out?

I was too tired even to pull out my notebook. I'd probably remember it in the morning.

Chapter 16

I woke up a little after ten o'clock. I still felt groggy and also vaguely anxious, though it took a minute or two to remember why. Christmas was only three days away, all my outgoing presents were already wrapped and under the tree, the comforting odors of bacon and baking bread were teasing my nose—why wasn't I feeling more holiday spirit?

Ian. Memory came flooding back. I'd spent much of yesterday dealing with Ian. Running interference between Ian and the people he ran roughshod over. Gathering information about Ian's misdeeds to help Festus terminate the contract with AcerGen. Or, more accurately, to help us convince Rob that we needed to terminate the contract. Festus already seemed to have enough information. And now Ian's death threatened to cast a blight over the entire holiday season.

There was a small silver lining. We still needed to deal with AcerGen. But not with Ian. Although unfortunately dealing with AcerGen would probably have to take a back seat to finding Ian's killer. For that matter, would Ian's murder hamper our efforts to break things off with AcerGen? Would it look heartless, ending the project while AcerGen was already dealing with the loss of its CEO? And worse, could AcerGen claim that Ian was the cause of our problems, and that his death meant we no longer had grounds for termination?

Probably not. Ian might be—almost certainly was—the cause of AcerGen's financial problems, but his death wouldn't make them go away. And the company would still be liable for any bad actions Ian had committed while CEO—like releasing DNA data without proper permission. What if Cyrus Runk wasn't the only felon with a grudge against Ian?

Just for a moment I wanted to burrow back under the covers, dial the electric mattress pad up a notch, and forget about everything connected with Ian and AcerGen. But it was ten. Which meant that in theory, even allowing for the time when I'd been tossing and turning, I'd probably managed nearly my target eight hours. It didn't feel that way, but I doubted I'd get back to sleep. And I was curious to see what had been happening while I was asleep. For all I knew the chief might already have caught the killer. So I threw on some clean clothes and headed downstairs.

I found Rose Noire sitting cross-legged in the front hall, eyes closed, breathing slowly and deeply. Either she was deep in meditation or she'd finally mastered the art of sleeping vertically. I was about to slip past her and head for the kitchen when she opened her eyes.

"Morning," she said.

"Where is everyone?" I asked.

"Horace is still working the crime scene," she said. "Since they're still under a deadline, the Canadians all went to the Mutant Wizards office, and the chief is interviewing them there. Your father took most of the relatives down to the zoo for a VIP tour."

A brilliant idea, that last part. With any luck, by the time they all got back from watching the meerkats and koalas, the chief would release the ice rink. Except—

"Even Cordelia?" In the interest of family harmony, she and Grandfather had forged a kind of truce, but it worked much better when they stayed out of each other's way.

"Of course not. Your mother took her over to Trinity to help Robyn with a project. I saved some breakfast for you—do you want me to come and heat it up?"

"I'll manage."

"Then I'll run my errands." She stood up in one graceful motion and began putting on her wraps.

I confess, I was a little disappointed. I was hoping she'd announce that while I had been sleeping, the chief had solved the case and arrested Ian's killer. Ah, well.

In the kitchen, I found Cousin Nora chopping up a mountain of onions into bits of remarkably small and consistent size. I could feel my eyes watering slightly from afar, but the onion fumes didn't seem to affect her in the slightest. Clearly nature had endowed Nora with superhuman culinary powers, and I should stop feeling guilty about my lesser skills.

"Morning," I said.

"Breakfast in the fridge," she said.

I nodded, hunted out the covered plate with my name taped to it, and stuck it in the microwave. While I was waiting for it to finish, I looked out the window. All seemed quiet out at the rink. I could only just spot Horace moving slowly across the ice on his hands and knees, holding a magnifying glass to the surface. His figure was tiny at this distance and nearly round thanks to all his wraps. It occurred to me that even after the chief released it, the rink would need a little bit of cleanup to remove the blood. Should I—

The doorbell rang. Nora glanced at me with a slight frown,

as if to suggest it was distracting her from her work, and I should do something about it.

"I guess Rose Noire took off," I said. "So I should go answer that."

She nodded and went back to her rapid chopping. By the time I reached the front hall, our impatient visitor had rung the doorbell again. Tinkerbell had roused herself from her usual warm spot by the fireplace and was standing in the archway between the hall and the living room, staring at the door. Was there something about our visitor that roused her suspicions, sight unseen? Or had the fact that the house was almost completely empty activated her protective instincts?

Maybe she was just annoyed at being awakened by the doorbell.

"Good girl," I said. Since there was still a killer on the loose, I rather liked having a real, live Irish wolfhound sitting there, visible to anyone who stepped in, ready to play protector.

I peered through the peephole. Our visitor was a tallish, clean-shaven man. I could see pin-striped trousers below his bulky down jacket. Probably in his thirties. His hair was blond and carefully groomed, and he had a long face and a thin nose. Not quite handsome, but more than presentable. His cheeks and nose were slightly reddened by the cold. If he had his DNA analyzed, I'd expect his profile would show a lot of Scandinavian ancestry. Not exactly a threatening figure—especially not with Tink at my elbow. So I opened the front door.

"Can I help you?"

"You must be Mrs. Waterston." He smiled what I'm sure he intended as a charming, ingratiating smile. But it came across as insincere.

So I didn't say yes or no—I just looked expectantly at him. And decided that for the time being, he could go on staying on the other side of our threshold. After all, unlike me, he was dressed for the arctic air.

"I'm sorry to bother you," he said, when he realized I wasn't going to divulge my identity. "But I heard that Mr. Ian Meredith was staying here, and I really need to get in touch with him."

"Sorry," I said. "No Ian Meredith staying here."

"But you know who he is, right? The CEO of AcerGen—they have a team in town working with a local software company, and I heard he might be staying with you."

"Sorry," I said. "He's not."

"Do you know how I can get in touch with him?" he asked.

"Have you tried contacting him through the local software company you think he's working with?"

"Mutant Wizards? Yes, and they just gave me the runaround. They'd be happy to take a message for him, but no, they can't tell me where he is."

I made a mental note to praise Kristyn the next time I saw her, and maintained my polite, inquisitive expression. I'd read enough of Dad's beloved mystery books to know that the best way to get information out of people was to shut up and let them talk to fill the silence.

"And I really need to talk to him," the man added, with another oddly off-putting smile.

"I'm afraid I can't help you, either." It wasn't entirely a lie. I didn't know exactly where Ian was by now. Probably in the morgue at Caerphilly General. They'd eventually get the Caerphilly Funeral Home to arrange shipment back to Canada, and they might already have transferred him over there, but I had no way of knowing. And as for talking to him—maybe a Ouija board could help with that, but I certainly couldn't.

"It's— Sorry." The man took a breath and smiled again. "I should probably introduce myself. My name is Alfred Sloan. I'm an attorney representing a party who's brought a legal action against Mr. Meredith and AcerGen, and I'm kind of afraid my client has gone off the deep end and come down here to . . . um . . . accost him."

Now this was interesting.

"Are you suggesting that your client could be dangerous?" I asked. "To this Ian Meredith or anyone else?"

Sloan looked uncomfortable.

"I wouldn't say that she's exactly dangerous," he said. "She doesn't have a history of violence, if that's what you mean. But she's very . . . emotional. Confrontational. I'd really rather avoid having her come into contact with him."

An idea popped into my head.

"What's the name of your client?" I asked.

"Katherine Anne Koenigslutter."

My face must have shown some reaction.

"You've met her?" He sounded hopeful.

"No." I allowed myself a chuckle. "I think I'd remember being introduced to someone with a name that . . . unusual. You said you were afraid she'd 'come down here'—where is your client from?"

"Wisconsin," he said. "Little town near Lake Superior. And maybe I'm worrying in vain, but it's hard to imagine someone coming over a thousand miles to see someone she's mad at and just . . . telling him off, you know? I only want to make sure nothing happens."

Which suggested that he'd lied—that maybe he really *was* worried about the possibility that his client might be dangerous.

"Why is your client so mad at this Mr. Meredith?" I asked.

He frowned and compressed his already thin lips. I'd seen this reaction before, from Festus and the several other attorneys in the family. I was expecting him to say that was attorney/client privilege. Then he sighed.

"It's a matter of public record now, I suppose. Now that we've filed our suit, that is. Ms. Koenigslutter submitted her

DNA to AcerGen for testing. AcerGen notifies its clients of any DNA relatives who are also in its database, so they can contact them if they so choose. My client maintains that she did not want to be contacted by any DNA relatives and that AcerGen violated her privacy by giving them her contact information."

"Sounds as if she might have a good case," I said.

"We think so." His quick tight smile was just a little on the smug side, but maybe that was understandable. "Our situation is complicated by the fact that Ms. Koenigslutter is very upset about the possibility that her half brother will succeed in claiming a share of the substantial estate she inherited from her late father. The idea of having to give him anything—well, she reacts very negatively to that. I just don't want her to do anything that would complicate matters. Or get her in trouble."

"I wish I could help you," I said. "But as I told you, Mr. Meredith isn't staying here and I don't know how you can contact him. Is there a way I can let you know if I do run into him or Ms. Koenigslutter?"

He frowned. Then he reached into his pocket and brought out a pen and a business card.

"I'll give you my cell phone." The porch pillars were wrapped with holly and ivy, but he managed to find a space big enough to write on the back of the business card. "If you see her or Mr. Meredith, please call me. Any time. I'd really appreciate it."

"You might want to get in touch with the police," I said. "I think they'd share your interest in preventing any kind of confrontation between your client and her nemesis. Of course, you've probably already done that."

"Not yet," he said. "I didn't want to alert law enforcement if I could find her and calm her down myself. I thought I'd be able to find her by checking the hotels, but she's not at the Caerphilly Inn—is that really the only hotel in town?"

"Yes," I said. "There are quite a few bed-and-breakfast places. You should be able to pick up a list of them at almost any shop in town."

"I'll do that." He shook his head slightly. "They seem to be full up at the Inn, and if I don't find her pretty soon I'll be looking for a place myself for tonight. I also asked about Mr. Meredith at the Inn, but he wasn't there, either."

And maybe that was how Mr. Sloan found his way to our doorstep—by talking to an Inn employee who was more gullible than I was. I'd have a word with my friend Ekaterina, who managed the Inn. It was one thing to have respectable lawyers showing up on our doorstep. What if someone like Cyrus Runk showed up asking about Ian's whereabouts? Or Katherine Anne Koenigslutter?

"I'd appreciate it if you didn't share this address with your client," I said. "Obviously I couldn't be of any more help to her than I can to you, and if she's inclined to be confrontational—"

"Of course not," he said. "I can't promise she won't find out on her own, you understand—although I will certainly be trying to convince her to go back to Wisconsin and let the justice system do its work. But if she does show up—"

"I won't blame you."

"Thanks." He looked harried, as if suddenly worried about the possibility of his client confronting innocent bystanders along with Ian Meredith. I felt a sudden surge of sympathy for him.

"Look, maybe it's none of my business and maybe you've already thought about this, but you know what I'd do if she were my client?"

He shook his head.

"I'd get new DNA tests," I said. "On your client and her supposed half brother. From some other DNA company—the most reputable you can find. I mean, this is AcerGen, right? How do we know they're even doing the testing right?"

"I think they send it out to a lab." Sloan frowned and stiffened as if my suggestion upset him.

"To the cheapest lab they can find," I said. "And I've heard rumors they're having quality control issues with whatever lab they're using. Do you really want to trust whatever cut-rate lab AcerGen found? Remember how John Glenn felt when he went into orbit, knowing every single part in his spaceship was supplied by the lowest bidder."

Sloan didn't find that amusing. And didn't seem to like my idea.

"DNA tests are expensive," he said. "What if we spend all that money only to get confirmation of exactly what AcerGen told us?"

"Then would you be any worse off than you are now? And DNA tests only cost a few thousand dollars—wouldn't a trial be a lot more expensive?"

He nodded absently, while staring at me as if he wasn't particularly happy with my suggestion. Maybe he was annoyed that he hadn't thought of it. Or maybe he was one of those attorneys who didn't find a case interesting if there wasn't going to be a trial involved.

Or one of those less-than-ethical attorneys who only cared about running up the client's bill. He didn't come across that way, but I only had his appearance and a few minutes of conversation to go by.

"Just an idea," I said. "Your case, after all. Good luck with your search." I stepped back to close the door. He looked as if he wanted to stick out a hand or a foot to keep me from closing the door and thought better of it.

Possibly because Tinkerbell had edged closer and was now leaning against my hip, eyes glued to him until the second the door was closed.

I rewarded her with a treat from the supply we kept in the closet. Then I peeked outside to see how Mr. Sloan dealt with disappointment. He was standing at the other end of our front walk, looking up and down the road. Looking for Ian's car, perhaps? Which might actually be parked here. Then he got into a car that was parked right in front of the walkway, in the space we'd marked off with official-looking HANDICAPPED PARKING ONLY signs to remind people to leave it open for less able fellow guests. I noted the license number on his dark-blue Ford Taurus.

Then I settled down by the fire and dialed the chief.

Chapter 17

"Yes, Meg." He didn't sound impatient. In fact, he sounded expectant, as if hoping I had some useful bit of information. I hoped so, too.

"I just got a visit from a lawyer who's looking for Ian," I said. "I thought you might be interested in knowing about it."

"I would indeed."

While I relayed the gist of my conversation with Sloan, I multitasked and took pictures of the front and back of his business card. His law firm was in Green Bay, Wisconsin, and Sloan wasn't one of the four Scandinavian-sounding last names in its title, only a staff attorney. But it was a nice, elegant, expensive-looking card, printed in a slightly old-fashioned typeface on heavy, textured cream card stock. I texted my pictures to the chief.

"Interesting," he said. "Given that his client was observed several times in the area of your house only a few hours before the murder. You didn't mention that to him, I assume."

"No," I said. "A stranger shows up at my door asking to speak to a murder victim—call me paranoid but I'm not going to tell him anything I don't have to until I figure out what he's after."

"Very wise," he said. "Thanks for the heads-up. I will be interested to talk to Mr. Sloan."

"If either he or his client shows up here again, I'll let you know. By the way—I disavowed any knowledge of Ian's whereabouts, but for all I know his car is still here, and if this lawyer happens to know the make, model, and license number—"

"It won't do him much good, since Mr. Meredith's car is now safely stowed in our impound lot."

"We have an impound lot now?"

"That old shed behind the jail—the one where they used to store the coal before they put in the new heating system."

"Oh, right." The shed also served as Horace's overflow evidence locker. With luck they'd already given it a thorough cleaning after last month's exciting alpaca-rustling case.

"I had Osgood Shiffley tow it away around dawn this morning, so unless Mr. Sloan started casing your house in the middle of the night, he won't know it was there. But I suppose his client might have seen it. Nothing we can do about that."

We said our goodbyes and hung up.

And then something occurred to me. How had Ian's killer found him back there at the ice rink? The ice rink whose very existence had been a secret until a few hours before his murder. Given the effectiveness of Caerphilly's grapevine, most of the town would probably know about it by nightfall today, but last night the only people who knew about it were my family and the Canadians—two groups of people I didn't want to think about as possible suspects.

Of course, if someone had it in for Ian they could have been stalking him. Could have followed him, either from the house or, more likely, from the Mutant Wizards parking lot.

The chief would already have thought of all this, I reminded myself. He wouldn't overlook the possibility of a stalker. And he was probably able to be a lot more impartial about whether the Canadians—or my relatives—were viable suspects. I should stop worrying about it.

But I probably wouldn't.

Just then, the doorbell rang again. Tink, who had settled down by the hearth, lifted her massive head and contemplated the front door. I scowled, feeling a quick twinge of annoyance. If that was Sloan again—

No reason for it to be, I reminded myself. And if it was, I'd deal with him. I returned to the front door and looked out through the peephole. No one on the front porch. No car at the end of the front walk. I opened the door to find a huge bouquet of red roses sitting on the doormat. More than a dozen. More than two dozen—probably forty or fifty perfect red blossoms.

There was no card on the vase or under it.

And no one in sight.

I stepped outside and looked up and down the porch. No one peeking around the corner of the house. I strode down the walk to the road. No cars disappearing into the distance. No one hiding behind the hedges.

Perhaps there was someone hiding in one of the cars parked by the side of the road. Or someone sprinting through the woods. I wasn't about to risk frostbite to find out—I was shivering already.

I hurried back to the house, picked up the flowers, and took them inside.

Tink and the Pomeranians barely reacted to my return. Well, if the dogs weren't worried, I'd try not to be. Sooner or later I'd figure out who'd left them.

I set the roses on the coffee table. They fitted in perfectly with Mother's holiday decorations. Maybe that was the answer to the riddle. Maybe she'd arranged to have someone drop them off.

Back in the kitchen, Nora had moved on from onions to green peppers.

"Your breakfast's gone cold."

I nodded and punched the microwave buttons again. While waiting, I watched Nora at work. Amazing how fast she could chop. At half that speed, I'd already have added parts of several fingers to the peppers.

"I assume if you could use my help you'll ask," I said.

She nodded in time with her busy knife.

"I'll stay out from underfoot, then." I began putting on my wraps so I was ready to move when the microwave dinged. "I'll be in my office."

When I stepped outside, I frightened away rather a lot of birds that had been swarming the several bird feeders now occupying our backyard. Including several birds with a gray upper body and a white belly—were they juncos? If memory served, that was what juncos looked like. Maybe I'd do a little bird-watching when I got back to the house, and take a picture of anything that looked as if it might be a harbinger of snow.

Out in my office I nibbled at my breakfast as I sent my pictures of the front and back of Sloan's business card to my computer. Luckily Rose Noire had included a lot of bacon, which survived its double nuking splendidly. The sausage, eggs, and hash browns didn't suffer much, either, and I realized I was actually pretty hungry. I continued to munch while I opened up my email program, wrote a short description of my encounter with Sloan, and sent it to Festus and Stanley.

And then, since I was at my computer and still only halfway finished with breakfast, I did a few internet searches.

Katherine Anne Koenigslutter didn't bring up any useful results under any of the variant spellings I could think of for her first, middle, and last name.

Cyrus Runk brought up a fair number of articles. Not a lot about his conviction, which seemed to have passed largely unnoticed except in the remote rural county in which his victim had lived. Quite a few about the surprising decision by the Court of Appeals to overturn his conviction. Much discussion about whether or not the Supreme Court of Virginia would hear the prosecution's appeal, and a general consensus that a new trial, even with a change of venue, was unlikely to result in a different verdict. Not a single article mentioned the possibility of the DNA evidence being challenged, though, so evidently Runk's lawyer was keeping his new tactic a secret for now.

More interesting were the pictures, especially of the defendant and his appellate lawyer. Cyrus Runk was nondescript, except for a broad nose that looked as if it had been broken a time or two. At twenty-two his hair was already receding at both temples, making his forehead rather M-shaped, and in the picture his small eyes looked hurt and anxious. I could see myself feeling sorry for him if he hadn't been proven by DNA to have whacked a seventeen-year-old girl over the head with a foot-long flashlight. William T. Morgan, Esquire, was tall and arguably handsome, although not my type—I much preferred Michael's lean, rangy look to Morgan's beefy frame. I suspected his pin-striped suit was well tailored to disguise a once-athletic body slowly losing the battle against time and business lunches. Maybe it was just my imagination that made him look rather smug and self-satisfied. Or maybe I was prejudiced by the fact that he was trying to free a killer.

I studied them both. I'd know either of them if he showed up on my doorstep.

Although I really hoped neither of them would. And after all, with Ian no longer living here, why would they?

In fact, why would they even while Ian was still alive? Surely they'd be seeing him in court soon enough. Of course, if they did want to confront him in person, it would make sense that they'd take advantage of the fact that he was more accessible here than he would have been back in Canada. Runk didn't look like the sort of guy who could afford to do much international travel, so he might not even have a passport. But what if he had been eager to confront Ian, and decided to take advantage of his enemy's temporary stay here? The one substantive article I'd found suggested that Runk hadn't planned the murder he'd been convicted of—that he'd done it after losing his hair-trigger temper. I could see the attack on Ian happening the same way, with the hockey stick—like the flashlight—a weapon of opportunity. So I assumed Runk would be high on the chief's suspect list. Unless he was in jail. None of the articles said whether he was still locked up or out on bail. I jotted down a note to ask Festus and Stanley to find out. Or the chief. Surely he'd think that a reasonable request, so we could know whether we should be looking over our shoulders for Runk.

Morgan, his lawyer, could afford a jaunt to Toronto, but probably wouldn't want to rack up big travel expenses on what I gathered was a pro bono case. Mason, Morgan, and Friedman was located in Richmond, so if he wanted to confront Ian for any reason, a trip to Caerphilly would be a lot cheaper and faster than an expedition to Toronto. But why would a high-powered attorney just show up here? Wouldn't he be much more likely to make an appointment? Or at least try to?

And how would either of them have known Ian was here in the first place?

I snagged the clearest pictures of Runk and Morgan and sent them to Michael, Rose Noire, and Kevin, with a note explaining who they were and a suggestion that they call 911 ASAP if they saw either one.

I'd finished my breakfast by this time, so I shut down my

computer, locked my office, and jogged across the backyard to the kitchen door, scattering juncos in my wake.

"You're low on baking soda," Nora said when I arrived in the kitchen. "And out of powdered sugar."

"I'll make a grocery run, then." I had no desire to foil any plans Nora had that involved powdered sugar. "Can you jot down a list of everything you'd like me to get?"

"Already have." Nora handed me a list. A rather long list.

Well, I needed to go into town anyway. I could check the cat traps at the Methodist church. And drop by Mutant Wizards to fill the bird feeders. With luck I could manage to overhear something that would justify dropping by the police station to tell the chief, which might let me pick up a little information on how his investigation was going.

"Call me if you think of anything you've left out," I said.

Nora raised one eyebrow, as if to suggest that her grocery lists were never incomplete, and nodded slightly. Then she turned back to whatever she was working on—probably pie crusts. She had a lump of dough on a marble pastry slab with a rolling pin nearby.

I tore myself away and headed for the front hall.

As I left the kitchen I heard the front door open and close. I quickened my steps so I could see who was entering. Even as I did it, I wasn't entirely sure why. No one could have gotten in without a key. And it wasn't as if I felt obliged to play doorman, what with a dozen visiting Canadians and an ever-increasing number of relatives coming and going with their own keys. Maybe having a murder in the backyard had made me slightly on edge.

I saw Rhea standing in the hall—Rhea, who had been so excited at the idea of owling with Grandfather. How long ago that conversation seemed. I wondered if Caroline had organized the expedition—and whether they'd go forward with it in spite of Ian's death. And it also occurred to me to wonder what Rhea was doing here in the middle of the day. Perhaps Ian's death meant the Canadians would no longer be working such killer hours. Although I had the impression that they needed to work those hours to have any hope of finishing the project by the deadline Ian had committed them to. Had some of the Canadians figured out that the project was about to be canceled?

If it was, the owling trip would be an even more useful distraction, I decided, as I approached Rhea. She had unbuttoned her puffy coat but was still wearing it, as if she planned to leave momentarily. She looked tense and anxious. They probably all were. From what I had seen the Canadians seemed united in their intense dislike of their boss—but that didn't necessarily mean that his death would improve their morale. At the very least, they had to be worried about their jobs—especially any of them who knew about Cyrus Runk's lawsuit or the backlog of untested DNA kits piling up thanks to the lab that had the temerity to want payment for processing them. How many of them actually knew? And what other corporate dirty laundry were they aware of?

Rhea suddenly became aware of my approach. She started and turned around with a little gasp.

"I'm sorry," I said. "I didn't mean to startle you."

"Not your fault," she said. "I think we're all a little on edge because of . . . you know."

I nodded. Yes, I knew.

She glanced up the stairway and then back at me.

"Sorry," she said. "I'm impatient for Angela and Maeve to come down so we can head back to the office. Maeve left her migraine medicine here, and with everything that's going on she didn't want to come back for it all alone, so Angela and I came with her for moral support. But I don't want to be gone too long. Which is silly, I suppose—it's not as if anyone's going to be counting the minutes we're away from our desks—not with Ian gone."

"I noticed he was a tough taskmaster," I said.

"More of a petty tyrant," she said. "A taskmaster would be trying to make sure we were getting our projects done—Ian just wanted to see us at our desks looking busy. Especially if he was giving a tour to potential investors."

"You're reminding me of all the reasons I'm self-employed," I said.

She smiled at that and glanced up the stairs again.

"He didn't see that sometimes staying chained to your desk is counterproductive," she went on. "Sometimes if you can't figure out the answer to a programming challenge, what you need is not to keep plugging away at what hasn't been working. Sometimes, if you go outside for a brisk walk, your brain will solve the problem as soon as you stop trying to force it. And sometimes what you need to do is go down to the break room and talk the problem over with a couple of other programmers—you'd be amazed how often you solve your own problem when you're trying to explain it to someone else. Ian never did understand that if he found a handful of people in the break room talking, they just might be working, not goofing off."

I nodded. I'd heard Delaney and Kevin explain the same thing more than once. And I'd experienced it myself. Sometimes, if I had a thorny dilemma or a puzzling problem, the best thing to do was to spend some time at my forge. I'd emerge from a blacksmithing session tired and dirty but with a solution to my problem.

"And it's the same for the genealogists like Angela and Maeve," Rhea continued. "Sometimes they need to talk over their work with their colleagues or get away from it entirely so they can come back with fresh eyes. And he was particularly hard on Maeve. He never understood that if she felt a migraine coming on, she might be able to fend it off if she took her meds and lay down for a little while. And then she'd make up the time. She always did. He never understood that."

I nodded. She glanced at me and winced slightly.

"Listen to me," she said. "Telling you all the reasons why I disliked him. You're not supposed to speak ill of the dead."

"But you're not obliged to lie about them, either," I said.

"No," she said. "And right now I don't trust anyone who's pretending to be all broken up about Ian's death. Not that anyone's celebrating, of course, but even though we feel guilty about it, I think a lot of us are feeling a sense of relief."

"Mixed feelings are totally natural," I said.

"And most of us are working on expressions of dignified sympathy for when Mr. Meredith arrives. Mr. Meredith senior," she added, seeing my puzzled expression. "Ian's father. He's flying down later today."

"Ah," I said. "Good to know."

"Oh," she said. "You mean because he might end up staying here—I never thought of that."

"Actually, if he needs a place to stay, I'll probably send him over to Mother and Dad's." It also occurred to me that for one old man, and a bereaved one at that, Ekaterina might be able to arrange a room at the Inn for a night or two.

"He's actually very nice," Rhea said. "A sweet old gentleman. Maeve and Angela adore him—they've been with the company a lot longer than I have. It's just that he has a blind spot when it comes to his son."

"But I imagine he won't want to stay this close to where Ian was killed," I said. "And besides, Mother's an expert at taking care of grieving survivors. I remember when she went to the funeral of a perfectly horrible woman, someone she considered her worst enemy. She managed to offer her condolences to the family with such touching sincerity that they asked her back to the house for the private lunch they were giving for just the family. And she wasn't being insincere," I added. "She didn't tell a single lie about how fond she was of the dead woman—just expressed how genuinely sorry she was for their loss."

"Let's invite her over to the office when Mr. Meredith gets here," Rhea said. "We all want to be sympathetic, but it's hard not to be worrying about our own futures. Will we all have jobs by the end of the week? What if he shuts down the project? Or decides to sell the company?"

I wondered if all the Canadians felt this way. If so, it made them a lot less likely as suspects. "Do you think that's a possibility?" I asked.

"Who knows?" she said. "I know there was a pretty solid rumor a while back that they had an offer from one of the big companies in our field. And most people were glad when it was turned down, because we liked working for a small company with a nice boss. That was when Mr. Meredith senior was in charge. But I'm not sure how much luck they'd have selling it now. Things haven't been going all that well lately."

"Since Ian took over?" I ventured.

She tried to look as if she didn't quite understand, then gave in and nodded.

"Look, this is probably none of my business," I said. "But I hope you were honest with Chief Burke about how you felt about Ian. Stuff like this always ends up coming out, you know."

"And he'll probably be a lot more suspicious of anyone who pretends they liked Ian," she said. "I mean, he's met him once or twice. I think most of us were pretty honest. I know I was. I just wish I'd managed to leave before now. I had my résumé out, and I had some nibbles. But Ian made it so hard to get away for an interview, and then he brought us down here and made it impossible. But I was planning on quitting on Friday. I talked to my parents, and they said they'd help out if it took a while to get a new job, and maybe I'd even be able to come home for Christmas. I've got my resignation letter in my laptop, ready to print out. I was going to do that either today or tomorrow. Maybe I still should."

I couldn't decide whether to be cheered or saddened by the look of pure happiness that crossed her face at the thought.

And did being on the brink of leaving make her less of a suspect for Ian's murder? Or did his mistreatment of her—and all the rest of his staff—and the way he'd made it hard for her to find another job make her more suspicious?

Just then Angela and Maeve appeared at the top of the stairs. They stopped, and while I couldn't see Angela's face, Maeve's showed a brief flicker of—fear? Anxiety? The expression passed, and her face returned to its usual look of kindly, thoughtful intelligence as they came down the stairs.

I liked Maeve and Angela. And I could relate to them better than to most of the other Canadians, who in addition to being much younger, were from the tech side of the company. Perfectly nice, all of them—I just hadn't found that we had much in common. If I'd had to guess Angela and Maeve's profession, I'd have said that they were either teachers or librarians—two of my favorite kinds of people. I wasn't surprised when I learned that they were genealogists.

What had surprised me was the close friendship they appeared to have formed with the much-younger Rhea. But with what I'd learned about Ian in the past twenty-four hours, I was definitely wondering. Was this a friendship that had arisen naturally out of shared interests and congenial personalities? Or were Maeve and Angela being protective of Rhea? Never leaving her alone in situations where a known sexual harasser was present? Gently but persistently fending off Ian?

I considered this idea while they descended the stairway.

Yes, I thought. It was the sort of mission I could imagine them taking on.

"How's your head doing?" I asked Maeve.

"My head?" She looked briefly puzzled.

"I thought it was okay to mention your headache to Meg," Rhea said.

"And it's not a headache yet, and probably isn't going to be," Maeve said. "It's amazing how well Depakote works when you manage to take it in time."

"I'm glad I insisted on coming back for it," Rhea said. "I mean, it's not as if anyone expects to get a lot done today."

"Still, we should be getting back." Angela glanced at her watch. "If you think you're up to it," she added to Maeve.

"I'm sure it will be fine." She gave a reassuring smile. "See you this evening," she added to me.

They buttoned up their coats, pulled on their hats and gloves, and went out into the cold with the brisk steps of people for whom protracted temperatures in the twenties were merely a feature of life, not a rare and horrible event.

But there was something slightly furtive in their manner. Maybe they were still unused to being able to come and go from the office without being reprimanded. Maybe what I was seeing was guilt about how relieved Ian's demise made them feel. Relieved—maybe even happy.

Still, I couldn't help feeling that they were up to something. That I should call the chief and tell him about their thinly disguised relief and cheer. That I should rush upstairs and search all their rooms—for what? My curiosity warred with my self-respect.

Self-respect won—barely. It wasn't as if I could expect to find a blood-soaked murder weapon in one of their rooms— the chief already had that. But they might not be the only Canadians feeling free to sneak away from the office with

Ian gone, and I didn't want to get caught snooping. Besides, Rose Noire would be tidying their rooms and maybe even changing their linens sometime this afternoon. I could let her do the snooping. Better yet, I could volunteer to help her. It wouldn't count as snooping if I merely kept my eyes open while there on legitimate business, right?

In the meantime, I had errands. Shopping for groceries. Filling the bird feeders down at Mutant Wizards. Checking the cat traps. Maybe even taking the pregnant feral to Clarence's if we caught her. I opened the closet and began bundling up against the cold.

Chapter 18

I checked the weather app on my phone. Alas, it wasn't going to get above freezing today. But on the positive side, the chance of precipitation had changed from 0 to 30 percent. And any precipitation that fell today would almost certainly be snow. Maybe a white Christmas was possible after all.

On my way into town I tried to appreciate the surrounding holiday decorations and let them coax me into a holiday mood. So far it wasn't working all that well, but still, I would keep trying. Deliberately make myself notice everything that would cheer me up.

Nice to see that the tourists seemed to enjoy the Dickensian theme of Christmas in Caerphilly. In fact, more and more of them were showing up dressed in Victorian finery of their own. I made a mental note to suggest to Randall that a costume shop might be a revenue generator if someone wanted to open one.

I took a slight detour to cruise by a yard that always

featured some of my favorite decorations. It belonged to a couple who were so enamored of Halloween that they repurposed their over-the-top Halloween decorations into a Christmas display, thanks to strategic use of Santa hats, tinsel, and strings of Christmas lights. A skeleton Santa rode in a rickety sleigh pulled by eight skeleton reindeer. A wreath made of bones festooned their front door. All the bony arms coming out of the ground now held bits of mistletoe or shiny glass balls. And this year the skeletal friendly beasts approaching the bony Holy Family included a flock of bats wired to look as if they were coming in for a landing.

"'Still through the cloven skies they come,'" I quoted. "'With peaceful wings unfurled.'"

That was one thing about living in a town that celebrated an over-the-top Christmas festival every year—by now I knew all the words to all the verses of even the most obscure Christmas carol. Unfortunately, there was no one around to be impressed with the fact that I knew the opening to the second verse of "It Came Upon the Midnight Clear." If I tried I could probably even dredge up most of the lyrics to "Whence Comes This Rush of Wings." Maybe I'd work on that before I drove some of our visitors past what most locals had taken to calling *The Nightmare Before Christmas* yard.

I was still humming and retrieving words when I pulled up at the gate of the Methodist parking lot. Luckily, a volunteer from the congregation was minding the phone in the office, which meant I gained admission to the parking lot with a lot less hassle than if Mrs. Dahlgren had answered. I pulled on my work gloves, grabbed the paper bag of cat bait Clarence had given me, and began making the rounds of the humane traps.

The first trap showed no signs of being disturbed, except that the little food trails leading to it had disappeared. I laid new trails and moved on.

The second trap contained an annoyed squirrel who chittered angrily and flicked his tail at me when I peered inside. I opened the door of the trap and he ran off, still looking vexed.

"You're lucky I'm not fond of Brunswick stew," I told him. He ignored me, so I focused on rebaiting the trap and laying nice trails to it.

The third trap was missing. I could see a faint imprint where it had rested, and also a few places where something had scarfed up all the little bits of bait in the trails. But no trap.

The fourth trap was undisturbed. After I refreshed its bait trails, I went back to where the third had been. I searched the nearby bushes, since it occurred to me that someone—Mrs. Dahlgren, most likely—might have thought it was a little too visible and moved it to a more discreet location. No luck.

Mrs. Dahlgren had returned while I was working, so I should probably go inside to ask if she'd seen anything.

"The things I'm doing for you, little mother cat," I muttered.

Mrs. Dahlgren was there in the church office, casting stern glances at a trio of women who were stuffing envelopes with frantic speed. Over at Trinity Episcopal this activity would be done at a much slower pace and accompanied with much gossip and laughter, but Mrs. Dahlgren's presence probably cast a pall over things. The three women glanced up, gave me quick smiles, and then put their heads down over their work.

"Good morning," I said to Mrs. Dahlgren. "My grandmother and I helped Clarence Rutledge set out some traps yesterday, to remove the feral cat that's been hanging around your grounds. One of the traps is gone—do you have any idea what happened to it?"

"I assumed you had already caught the stray," she said. "And that was why you carried the one trap away this morning. Does this mean you're not here to remove the other traps?"

"Carried the trap away?" I echoed. "I haven't been here since yesterday. What—"

"I didn't mean you *personally,* of course." Mrs. Dahlgren frowned slightly. "One of your other cat people."

I suppressed a smile at the image this conjured up, of slinking around with a group of fellow feral rescuers, all of us dressed in furry polyester jumpsuits like refugees from a low-budget production of *Cats.*

"If the cat's been caught, I haven't heard about it," I said. "What time did this happen? The people removing the trap, I mean."

"At ten fourteen." Her precision was reassuring.

"Did you see who took the trap? Was it anyone you knew?"

"I only saw their backs," she said. "Two people in coats and hats."

Since only a lunatic would be out in subfreezing weather without wraps, this wasn't particularly helpful. So much for precision.

"I'll ask around," I said. "And if the cat's been caught, I'll come over right away to remove the rest of the traps."

Mrs. Dahlgren nodded, and her face said "Of course you will."

I made my way back to my car. After thinking about it for a second or two, I called the Caerphilly Veterinary Hospital and got Clarence's assistant.

"Morning, Lucas," I said. "Did anyone bring in that pregnant feral cat this morning?"

"Not yet," he said. "I checked the traps when I came in this morning, around seven, but I've been too busy to get over there since. Can you—"

"I'm there," I said. "I rebaited three of the traps, but Mrs. Dahlgren saw someone hauling away the fourth at ten fourteen."

"You sure she didn't just chuck it in their Dumpster?" he asked.

Evidently he had also met Mrs. Dahlgren.

"I'll check before I leave, but I doubt it," I said. "I can see her doing that, but why would she stop at one? Besides, she wouldn't lie about it afterward. She'd have some rationale for throwing them away that would make it seem totally justified. Look, I'm worried about this. If anyone brings the cat in—a very pregnant yellow tabby—can you let me know?"

"Sure thing."

I got out of my car and checked the Dumpster. Luckily it didn't have that much in it, so I could tell without digging into the contents that the humane trap couldn't possibly be there.

"Here, kitty-kitty-kitty," I called into the Dumpster. And then I repeated it a couple of times nearby. Not that I really expected to find the cat there—but I didn't want Mrs. Dahlgren to make a fuss in case she was watching me and wondering why I was snooping in the Methodist Dumpster.

Back in my car I called Cordelia.

"Feeling better after your nap?" she asked.

"Much better," I said. "But I'm worried—you haven't been by to check the cat traps, have you?"

"I was planning to drop by this afternoon," she said. "Your mother and I are over at Trinity helping Robyn wrap all the toys donated to the Christmas drive, but we should be finished soon."

"No need," I said. "I came over to check and rebait the traps. And someone stole one of them."

"With or without the pregnant cat?"

"No idea."

"Worrisome. Of course, it could be some kindhearted person who saw that the trap was full and didn't want to leave the poor creature out in the cold."

"Maybe," I said. "But then why didn't they haul it over to have Clarence check it out? Because that's the first thing any local animal lover would do. Look, if you're still over at Trinity, tell Robyn to put the word out on the parish grapevine to keep an eye out for the cat."

"Will do. By the way, your mother wants to know if you can come to Mutant Wizards at two for a board meeting."

I glanced at the corner of my phone that displayed the time. Nearly noon. I should be able to do the grocery shopping and drag it home by two. Especially since I could delegate putting things away to Rose Noire and Nora.

"I'll be there," I said.

After I exited the Methodist parking lot I was momentarily distracted by spotting a familiar-looking car in my rearview mirror. A dark blue Ford Taurus. Was it the same Taurus Katherine Anne Koenigslutter's lawyer had been driving? Was Sloan following me?

More likely he was scouring the town in search of his client, and if he was doing that, the odds were good that we'd cross paths sooner or later. Though if I were him, I'd try lying in wait near Mutant Wizards. If Ms. Koenigslutter had found out that Ian was staying at our house, she had to know he was working at Mutant Wizards. Maybe I should call Sloan and suggest it.

Then again, he hadn't been particularly receptive to my suggestions earlier. Maybe I should save my advice till I was asked.

I headed over to the Caerphilly Market. Normally I'd have tried to take the boys with me to handle the hauling, but they wouldn't be out of school for a few more hours, and I wanted to get the shopping over with as soon as possible. I had no intention of impeding whatever culinary wonders Nora had planned for this evening.

But it took me longer than planned, so I decided the groceries would have to wait in the car while I attended the board meeting. Instead of heading home I wound my way through the throngs of tourists to the Mutant Wizards building.

And as I passed near the town square, I noticed something odd was afoot. A number of women appeared to be looking frantically for something. Some of them were dressed in the Victorian finery Randall encouraged us all to wear if we were wandering about downtown—to add to the festive Dickensian atmosphere of Christmas in Caerphilly. Some were dressed more suitably for the arctic temperature. Most of them I recognized as members of St. Clotilda's Guild, Trinity Episcopal's main women's organization for carrying out good works. And all of them were looking under shrubbery and into trash cans and generally giving the impression that they'd lost something important.

A lost child, probably. Which would certainly be an emergency in this weather. I pulled over to where one lady I knew from church was searching an overgrown hedge and rolled down my window to ask what was going on and how I could help. I was about to call out to get her attention when—

"Here, kitty-kitty-kitty-kitty!" the woman called, thrusting her head into the hedge again. She was waving a chunk of sardine—even at a distance of six feet I could smell the oily, fishy odor of it.

They were looking for the cat.

The woman extricated herself from the hedge, spotted me, and strode over to my car.

"Robyn's got us looking for a missing cat," she said. "Have you seen one? She's—"

"A yellow striped tabby," I said. "Very small and very pregnant. And no, I haven't seen her since yesterday."

"A pity," she said. "But never mind. We'll find the poor thing, never fear!" She shook the chunk of sardine fiercely, and I winced as a few drops of oil landed on my face.

"Good work," I said, and left her to continue peering into the hedge.

Maybe I'd come back later to help. Then again, if Robyn had enlisted the entire Guild, maybe they didn't need my help.

No, they definitely didn't need my help, I decided, as I spotted two members of the New Life Baptist Choir waving sardines at a hedgerow. If Robyn enlisted the choir on top of the Guild, half the town would soon be searching for the cat.

I arrived at Mutant Wizards at one forty and parked near the front door. As soon as I stepped out of my car into the icy air, any worry I might have had about the groceries spoiling vanished. Things might freeze, but they certainly wouldn't spoil. I did a quick mental inventory to reassure myself that my grocery haul didn't include anything I needed to bring inside to keep warm.

When I stepped inside I took a moment to appreciate the very modern holiday decorations Mother had come up with for the great open space of the Mutant Wizards lobby. Holiday, rather than Christmas, since the staff was pretty multicultural. Rather than work in references to the dozen or so holidays various staff members would be celebrating, Mother picked a favorite color scheme of purple and gold and decked the halls with garlands, ribbons, and banners in one or both of those colors. Employee reactions were mixed—some people missed the usual evergreen and Christmas colors. But every time I stepped inside I could almost imagine a team of trumpets performing a joyous fanfare.

On my way past the reception desk, I stopped to greet Kristyn. She handed me the envelope containing the torn subpoenas with an air of utter nonchalance.

"Mr. Meredith is here," she said. "Senior. Ian's father."

"So soon?"

"He was already in Washington when they reached him,"

she said. "He rented a car and headed down as soon as he heard. He's in with the chief now."

She nodded toward a small glass-fronted conference room off the lobby. The chief's back was to me, so I could see Mr. Meredith. I was relieved to see that he didn't look like an older version of Ian—I think that would have shaken me. He was a small, neat man with a carefully trimmed mustache and thinning gray hair. Older than I'd expected. Or did he just look that way because he was in grief and shock over his son?

"That's why we've gone old-school on the music," Kristyn said, pointing up at the speaker over her head. The soft notes of an orchestral version of "Lo, How a Rose E'er Blooming" emerged from it. The usual holiday fare here at Mutant Wizards ran more to rock or hip-hop, with the occasional addition of "Run, Rudolph, Run" "Jingle Bell Rock," and Bruce Springsteen's version of "Santa Claus Is Comin' to Town" as a nod to the season.

"Thoughtful," I said.

"I just hope we don't have to postpone the big holiday taco feast," Kristyn said. "That's still on for the day after tomorrow, but I'm worried."

"I'll talk to my mother," I said. "If Mr. Meredith is still in town by then, she and I can figure out a plan to keep him away from the office while the feast is going on."

"Great." Kristyn looked relieved.

"I'm going to head up to the conference room," I said.

"Rob's already up there," she said. "And Caroline Willner. I'll page Delaney and send up the others as soon as they get here."

I found Rob in the vast employee lounge indulging in a desultory game of billiards on the black-and-purple pool table.

"Ready for the meeting?" I asked.

"You're breaking the rule, you know." He jerked his head

toward the wall where a large sign said EMPLOYEE LOUNGE: NO SHOP TALK!

"Sorry," I said. "I was going to ask you if Delaney filled you in on all the dirt we found out about Ian, but I don't want to flout corporate policy."

"He really turned into a jerk, didn't he?"

"I think he always was one," I said. "He just stopped pretending."

He nodded and returned to his game. I watched him miss two relatively easy shots in a row—clearly he was troubled.

"See you in the board meeting," I said.

I was about to head for the conference room when I noticed a man and a woman standing by the glass back wall of the room, staring out through binoculars, while another woman was frowning as she flipped through a book. Mutant Wizards employees, I realized, and if I worked at it I might be able to remember their names. I strolled over to see what they were watching.

"I give up," the woman with the book said. "There are just too many nondescript-looking birds."

Her book was a copy of Dad's favorite birding manual. Of course his was battered, well-thumbed, and water-stained while hers was pristine and still had the tip of a sales receipt from the Caerphilly Bookstore sticking up out of its pages like a bookmark.

"Don't worry about the nondescript birds if you're just getting started at bird-watching," I said. "Enjoy the decorative birds like cardinals and blue jays and woodpeckers, and let all the little nondescript brown birds take care of themselves."

"We've got nothing but nondescript birds at the moment," the man said. "Only these aren't brown—they're gray and white."

"You could—wait. Gray and white? May I take a look?"

The man handed me his binoculars. I pointed them at the feeder, adjusted the focus, and suddenly I was looking at the beady black eye of a bird. A bird with a dark gray body and a white belly.

"That," I said, "is a junco. A dark-eyed, slate-colored junco. I will not inflict its Latin name on you." And I hoped they didn't ask, because I couldn't quite recall it. I pulled the binoculars away from my eyes so I could get a broader view of the back garden. The half dozen feeders were swarming with juncos. Dozens of them. "This is good news. Very good news."

"Are they, like, extinct or something?" the woman with the bird book asked.

"No, but the old-timers consider them harbingers of snow," I said. "Our odds of having a white Christmas just got better."

The two with the binoculars began wielding them again with greater enthusiasm. I showed their companion where to find juncos in her manual. She began reading out its description to the others. I left them to it.

As I turned to go to the conference room, I caught sight of a couple of familiar faces—Maeve and Angela. They entered the lounge, then froze, exchanged a few words, and retreated, looking back over their shoulders with anxious expressions.

Odd. Were they hoping to find the lounge empty? Surely they'd been here at Mutant Wizards long enough to know better. More likely, they had spotted someone they wanted to avoid. And at the moment, that would be Rob, the three bird-watchers, or me.

I should definitely check them out more carefully. Search their rooms or interrogate them or maybe ask Kevin to see what he could find.

But that would have to wait until later. I headed for the conference room.

When I entered I found that Caroline had already arrived

and was seated at the conference table doing something on her laptop.

"Blast the man," she exclaimed. She looked irritated, and just a little frazzled. She smiled when she saw me, but then went back to frowning and staring at her computer screen.

"What's wrong?" I asked.

"Your grandfather can be so irritating sometimes."

"No argument," I said. "What's wrong now?"

"Is there a bowling alley in town?"

"A bowling alley?" I echoed. "Actually, there is as of last year. Two of Randall Shiffley's cousins opened one. Does that question have something to do with Grandfather?"

"Unfortunately, yes," she said. "It appears he will be competing in a bowling tournament, if we can organize one."

"Is he an expert bowler?" I asked.

"He doesn't recall ever bowling in his life." She rolled her eyes. "But—and this is a direct quote—'how hard can it be?'"

"Should be interesting," I said. "How did this all come about?"

"He tried to post something on the Facebook page for Blake's Brigade," she said.

I nodded. Blake's Brigade was the informally organized group of nature and environmental enthusiasts who regularly volunteered to help Grandfather whenever he went out to rescue an endangered species, tackle an animal welfare issue, or confront corporate polluters. I hadn't realized they'd set up a Facebook page for themselves, but it wasn't surprising.

"Your grandfather should not be allowed on social media," Caroline went on. "He just did a quick and dirty post asking if anyone wanted to go owling with him, and never noticed that autocorrect changed 'owling' to 'bowling.' And before I noticed it and posted a correction, several dozen people signed up."

"Good grief," I muttered.

"And once I corrected it, we started hearing from any number of people saying how deeply disappointed they were about our canceling the bowling—as if you could cancel something that wasn't even scheduled in the first place. So he told me to go ahead and organize some kind of bowling event. Open to anyone in the Brigade, no cost, but donation to one of the Blake Foundation's environmental projects suggested. Brigade members love events like that. We're sure to get way more donations than it costs to rent a few bowling lanes. Now I just need to figure out how to deal with his other typo, which won't be quite as easy."

"Why?" I asked. "What was the other typo?"

"He intended to say that we'd wrap up the event by singing around a campfire," Caroline said. "I have no idea why autocorrect changed 'campfire' to 'vampire.' Or why anyone would suppose he'd be planning to serenade one. Am I really expected to provide a vampire on top of the bowling?"

"We could see if Dr. Smoot is in town," I suggested. "Remember, he was the local medical examiner before Dad."

"The one who used to show up at crime scenes in fangs and a cape?"

"Yes," I said. "I'm sure he'd be happy to oblige. And Dr. Smoot is passionate about bats. How about if you made it an event to benefit rescuing endangered bats? Assuming there are any."

"Plenty of them." Caroline brightened. "Including several species right here in Virginia—the gray bat, the Indiana bat, and of course the Virginia big-eared bat. Your grandfather's particularly fond of the big-eared bat. What a good idea. Can you find this Dr. Smoot?"

"I'll call him today," I said. "And if he's not in town—he spends a lot of time in Transylvania these days—I'm sure I can find you a substitute vampire. One of Kevin's Dungeons & Dragons players. Or one of Michael's drama students. Or all of the above—the more the merrier. I'm sure we can provide as many vampires as you need."

"Do, please," she said. "A platoon of vampires would annoy your grandfather no end, but he'll shut up and play along if it's to benefit his beloved *Corynorhinus townsendii virginianus*."

"Can you write that down for me, please?" I said as I pulled out my phone to call Dr. Smoot. "It's always easier to calm Grandfather down if you start by throwing a few Latin names at him."

"Of course." She pulled over one of the Mutant Wizards notepads from the middle of the table and scribbled down the name.

Just then the rest of the board members walked in. Mother led the way, followed by Minerva Burke and Uncle Tut. Then Rob scurried in, followed by Delaney. Festus brought up the rear. I scribbled a quick item in my notebook to call Dr. Smoot later and focused on what I hoped would be a typically quick and congenial board meeting.

Chapter 19

"Let the minutes show that I called the meeting to order at two o'clock precisely," Mother said.

Uncle Tut, who was secretary, started, then grabbed a notepad and scribbled a few words on it.

I took a discreet glance at my phone. It was actually two minutes past the hour, but Mother believed that the minutes should uphold a high standard of punctuality, even if her all-too-human board members fell slightly short of it.

"I think by now you've all been briefed on what Festus and Meg have learned about AcerGen." Mother glanced around the table. "They misrepresented their financial position, and they're conducting their DNA operations in a way that could cause serious liability for Mutant Wizards. Festus assures me we have cause to terminate the contract. Does anyone have any questions?"

"Do we know if any of this has anything to do with the murder?" Uncle Tut asked, in his usual blunt manner.

"We don't yet know," Mother said. "While I understand our very able local law enforcement are making rapid progress on the case—"

She gave a gracious nod to Minerva Burke, who returned it in kind.

"We have to remember that Mr. Ian Meredith's body was discovered a mere twelve hours ago," Mother went on. "It would be completely unrealistic to expect a resolution so soon."

"True," Uncle Tut said. "Which gives us a problem— obviously there's going to be speculation whether Meredith's murder has anything to do with his company's operations. And then word gets around that we're dumping them while the murder investigation is still going on? Could have a very negative effect on the company. They might have grounds for an action against us."

"We wouldn't be terminating the contract because of the murder—" Festus began.

"'Course not," Uncle Tut said. "I'm not arguing about whether we should terminate it. I know we have to take a formal vote on it, but it's a no-brainer as far as I'm concerned. It's the timing I worry about. It looks bad for us, like we're kicking them when they're already down."

"If we're going to terminate, the sooner the better," Delaney said. "Every day we wait we spend thousands of dollars— theirs as well as ours—on a project that we now know won't really happen."

"Could cost a whole lot more if they get mad and try to sue us," Uncle Tut said. "And never mind that they probably wouldn't win. They could try, and we'd burn up a lot of legal time making it go away."

"May I make a suggestion?" I said. "Assuming we vote to terminate the contract, we don't have to tell AcerGen, much less the public, right away. Why don't we announce that we're putting the project on hold for the time being. Out of respect for AcerGen's loss, and to allow time to bring a new project leader up to speed, or whatever corporate-speak our lawyers think sounds good."

Festus suppressed a smile at that.

"We'll need to clear it with AcerGen," he said. "But I suspect they'd be agreeable."

"I like it," Delaney said. "Bring everything we're working on to a good stopping point and send the troops home to recuperate and spend the holidays with their families."

"Good solution," Uncle Tut said. "And when the time comes to announce the termination, AcerGen can spin it that without the vision and leadership of their late CEO they no longer want to go forward with the project."

"Exactly." Festus smiled at Uncle Tut. "Shall we offer to let them borrow you to draft the press release?"

"Happy to oblige." Tut leaned back and laced his fingers over his belly.

"Actually, no one who knows Ian will buy that," I said. "They'll all figure out that his death gave the company a good excuse to cut their losses and end what would have been a disastrous project."

"They're welcome to their own interpretation," Festus said. "As long as we're not on record dissing the project."

"Hey, our code would have been outstanding," Rob protested.

"All the more reason you wouldn't have wanted Ian to misuse it," I said.

"Meg's solution will give AcerGen a way to save face," Festus said. "I like it."

"Motion that we terminate the AcerGen contract per our general counsel's advice," Uncle Tut said. "And authorize the chair and the general counsel to carry out Meg's suggestion. I can put that in legalese if you insist."

"Second," Caroline and Minerva said, simultaneously.

"Let's start by voting on the first part," Mother said. "All in favor of terminating the contract?"

"Aye," we all chorused, before she'd actually finished her sentence.

"Now—"

We heard a knock on the door.

"Come in," Mother called, but since the boardroom was well soundproofed, I jumped up to open the door and see who was there.

It was Kristyn. She looked solemn—almost anxious. Unusual for her.

"Mr. Meredith's here," she said. "Mr. Gordon Meredith. He heard the board was in session, and wanted to know if he could speak to you."

I glanced back at Mother.

"Of course," she said. "Meg, show him in."

So I opened the door a little wider and Kristyn gestured for Ian's father to go in.

Mr. Meredith walked in and stood for a moment, glancing around the room before taking the chair I had pulled out, at the end of the table closest to the door. He looked as if even walking was an effort, and I couldn't decide whether he was suffering from some kind of physical weakness or whether he was just weighed down with grief. Probably a little of both. He was definitely older than I expected—clearly he hadn't become a father at a young age. He smiled slightly as Mother introduced—or reintroduced—the various members of the board.

"Thank you for seeing me on such short notice," he said.

"Of course," Mother said. "We're so sorry for your loss."

"Thank you," Mr. Meredith said. "I know Ian's stay here wasn't entirely tranquil—"

"But all of that is water under the bridge," Mother said, waving her hand as if shooing away a flock of pesky gnats. "I can only imagine how terrible this is for you. I assure you, we're all doing everything we can to help Chief Burke apprehend the guilty party. And if there's anything we can do for you, please let us know."

"Actually, there is something." Mr. Meredith looked uncomfortable.

Mother clasped her hands and leaned forward, as if nothing in the world could keep her from making his slightest wish come true. I hoped he wasn't about to beg for us to keep the joint project moving ahead on schedule.

"I'm not quite sure how to explain this," he said. "But . . . well, I've decided I don't altogether approve of DNA. Not DNA itself, of course—nothing wrong with science—but the fad for consumer DNA testing."

I liked the sound of that.

"A lot of good things are coming out of the explosion of interest in DNA," Rob said. "Dangerous criminals being caught. John and Jane Does being identified so their families get closure."

"Yes," Mr. Meredith said. "Those can be good things. Although even the use of DNA by law enforcement has its perils. I understand from my conversation with Chief Burke just now that one of the chief suspects in my son's murder is a man who was convicted of a previous murder in large part due to familial DNA that AcerGen provided."

Most of my fellow board members nodded, even those I suspected might not yet know that much about Cyrus Runk. I had a feeling we'd be doing an in-depth briefing as soon as Mr. Meredith was out of earshot. Unless Mother had already taken care of that. And maybe this wasn't a good time to mention our suspicions that AcerGen—or Ian, as its CEO— had brought on their own problems by violating their privacy policy in the Runk case. But didn't we have to bring it up eventually? Evidently Festus had the same idea.

"Providing data to law enforcement isn't usually a feature that comes under the heading of consumer DNA testing," he pointed out. "You could establish a corporate policy against releasing any data except to the owner of the DNA."

"I rather thought we had." Mr. Meredith's tone revealed a note of dry precision that I liked. I suspected he'd have been good to work with when he wasn't in mourning—in mourning and maybe even still in shock. "It was news to me that we were letting law enforcement search our databases," he went on. "And not good news. I was actually planning to have a frank discussion with Ian today on that very issue—that's why I came down to Washington last night."

More nods around the table.

"But it's not just that we shouldn't be sharing DNA with law enforcement," Mr. Meredith went on. "I'm starting to think maybe we shouldn't be in the DNA business at all. It has so much potential for tearing families apart."

"But what about—" Rob began. Then he subsided, probably because both Mother, on his right, and Festus, on his left, had each placed a hand gently but firmly on his arm.

Mr. Meredith didn't even seem to notice the interruption.

"We're already dealing with one lawsuit—we put a woman in touch with her half brother, who has apparently turned out to be a dangerous sociopath."

Evidently he'd heard about the elusive Katherine Anne Koenigslutter.

"How many more families will be ripped apart when old secrets are revealed by DNA?" he went on. "People will find out that their spouses were unfaithful. Children will learn about their parents' misdeeds. What about women who gave up babies for adoption and were promised confidentiality? Couples who conceived through sperm or egg donations and didn't want to tell their children? Children whose parents chose not to tell them they were adopted?"

"Those are certainly potential unwanted consequences of making DNA information available to the consumer." Festus's tone was careful.

"It tore our family apart," Mr. Meredith said. "We never told Ian he was adopted. I didn't exactly think that was a wise decision, but the idea of telling him upset my wife so much that I went along with her preference. When he found out a few years ago—thanks to DNA testing—he was very angry. He thought we'd betrayed him in some way. I don't think he ever forgave us."

We all sat in silence. I wished I could think of something to say. But nothing I could think of was likely to comfort Mr. Meredith. Maybe hiding Ian's adoption from him was unwise. But no matter how negative Ian's reaction was to finding out, was tearing the family apart necessarily the result? Of course, I had nothing like that in my experience. Dad had known all along that he'd been adopted as an infant. He had adored the Langslows, his adoptive parents—he didn't love them any the less because he didn't share DNA with them. And he didn't honor their memories any the less when he later found Grandfather and Cordelia—thanks to DNA. The only effect being adopted seemed to have on him was to make him more tolerant—in fact, downright appreciative—of Mother's enormous family.

Maybe he'd have reacted negatively if he hadn't learned the truth until he was an adult.

Then again, Dad was Dad, and Ian was Ian.

"And what's been happening with the company is partly my fault," Mr. Meredith was saying. "Largely my fault. I knew he wasn't really ready to run the company. I knew I should have kept more control. But whenever we disagreed over something, he'd throw his adoption in my face. He seemed to have the crazy idea that I didn't trust or respect him because he wasn't my biological son. That's just not true. I was only reluctant because he didn't yet have the maturity or the experience to run the company. But I let him anyway. Because he's my son. And it was either that or continue to have our family torn apart."

We all sat in silence for an eternity while Mr. Meredith visibly struggled to control his feelings. I wasn't sure whether to hope he didn't break down and cry—or hope he did, because maybe he needed to.

And I found myself thinking that if Ian hadn't known about his adoption—if he hadn't even been adopted at all—he'd have found something else to throw in his parents' faces. Something to make them feel guilty and get his own way. But I didn't think Mr. Meredith would want to hear that.

Festus finally broke the silence.

"The project AcerGen and Mutant Wizards are engaged in is directly related to your company's planned expansion in the consumer DNA market," he said. "Are you suggesting that you no longer wish to pursue it?"

His tone was carefully neutral. I was glad he was the one doing the talking. I couldn't have kept the "yippee!" out of my voice.

"That's exactly what I'm suggesting," Mr. Meredith said. "I was already uncomfortable about some of the problems that were starting to happen because of our involvement in consumer DNA testing—already thinking we should have stuck to genealogy. And now that damned DNA testing has contributed to the death of my son. My only child. I don't want anything to do with it. I want to kill the project. Immediately. I know this request probably comes as an unpleasant surprise to you—I've been very impressed with the talent Mutant Wizards has brought to the project and the progress you've already made. I'm sure you'd deliver an excellent product for us. But we don't need it any longer. I'm taking us out of the consumer DNA testing market."

I glanced around the table and was impressed with everyone else's poker faces. They were all looking sad and sympathetic, with no sign of the immense relief they must be feeling.

Festus glanced at Mother, who nodded slightly.

"I think we all understand how you feel," he said.

"I know what a disappointment this must be," Mr. Meredith went on. "And I don't want Mutant Wizards to be the loser in this. Can we . . ." His voice trailed off.

"Mr. Meredith," Mother said. "I think we completely understand your concerns. Understand, and perhaps even share them. Why don't we agree in principle to terminate the contract, and let our attorneys work out the details? In a way that minimizes the negative impact on both of our companies."

"Thank you." Mr. Meredith looked relieved. "I'm just concerned that . . . do you think we can wrap this up relatively soon? I'd like to bring my people home for Christmas."

Okay, it was definite. I liked this man.

Festus nodded slightly.

"Meg, I think you had an idea about that," Mother said.

"I already suggested putting the project on hold," I said. "We tell the employees of both companies that it's just for the time being. To give everyone involved time to grieve and recover from the shock. And spend some time with their families over the holidays."

"And once we've had time to work out the details, we break the news to both sets of employees that the project has been canceled," Mr. Meredith said. "Perfect."

He beamed at me, looking—just for a moment—almost cheerful.

"Assuming Chief Burke is okay with having a dozen of his witnesses leave town before the investigation's over," Uncle Tut said, glancing at Minerva Burke, who nodded slightly.

"I rather got the impression that he's identified the culprit," Mr. Meredith said. "And it's only a case of apprehending him."

"Here's hoping," Rob said.

"I'm sure Henry will do everything he can to avoid spoiling everyone's holidays," Minerva said.

"Just to keep things official," Festus said. "Would someone like to make a motion to authorize me, as your general counsel, to negotiate with AcerGen to determine the terms for ending the project?"

"So moved," Caroline said.

"Second," Minerva put in.

"All in favor?" Mother asked.

We all gave our ayes with a suitable show of dignified regret, as if we hadn't already done so a few minutes before. I tried to make mine sound bittersweet and reluctant this time instead of relieved.

Mr. Meredith beamed as if we'd all just done him an enormous favor. And maybe we had.

"I can't thank you enough," he said. "Any chance we could work later today on what to tell both sets of employees? I can get my attorneys on the phone any time."

"How about if I meet you downstairs in the project office as soon as we finish the rest of our meeting agenda?" Festus suggested. "It won't take long."

"That would be perfect." Mr. Meredith stood. "I'm sure I can find my way."

But Kristyn was still waiting outside the door, so I could turn him over to her to escort downstairs.

I shut the door behind him and heard the room's other seven occupants breathe simultaneous sighs of relief.

Chapter 20

"That went better than we had any right to expect," Uncle Tut said.

"Anything in particular I should insist on in our negotiations?" Festus asked.

"We keep all the code we've written," Delaney said promptly. "With no constraints on what we do with it. Some of what we came up with is pretty sharp—we might be able to sell it to some other company. One that's staying in the DNA business."

"One of AcerGen's former competitors, you mean," Festus said. "Shouldn't be a problem."

"And make sure there's nothing in the agreement that prevents us from hiring any of their ex-employees," Delaney added. "Not that we want to steal their whole staff, but I'd like to be able to tell a couple of their people that if canceling the project eliminates their jobs or makes them less interesting, our doors are open."

Festus nodded.

"If there's nothing else on our agenda," Mother said.

"A motion to adjourn is always in order," Uncle Tut said. "So moved."

"Second," Caroline and I both said.

"All in favor?"

Another relieved round of ayes.

"I don't have to tell you to keep this confidential for now," Mother said. "Thank you all."

The board members began drifting out. Well, Delaney and Rob dashed out, since for now they had to at least pretend to be moving full steam ahead with the project, and Festus followed on their heels to start his meeting with Mr. Meredith and the AcerGen attorneys. Caroline, Uncle Tut, and Minerva strolled out together, apparently brainstorming on things they could organize to amuse the assembled relatives and visiting Canadians until the skating rink was available again. I stopped myself from suggesting that the relatives had managed to survive any number of rinkless visits in the past. And that the Canadians might not be in the mood for amusement. No sense in discouraging anyone who would make my life easier by entertaining the multitudes.

I looked over at Mother, who seemed to be scrutinizing the décor of the boardroom. Decorating was to Mother what my notebook was to me—a source of comfort when she felt stressed. A very present help in time of trouble, as she would put it.

But surely the results of our meeting should make her less stressed, not more.

"Having second thoughts about anything we just did?" I asked.

"No, dear," she said. "Just hoping we can announce the project halt this afternoon."

"Worried about Rob's ability to keep a poker face?" I asked.

"He does take after your father in that respect." Mother's

fond tone softened the words a bit. But she was right. I hoped Festus would hurry.

"I just can't help thinking how relieved I'll be when the Canadians are all safely back at home," she said.

"Are you worried that they're in danger?" I asked. "Or that they are a danger?"

"Either," she said. "Both. I can't imagine any of them as the killer, but then they've been here less than a week. We really don't know them very well, do we?"

"No." I shook my head. "Of course, it's hard to think of a motive that any of them would have for killing Ian."

"Not that hard if you ask me." She frowned at me as if disappointed in my lack of imagination. "All three of the young women in the group are quite personable. Well, so are the older ladies, but I don't see Ian as someone who's apt to be attracted to an older woman. What if Ian has been harassing one or more of them?"

"Quite possible." Perhaps she had also noticed how inseparable Maeve, Angela, and Rhea were. They seemed like friends—now, anyway. Had their friendship started out of Rhea's need for protection?

"And of course any of the young men could be interested in one of his colleagues," Mother went on. "And resentful of Ian's attentions to them."

"That's a possibility," I said. "I think it's more likely that the killer is someone from outside. Someone with a grudge."

"Against Ian?" Mother asked. "Or against AcerGen?"

"That's the problem, isn't it?" I said. "If someone has a grudge against Ian, mission accomplished. Ian is no more. We can all relax. But if their grudge is against AcerGen, what if killing Ian doesn't satisfy them?"

"Then the rest of the Canadians would be their logical targets. I think the sooner we send them home the better."

"Yes," I said. "But I just thought of something. Maybe we

shouldn't announce the project halt until the chief is okay with sending them home. Right now they mostly spend all day here together in that great big open room, and then they all come home to our house at night. Safety in numbers. But if we cancel the project before the chief lets them leave, they'll have all the time in the world to wander off."

"Getting into trouble or causing it." She nodded. "I'll talk to Festus. Thank you, dear. That's a very good point."

"I hope by the time the chief lets the Canadians leave I can come up with a good reason for them to take all their stuff with them," I said. "If they think they're coming back, they're going to want to leave it all the way it is and we'll eventually have the hassle of packing it up for them."

"You could say that it would be nice if you could use the bedrooms for family members over the holidays," Mother suggested.

"That would work," I said. "You don't think it sounds a little cold?"

"It sounds very practical," she said. "I can't imagine they would quarrel with practical."

"And if we emphasize that the timetable for their return hasn't been worked out yet, maybe most of them will want to take their stuff with them."

"I know—we can tell them they have to pack up their things because while they're gone we will be negotiating to get them rooms at the Caerphilly Inn." Mother's tone was triumphant. "Not that you haven't been making them perfectly comfortable, but the Inn! They will have bathrooms en suite! And room service!"

"And it's much closer to the office."

"They can use the spa!" Mother exclaimed. "They will have access to a restaurant with two Michelin stars!"

"Which might possibly measure up to what Cousin Nora can provide," I said.

"The use of the golf course!"

"You do remember that this isn't real, don't you?" I said, starting to feel a little anxious. "That they won't really be coming back and staying at the Inn."

"Of course, dear," she said. "I'm getting into the right frame of mind to convince them."

Who knew that Mother was a Method actor?

"Good idea, then," I said.

"I'll go have a word with Festus."

"Before you go," I said. "Can you translate some French for me?" It had suddenly occurred to me that I had never found the time to get anyone to translate the results of my eavesdropping on Claudine. I'd sent it to the chief, along with my recordings of Ian, but I had no idea if he spoke French. Or, for that matter, if anyone in the department did. What if Claudine's words revealed some important clue?

"I'd be happy to translate." Mother held out her hand as if expecting me to hand her a document.

"Spoken French." I pulled out my phone, opened the voice recorder app and began to play back the recording I'd made of Claudine.

She frowned as if concentrating, then held up her finger. I interpreted that as a request to stop, so I pressed the PAUSE button.

"It's a little muffled," she said.

"I was eavesdropping at the time," I said. "Want me to rewind?"

She nodded. I started the recording over. This time she listened intently to the end, then looked up.

"Do you need a word-for-word translation?"

"Probably not," I said. "The gist will do."

"She was chastising someone for giving out her cell phone number to disgruntled AcerGen clients," Mother said. "Evidently the person on the other end denied doing so, at which she exclaimed that someone was, and yes, it was probably Ian. And then she went on a rather impassioned rant about the incompetence of the laboratory Ian Meredith had chosen to process their customers' DNA test kits. Apparently the lab wasn't even capable of keeping the labels on the test tubes straight—they'd switched the label from a Polish Canadian man's sample with one from an Afro-Cuban woman—"

"Good grief," I muttered. "If they can't even keep the labels straight, who knows how incompetently they're processing the samples."

"Exactly what she said, dear. She said the only honest thing to do would be to refund their clients' money and let them get a new DNA test from a reputable provider. And then she ended by saying she didn't care—maybe AcerGen *should* be driven out of business."

"Wow," I said. "Reassures me that we just made the right decision."

"Yes, dear." She shook her head. "Let's be very tactful in front of Rob, though. He was so proud of finding this project. Oh, one other thing Claudine said—she asked whoever she was talking to if they knew who Elias Boyd was."

"And did they know?"

"Evidently not. Do we know?"

"Not yet," I said.

She smiled at that.

"Although Ian may have mentioned the name in one of the conversations I overhead," I said. "But with no context, and I'd almost forgotten about it."

"She said it didn't matter, that it was probably just another of Ian's stupidities, and time would tell. And now I must talk to Festus. And then I'm going over to your house to add some mistletoe to the decorations, now that it's safe to do so. I didn't want to have any around your house before—not with that . . . impertinent young man around. But that's no longer a problem, is it?"

She sailed out, full of purpose again.

I sat for a minute or two. I was disappointed—I was hoping my eavesdropping on Claudine would reveal some new bit of evidence that would help the chief solve his case. If the name Elias Boyd was that new evidence, it wasn't exactly obvious to me. I'd sic Kevin on it.

"Find out who Elias Boyd is," I texted him.

"In what context?" he texted back.

"No idea," I answered.

He didn't reply to that, and I decided I'd save lengthy explanations for later.

I'd make sure the chief knew the name. And it was always possible that some nuance of what Claudine said would be useful to Festus if the AcerGen attorneys proved less amenable to the termination than Mr. Meredith. I forwarded the audio recording to Festus just in case. I was almost tempted to call Katherine Anne Koenigslutter's attorney and share the information with him. Reiterate my suggestion to have new tests done for both his client and the half brother she wanted to disown.

I'd worry about it if he showed up again. Or if she did.

I stayed in my chair for a few minutes. It was a very comfortable chair, and I knew that as soon as I left it, I'd need to drive home and deal with the immense load of groceries in the Twinmobile. Plus all the usual stresses of keeping peace and harmony in a house filled with a more diverse than usual batch of houseguests. I closed my eyes and began to take what Rose Noire called balancing breaths.

I was in the middle of my third breath when my phone rang. I glanced at the caller ID: Chief Burke.

So much for balance.

Chapter 21

"Good afternoon," I said. "Dare I hope that you're calling to tell me that you've arrested Ian Meredith's killer and we can have our skating rink back?"

"Well, I have a call in to Horace to see if he agrees that we can release the skating rink," he said. "You should have it back later today. But I'm afraid that's the extent of my good news."

"So is that all your news, period?" I asked. "Or do you also have bad news?"

"Not entirely bad news," he said. "Interesting news. Horace found fingerprints on the hockey stick."

"That's good news, isn't it?" I asked. "Unless they're Josh's fingerprints."

"They're not Josh's fingerprints, and we got a hit on them."

"In CODIS?"

"No," he said. "CODIS is DNA. For fingerprints you go to AFIS. We got a hit in AFIS."

"Don't tell Kevin I mixed them up," I said. "I should know better, and he'd never let me forget it. So who do the fingerprints belong to?"

"Cyrus Runk."

"Cyrus Runk?" I repeated. "I thought he was in prison."

"They had to let him out of prison when the court overturned the guilty verdict," the chief said. "By rights he should be in jail awaiting his retrial. But his attorney got him out on bail."

"Bet they'll revoke that when they find out he's been up here committing another murder," I said.

"They already revoked it when he failed to show up for a routine hearing yesterday morning." His voice sounded grim. "And when they went to fetch him, he'd taken off. There's been a three-state BOLO out on him since noon yesterday."

Since I regularly listened to Kevin's true crime podcast, I knew this meant that police in three states had been warned to be on the lookout for Runk.

"That's not good," I said. "Not the BOLO, of course—I'm all in favor of that. Not good that he's up here leaving fingerprints."

"No. Look, I can send you a picture of him—"

"I already know what he looks like," I said. "I looked him up online."

"Then keep your eyes open for him," the chief said. "Chances are he's long gone from here. I mean, logically, he should want to put as much distance as possible between himself and a murder."

"But he might not be a logical kind of guy," I said. "And what if he's got a grudge against the AcerGen staff in general? And wants to knock off a few more of them while he's here?"

"That notion had occurred to me," he said. "I've already assigned two deputies to guard the remaining Canadians. And we'll be getting some state troopers along with a few loaner deputies from Goochland and Essex Counties, both to take on some of the guard duty and to help us locate Runk. But if you see anybody you think looks even the least bit like him, call nine-one-one immediately."

"I will," I said. "Thanks for the heads-up. And by the way, since I have you on the phone—Minerva will fill you in on the details, but we're working out an agreement with AcerGen to put the big joint project on hold. Of course, once we do that, the Canadians will probably want to go home. Am I correct in deducing that you'd be okay with having them leave town?"

"I'd actually be relieved," he said. "I haven't definitively cleared all eleven of them, but it's not as if we don't have an extradition treaty with Canada. And they're pretty darned low on my suspect list, given that we know about both Runk and that woman who's suing AcerGen for mishandling her private information."

"Katherine Anne Koenigslutter," I said.

"Yes. We know she was here in town, too. And it beats me how either of them found out Mr. Meredith was here in the first place. I know there hasn't been any real publicity either locally or nationally—gossip, sure, but you'd only hear that if you were already in town."

"Social media?"

"No dice. I've had Sammy and Aida checking, since they're both pretty savvy about things like that. Most of the AcerGen staff are on social media, of course, and some of them have posted about how sad they are that they have to be away from home for the holidays, but none of them have said a word about where they were going. And anyone following Mr. Meredith's social media in the weeks leading up to his trip here would assume he was going to someplace tropical. Florida, or even some Caribbean island. You've never seen so many pictures of palm trees, sandy beaches, and piña coladas."

"Yeah, he was kind of clueless about geography," I said. "He was constantly complaining about the cold weather and the fact that we were over a hundred miles from the nearest beach. As if it was our fault he can't read a map. Unless—"

A wild thought struck me and I stopped to consider it.

"Unless what?" the chief prompted.

"Unless he was deliberately being obtuse about our weather. What if he wanted to make sure no one knew where he was. You have to admit it's pretty odd that none of the other eleven Canadians posted anything about where they were."

"Several of them mentioned that they were under orders not to. The only explanation they'd been given was that management didn't want the competition to find out their plans for the new, improved website."

"Somehow I don't think the competition's monitoring AcerGen's every move," I said. "I'm not even sure they know AcerGen exists. I bet Ian knew someone was after him and was using the project with Mutant Wizards as an excuse to disappear for a while."

The chief didn't say anything for what seemed like a long time.

"That's an interesting idea," he said. "And I don't mean that in the sense your mother uses the word. Even some of the AcerGen employees were skeptical about the idea that revealing their presence in Caerphilly would give away any big corporate secrets. But they complied, mainly because, as one of the young men put it, they didn't want Ian to go berserk. He rolled his eyes when he said it, as if he thought Mr. Meredith was being . . . overly dramatic."

"But maybe he wasn't," I said. "He told them the reason for keeping their whereabouts secret was to avoid corporate espionage. But what if in reality . . ."

I didn't have to finish the sentence. Obviously someone had given away the secret. Cyrus Runk and Katherine Anne

Koenigslutter had found Ian. Had they found out separately? Or were they in league together? In league—the term conjured up a bizarre vision of an organized group of people who felt themselves wronged by Ian and AcerGen. How many potential members did it have aside from Runk and Koenigslutter?

"I'm going to reinterview the Canadians before I give them permission to leave town," the chief said. "See if any of them can suggest any way that Mr. Meredith's presence here could have leaked out."

"Incidentally," I said, "Mother just informed me that she considers it safe to add some mistletoe to our holiday decorations, now that Ian is no longer in residence. Do you think there's any possibility his history of sexual harassment could have provoked someone to kill him?"

I was rather proud of how I'd phrased that—it sounded as if I knew chapter and verse about Ian's misdeeds.

"The woman who filed the complaint against him is definitely in Toronto," he said. "And was last night as well, so she's out. Of course, there could be others, but the general consensus is that he was more of a pest than a menace. And when Mr. Meredith senior heard about the sexual harassment complaint he had strong words with his son and issued an unwritten order that no woman employee was to be left alone with him. Apparently they operate on a sort of buddy system."

"I'd noticed that," I said. "Anyone else would have been fired."

"And maybe anyone else would still be alive," the chief said. "The sexual harassment angle isn't my prime theory of the crime, but I'm not overlooking it. If you come across any information on that front, share."

"Will do," I said. "Oh, by the way—you may have noticed that one of the audio recordings I forwarded you was in French.

Until I had Mother listen to it just now I had no idea what was on it—"

"Neither did I until Minerva translated it for me," he said.

"Then you already know Claudine was asking about someone named Elias Boyd."

"I do, and I'm already trying to figure out who the dickens he is and whether he has anything to do with Mr. Meredith's demise."

"Bother," I said. "I was hoping you already knew. And I just wanted to apologize for not warning you about the French."

"No harm done," he said. "And if you or Kevin learn anything about Mr. Boyd's identity—"

"We'll share."

"Thank you," he said. "I know maybe it's unrealistic, but I would really like to wrap this investigation up soon. I think we'll all have a merrier Christmas if we don't have an unsolved murder hanging over our heads."

"Amen," I said.

After we hung up I pondered for a few minutes. Maybe interviewing the Canadians would help the chief find out how his enemies had found their way to Ian. I had a better idea.

I sent a quick text to Kevin.

"Want to help the chief solve Ian's murder?" it said. "Find out how Runk and Koenigslutter knew he was here in town."

I was in the elevator on my way down to the lobby when his answer came in.

"Been working on it already. So far, nada."

Rats. I'd been hoping either that Kevin already knew, or that the answer was so easy I could have found it myself if I'd been at my laptop. Ah, well. At least Kevin was on the case.

I stopped by the front desk to thank Kristyn for her tactful handling of Mr. Meredith.

"Mr. Meredith senior seems like a very nice man," she said. "All the AcerGen people seem very fond of him."

I nodded.

"So maybe this is completely out of line," she said. "But do you think the chief has checked his alibi?"

"You think he could have killed his son?" I asked.

"No," she said. "He seems like the least likely suspect imaginable. But isn't that who always turns out to be the killer?"

"In books it is." Maybe I should ask if Dad had been lending her reading material. Most of my family were book enablers. "I think in real life the most obvious suspect often turns out to be the guilty one."

"Real life is dreadfully overrated," she said. "But think about it—he drove down here this morning."

"From Washington, yes," I said. "A two-hour drive—maybe two and a half."

"Actually, from the Hyatt Regency near Dulles Airport," Kristyn said. "He mentioned that when I asked if he was staying in town. And staying that far out of the city could cut at least half an hour off the drive. More like an hour if you were doing a round trip."

"He's a bit frail, and not exactly a spring chicken," I said. "If you ask me, the drive down here today almost did him in."

"The drive down here today?" she asked. "Or having to make it a third time in twenty-four hours?"

She might have a point.

"You really suspect him?" I asked.

She thought for a moment.

"My gut feeling is that he's just what he seems," she said. "A nice old man who's racked with grief. But that's not proof. I mean, isn't that what people always say when the police arrest some really horrible killer—that he seemed nice and quiet and they never would have suspected him?"

"But you do suspect him," I pointed out.

"Because he seems so unlikely," she said. "What if Mr. Meredith was torn between his love for his son and his knowl-

edge that Ian was up to no good and was going to ruin the
company he'd built and the lives of some of the employees
he also loved. Some of them have worked for him for over
twenty years."

Maeve and Angela, probably.

"So you think Mr. Meredith senior came down here to do
away with Ian for the good of his company and of the rest of
humanity?"

"No," she said. "Of course not. But what if he came down
here to reason with him—or even to fire him as CEO. And
they got into an argument and that turned into a fight and
Ian ended up dead."

"Tell the chief," I said. "Because even if your theory sounds
completely bonkers—"

"I was afraid you'd say that," she said with a sigh.

"Stuff that sounds bonkers has happened before," I said.
"Besides, if you can think of it, so can a good defense attorney, which means it would be a good idea to prove it impossible long before the real killer goes on trial."

"Ooh." She brightened. "So you think it might be useful?
I'll tell him when he leaves."

"Do we know if Mr. Meredith is going all the way back to
Dulles tonight?"

"No." She shook her head. "Your mother arranged for him
to stay with the Reverend Robyn."

"Perfect." If Mr. Meredith felt any need for spiritual con-
solation, the rector of Trinity would be the perfect person to
provide it. And if he didn't, she wouldn't try to foist it on him,
and would ply him with tea and homemade cookies instead.

As I headed out to the Twinmobile, I glanced up at the sky
and was surprised.

"It looks like snow," I said, to no one in particular.

The sky had turned that peculiar shade of gray, somewhere
between leaden and luminous, that almost always predicted

snowfall. My spirits soared—maybe the juncos were right and we'd be having a white Christmas after all. I checked my weather app. Apparently the weather service had raised the likelihood of snow to 60 percent. I felt a sudden urge to drop by Flugleman's Feed Store to see what the old-timers were saying. Most of the time their aching knees and shoulders were a lot more accurate than the weather service.

Of course, I already had the expert testimony of the town juncos, I reminded myself. And now I was curious to see if the many feeders now surrounding our house had attracted their own flocks of gray-and-white birds. So I climbed into my car.

As I headed for the exit I spotted a familiar car parked at the far side of the parking lot—the dark blue Taurus. And this time I was pretty sure it belonged to Sloan, the lawyer—I caught a brief glimpse of his blond head popping up in the driver's side window and then disappearing again. Evidently he was crouching down in the car and peeking out whenever he heard a vehicle pass. Hoping to spot his client, I deduced. I refrained from waving, since I assumed he was trying to be unobtrusive. Instead, I silently wished him luck.

When I pulled out into traffic I found myself following a small car with a very large Christmas tree lashed to its roof. And not all that well lashed—the tree trembled alarmingly whenever the car's speed reached twenty miles an hour. I had plenty of time to observe this, since we seemed to be following the same route through the outskirts of town.

Not a problem. I relaxed and did my best to enjoy the slow trip through town. Even though we still had some time before sunset, it was getting dark already, thanks to the solid cloud cover overhead, and everyone's holiday lights were on. Twinkling red-and-green lights. Dignified plain white lights. The occasional flash of blue and silver for Hanukkah. And I had to cheer the occasional rebel display of nothing but purple or every color in the rainbow.

And the Guild and the choir were still hard at work searching for the missing cat. Every block seemed to contain a few pairs of searchers, waving sardines or catnip toys, and most of them already armed with flashlights. I hoped they wouldn't keep it up if it started snowing. If the cat was this hard to find, maybe she'd already found a safe, warm shelter for the night.

A few blocks away from the Mutant Wizards building I encountered another harbinger of snow—Osgood Shiffley in his snowplow, trundling toward me in the opposite lane. As usual, he'd decorated the plow for Christmas, with a huge fiberglass reindeer mounted on the hood—although he hadn't yet hooked up the wires for the flashing red light on the reindeer's nose. He'd probably do that when he had something to plow—for now, he was probably taking his plow to whatever he considered the best starting position for what would no doubt be a long night of road clearing. I kept my eyes open, hoping to see Osgood's cousin Beau, the driver of the county's other snowplow. He wouldn't be hard to spot, since he decked his plow with at least a dozen strings of blinking multicolored lights.

A good thing I was bringing home plenty of groceries—I wouldn't want to be going out in the storm that I now considered almost a certainty. Osgood and his cousin Beau were also much better predictors of the local snowfall potential than the weather service.

We'd be having a white Christmas after all. And with any luck, a Christmas free of discontented visiting Canadians. Should I feel guilty for wanting them gone? Or happy that they were getting what I was sure they wanted?

I glanced in my rearview mirror, partly to watch Osgood chugging off into the distance and partly to make sure I wasn't collecting a rear guard of impatient tourists. Then I noticed the car behind me. A white Toyota Corolla. At least I was reasonably sure it was a Corolla. It was pretty small, and I could see the blue-and-silver Toyota emblem on the hood.

Was that what Katherine Anne Koenigslutter had been driving when she cruised by our house? Or was she in a silver Corolla? I couldn't remember. And in this light it was hard to tell the difference anyway.

I told myself not to be silly—there had to be millions of Corollas on the road, many of them white or silver. A few of them were bound to end up in Caerphilly.

That thought reassured me—until I reached the outskirts of town and took the road that led out into the country, toward home. The Corolla was still behind me, though it seemed to be deliberately leaving as much distance as possible between us. Trying not to be seen?

I broke my rule against using my phone while driving. When I got to a nice, straight stretch, I slowed down until I was only going about twenty miles an hour. And I called 911.

Chapter 22

"What's your emergency, Meg?" Debbie Ann asked.

"I don't know if it's an emergency," I said. "But I'm being followed by a Toyota Corolla—I can't tell if it's silver or white, but—"

"Where are you?"

"About two miles from my house," I said.

"Horace and Vern are both on their way," she said after the briefest of pauses. "I would ask if it looked like the same Corolla that was lurking in your neighborhood last night, but you'd only remind me that one car looks like another to you."

"Especially if they're both compact Japanese cars," I said. "I'm going to drive past my house. I can go all the way to where the road dead-ends and turn around. That will give Horace and Vern more time to get to the house before I have to get out of my car."

"Good idea," she said. "And stay on the line."

I deposited the phone in the little gadget designed to keep

it in view when I was using it to navigate by and drove on. Behind me the Corolla appeared over a hill and slowed down drastically.

I reported this to Debbie Ann.

"Not reassuring," she said.

I agreed.

I cruised sedately by the house. Not many cars there, and no humans in sight—not surprising, given the temperature, but it made my plan of driving on by seem all the wiser. I continued, well below the speed limit, until I reached where the road dead-ended at Caerphilly Creek. There was plenty of room to turn around, either in the parking lot of the Spare Attic or that of the Haven. The Spare Attic was self-service, like many storage facilities, so there was rarely anyone there. The Haven, which housed several dozen young Mutant Wizards employees, was a more likely prospect. If I'd seen any signs of life there I might have stopped, confident that its inhabitants would come to my aid. But this time of day most of them would still be at the office. And for that matter, although the place looked infinitely nicer than it had in its former life as a disreputable motel, it still wasn't exactly a garden spot, and its residents tended to spend most of their free time in town.

So I turned around and headed back the way I'd come. Half a mile from the dead end, I encountered the Toyota. Definitely white rather than silver. But also definitely following me. The driver braked hard when she spotted me. I only caught a brief glimpse, but I was pretty sure it was a woman.

"I just passed my stalker," I said. "She was definitely not happy to see me."

"Horace is at your house," Debbie Ann said. "Go ahead and park right beside his patrol car."

"Will do."

The house came into view. Horace's cruiser was in the driveway, in the spot closest to town. The spot my cousins had removed Ian's car from less than twenty-four hours ago. I parked in the spot closest to the house, leaving an empty space between us, so I could give Horace plenty of maneuvering room.

I waved at Horace. He nodded at me.

"Should I just stay here or what?" I asked Debbie Ann.

"Stay in your vehicle until the Corolla arrives."

It wasn't long, actually. The Corolla appeared in the distance. It seemed to speed up when it got near—speed up and then swoop into the middle parking space. Almost as soon as it came to a stop, the driver's-side door—which was on my side of her car—flew open. A woman scrambled out, covered the short distance between our two vehicles, and plastered herself against the Twinmobile's passenger-side window. Both of her palms were flat against the glass, and her face was almost touching it. She began shouting.

"Where is he? I need to see him! Where is he? I know he's here!"

Horace appeared behind her. I figured he'd keep her busy on that side of the car, so I cracked my driver's-side window so I could hear better.

"Put your hands in the air and step away from the SUV," Horace was saying. "Ma'am! Put your hands in the air!"

The woman ignored him.

"I know he's in there!" She began beating on my window with her right fist. "You can't keep us apart." She bent down, picked up one of the baseball-sized rocks that outlined the driveway area, and lifted it as if to smash the window.

Vern appeared at Horace's side. The two exchanged a glance. Vern nodded. The two of them stepped forward, and each grabbed one of the woman's arms.

She seemed startled, and struggled a bit, dropping the rock. But within a minute they had her handcuffed and sitting on the ground behind her car, with Vern standing guard over her.

I got out, the better to kibbitz on what happened next. She'd left the car door open. Horace was standing outside the car, peering inside, but not touching anything. I was about to ask why he was just standing there, when it came to me. She was a murder suspect. The contents of her car could be evidence. He wasn't going to rush in and risk having that evidence thrown out of court.

"You can't do this to me!" she was shouting. "It's not fair! I wasn't doing anything."

"You were following me, and when I stopped you started yelling at me and pounding on my car," I said. "Sorry, Vern," I said. "I shouldn't be butting in."

"No harm," Vern said. "We're just waiting to see if the chief wants us to search her car."

"You do not have my permission to search my car!" the woman said. "So there."

"So we wait for the chief," Vern said. "Or the judge. It'll keep."

"Just why do you want to see Ian, anyway?" I asked.

"Ian?" She frowned. "Who's that?"

"Ian Meredith."

She shook her head with what looked like genuine confusion.

"Aren't you Katherine Anne Koenigslutter?" I asked.

"Who?" She looked even more puzzled.

"I thought Koenigslutter was in a silver Corolla," Vern said. "This is white."

"See?" the woman said. "It's not me. You can let me go now."

"Hard to tell white and silver apart in the dark," I said. "And it was a rental car; you could have turned it in and gotten another.

"I'm not this Koenigslutter person," the woman said.

"Then who are you?" I asked.

"Her name is Jerosha Fawn," Horace said. "At least that's what it says on the rental papers on the front seat."

"Are you Ms. Fawn?" Vern asked.

"I have the right to remain silent," she said. "And a lawyer."

"You have a right to remain a lawyer?" I echoed.

"I mean I want a lawyer."

"Yes, ma'am." Vern was at his most courteous. "We'll take you down to the station and get you a lawyer."

"No!" she said. "I don't want to go anywhere."

"We can't drag a lawyer out here in this weather," Vern said. "You want a lawyer, I'm afraid we have to take you down to the station. That's the rule."

I drifted over to peer inside the Corolla. Apart from the papers on the front passenger seat, the car's only contents were a large-sized McDonald's cup in the cup holder and a backpack in the back seat. The backpack was made of a bright-colored anime-style print with dozens of cartoon cats in yellow, orange, blue, gray, tan, and white.

Enlightenment dawned.

"Oh, good grief." I turned to Jerosha Fawn. "You're Cat Lady, aren't you? CatLady517?"

Fawn's face set in a look of stubborn resistance.

"You know her?" Vern sounded puzzled.

"No, but if she's CatLady517 I've heard of her," I said. "I suspect she's a fan of the *Virginia Crime Time* podcast. Kevin told me about a fan who's stalking Casey."

"I'm not stalking him," the woman said. "We've connected on a very real level."

"Then why's she looking for him here?" Vern asked.

"He lives here!" Fawn shouted.

"Not last time I heard," Vern said.

"He really doesn't," I said. "I should know."

"He accepted the roses," she said.

"If you mean that bucket full of red roses you left on the doorstep, I took them inside so they wouldn't freeze. Casey hasn't even seen them—because he doesn't live here."

"More lies to keep us apart." Fawn crossed her arms and clenched her lips together in a way that suggested she had no intention of moving or talking.

Vern sighed.

"Horace," he said. "You want to take her downtown or you want me to do it?"

"I'll do it," Horace said. "Let's assist her into my vehicle."

Since Ms. Fawn refused to move, assisting her into Horace's vehicle turned out to mean picking her up and gently stowing her in the back seat.

"I'll let them know you'll be needing a hand down at the station," Vern said to Horace. "And I'll have Debbie Ann see if there's a public defender available."

"And lock up her car," Horace said. "I'll arrange to have it towed down to the station, so I can process it there."

Vern and I watched Horace's car disappear into the distance.

"She's probably just a harmless crank," I said.

"Probably."

"You don't sound convinced."

"She's definitely a crank." He walked over to her car and closed the door, using his gloved hand at a spot very low on the door—I assumed he was trying to avoid smudging any fingerprints that might already be there. "What if she isn't such a harmless one? What if she accosted Mr. Meredith like that and he just laughed at her?"

"And she lost it and whacked him with his own hockey stick?"

"Stranger things have happened," Vern said. "She looks as if she could take care of herself in a scrap, especially with a whiner like Ian. Let's let the chief sort her out. You need anything else?"

"I'm good," I said.

Actually, I could have used help getting the groceries in from the Twinmobile, but I couldn't very well ask Vern to pitch in with that. He went back to his cruiser, which was parked a little ways down the road, and got in, but he didn't leave—he was probably guarding the car until the tow truck arrived. I was about to go around to fetch the wire mesh garden cart we used for hauling large loads of groceries when I suddenly noticed something I'd overlooked in the excitement of being stalked.

There were hardly any other cars here at the house.

Actually, I'd registered it when I first went past the house, since it meant that there weren't many potential rescuers there. But it only just now struck me how odd it was. This morning the road had been lined with cars on both sides for half a mile in either direction. For that matter, there had been quite a few when I'd run out in my attempt to figure out who'd left the roses. Where was everyone now?

I was about to go inside to see what was happening when my phone rang. It was Randall Shiffley.

"I just talked to the chief," he said. "He's releasing the ice rink for y'all to play with."

"Excellent," I said. "But last I looked there was still blood on the ice in a couple of places—I think we need to clean that up first."

"That's why I called," he said. "I'm going to send Janet and Fred over to take care of it. And while they're there, they can show you how to use your machine."

"Our machine?" I echoed. "We have a machine? Like a Zamboni?"

"Like a really small Zamboni, yeah." He chuckled at the idea. "And you don't ride around on it—I think you push it, like an old-fashioned lawn mower. Or maybe drag it along behind you. Fred and Janet will figure that out, and it'll do the job."

"Great," I said. "Tell them to let me know when they get here. I'll probably be in my office."

"Will do."

We hung up. I fetched the garden cart, managed to fit all the groceries on it, and dragged it around to the back door. I grabbed a heavy sack of flour and went into the kitchen. Nora was the only one there.

"Food's here" I said. "Where is everybody?"

"Out at your grandfather's zoo," Nora said. "Let me help you with that."

We made short work of emptying the cart. While we were doing so, I saw Osgood Shiffley's tow truck driving away with Jerosha Fawn's rental Corolla. Good riddance.

Nora hummed with pleasure at the renewed bounty that now filled the pantry. Actually, more than filled the pantry and overflowed into the kitchen. I'd haul some of it down into the basement later.

"So why has everyone gone down to the zoo?" I unbuttoned my coat, but I didn't take it off. I'd be headed outside almost immediately. "And shouldn't they all be coming home for dinner before too long?"

"We packed up all the food and sent it out there—a good thing coq au vin travels well. So they'll all be dining with the wombats and koalas and such. The Canadians, too. A couple of state troopers went there with them. For protection, I'm told. Are they protecting the Canadians, or protecting us from them?"

"I don't think anyone quite knows yet," I said. "Still, they should have fun. But they left you holding down the fort here?"

"I wanted to get a head start on tomorrow's dinner," she said. "Delaney suggested that maybe some of the younger Canadians might be just as happy eating pizza, so I'm going to make a few for tomorrow's dinner."

A few? The entire kitchen was filled with pizzas in all stages of their life cycle—huge mounds of doughs being allowed to rise, already-shaped crusts lying on the counter waiting to be decorated, crusts filled with unbroken lakes of red sauce, and pizzas in the process of being festooned with various combinations of ingredients from the bowls lined up on the counter. I spotted sausage, pepperoni, ham, bacon, anchovies, shrimp, chopped chicken, three kinds of mushrooms, four kinds of peppers, onions, black olives, green olives, diced tomatoes, minced garlic, minced basil, shredded spinach, diced cauliflower, half a dozen different cheeses, and even pineapple chunks, which didn't count as legitimate pizza toppings in my book, but I knew other people felt differently.

Luigi's, our local pizza joint, was going to suffer as long as Nora was here.

"They're all hoping the skating rink will be ready by the time they finish dinner," she said. "I'm supposed to let them know if I find out when that happens."

"Randall's sending two of his workers to condition the ice." I thought that sounded a lot better than "clean up the blood."

Nora nodded. Then she sent a chunk of dough airborne and began shaping it into a hand-tossed pizza crust.

"They're supposed to come to my office," I went on. "If they show up here at the house, send them out to me."

"Can do." She frowned. "If everyone's coming back here to the house, I should make a few more pies. We're running low on pies."

I liked her priorities. Anyone who considered an adequate supply of pies essential was welcome to take over my kitchen anytime. I buttoned my coat again and went outside, startling a great many birds from the feeders. Including juncos—at least a dozen of them.

And the juncos weren't lying to us. On my way to the barn I spotted several dozen tiny snowflakes. The weather app on my phone still had the likelihood of snow at only 80 percent, but maybe it was time to stop paying attention to the weather app and trust what my eyes were telling me. My eyes and the juncos that were already swarming the feeders and the ground around them, even with me still standing there. We were getting a white Christmas after all.

While I was eyeing the juncos, I spotted a Corolla slowly cruising by the road in front of the house. This one was silver.

I pulled out my phone and dialed 911.

Chapter 23

"You must be having a day and a half," Debbie Ann said. "More trouble?"

"Toyota Corolla slowly cruising by the house," I said. "Silver this time."

"Mercy. Vern only just left your house. He's making a U-ie and heading back."

"I'm going to go back inside," I said. "I don't want to leave Cousin Nora alone in there."

"Good idea. Stay inside."

We hung up and I went inside. Nora had finished with the pizza crust and was sprinkling toppings on some of the pizzas. She looked up as if surprised to see me back so soon.

"I saw someone driving up," I said. "Didn't want you to have to answer the doorbell."

She nodded slightly and returned to dispensing crumbles of cheese and sprinkles of oregano.

And then the doorbell rang.

I peered out through the peephole before answering. The silver Corolla was parked at the end of our front walkway, but I couldn't see whoever rang the bell. Maybe some people would be puzzled and open the door to see if anyone was there. I knew better, thanks to all those mysteries Dad kept shoving into my hands. I kept looking out. After ten seconds or so a figure came into view. A woman, in her forties or maybe fifties. Blond. About my height—maybe an inch taller, which would make her five eleven. And well bundled up against the cold, which made it impossible to tell if she was skinny or fat. She was broad shouldered, though. She looked sturdy. Capable.

The cheerful version of "Deck the Halls" coming out of the little hidden speakers in the hall added an incongruously festive note to the scene.

My visitor glanced at her watch and then at the door, as if wondering if she'd waited long enough that she could ring again.

I made sure the chain was on and opened the door as far as it would allow.

"Hello." She assumed a smile that struck me as insincere, although it was always possible that recent events had made me jaundiced. "I'm here to see Ian Meredith." She paused, and when I didn't respond immediately, she added, "He's expecting me."

Had he been expecting her? Or had he already encountered her out at the skating rink? If she were Ian's killer, the logical thing to do would be to put as much distance as possible between herself and the crime scene. Go home—back to Wisconsin, if she were Katherine Anne Koenigslutter.

Unless she knew there was proof she'd been in Caerphilly yesterday—proof like an alert deputy giving her a warning for running a stop sign. In that case, might she think her best tactic was to pretend she didn't know Ian was dead?

Either way, my best tactic was to stall her until Vern got here. Just keep her talking on the doorstep. Given how cold it was, that would be terribly rude if she were an ordinary guest, but I didn't think I was obliged to worry about the comfort of a prime murder suspect.

"You must be Ms. Koenigslutter," I said. "I hope I'm pronouncing that right."

"You're pronouncing it fine," she said. "Can you tell Ian I'm here?"

"Why do you want to see him?" I said. "You're already suing him. Wouldn't it be wiser just to let that play out in court?"

For a few seconds her face darkened, and I was expecting her to make a more forceful demand to see Ian. Then she visibly checked her temper and spoke in a calm, almost soft voice.

"I want him to know just what he's done to me," she said. "I need to tell him. He ruined my life."

"How?" I asked.

She set her jaw at first, and I assumed I wouldn't be getting any information from her. Then she blew out a breath in a great visible cloud and an eager look crossed her face. She was a woman with a grievance. And I'd just volunteered to play audience.

"The jerk helped my half brother find me," she said. "A half brother I never even knew existed. I knew Dad was no angel, and maybe I shouldn't have been surprised when Elias turned up and told me we were half siblings, but I was. And maybe it sounds like some kind of good thing, finding a brother you never knew you had, but Elias Boyd isn't anyone you'd ever want in your life. He's a psycho."

"I see." I hoped I'd managed to avoid reacting when she said the name Elias Boyd. "And you think Ian helped your brother find you?"

"Half brother," she corrected. "I don't just think it—I know he did." Her tone was suddenly sharp and fierce. Then she took a deep breath and smiled again. "Sorry," she said. "It's kind of an upsetting subject. Yes, Ian helped that creep find me. Maybe not deliberately. Maybe his company just wasn't careful about only showing people their own information. But Elias found me through the AcerGen website, and when I complained, Mr. Big Shot Ian Meredith just laughed and said 'What's the big deal?'"

Yeah, that sounded like Ian.

"And I'll tell you what's the big deal." Her voice was getting louder. "That creep is demanding money from me. He wants half the value of my farm. Not half the farm—half the value. He doesn't give a damn about farming. He claims if I don't pay him off, he'll go to court and sue me for it, and then on top of half the farm I'll also be out for all the legal fees and punitive damages. And I couldn't pay him half the value even if I wanted to—the farm is mortgaged to the hilt and I'm so broke I had to borrow money to hire a lawyer to fight him. That's what's the big deal. And it's Ian Meredith's fault—him and his company. They need to pay for what they did to me."

"I'm sorry," I said. "It sounds as if you were badly treated. But I can't help you. Ian's not here—"

"Then where is he?" she demanded.

Over her shoulder I saw Vern's cruiser. He went past the silver Corolla and parked in front of it. Another police cruiser parked right behind it, and my friend Aida Butler hopped out. Their cars were almost touching her front and rear bumpers. If my visitor wanted to go anywhere, she'd have to do it on foot.

Ms. Koenigslutter didn't seem to notice them, possibly because the orchestral version of "It Came Upon the Midnight Clear" drowned out what little noise their vehicles made. The move to go hybrid when replacing the county's aging police vehicles had been made with thrift and environmental consciousness in mind, but the new cruisers also appeared to be excellent for sneaking up on suspects.

I made a mental note to mention this to the chief. And another to tell Mother that the speakers on the front porch were a little loud.

"Just tell me where Ian is," Ms. Koenigslutter demanded.

"I don't know," I said. "But I think they can tell you."

She whirled around, and flinched when she saw Vern and Aida marching up the walk. I thought for a moment she'd turn and run. Then she apparently thought better of it.

"Thanks a lot." She gave me one last venomous glance before turning to face the approaching officers, arms folded across her chest.

Vern and Aida stopped at the bottom of the porch steps.

"Ms. Koenigslutter?" Vern said. "Could I ask you to come down to the station with us? Our chief of police would like to interview you."

"About what?" Her voice sounded petulant and impatient, the way a small child would react to being told it was bedtime. "You can't make me."

"Actually, we can," Aida said. "You can come voluntarily, or we can arrest you on suspicion of murder."

"Murder!" She uncrossed her arms and took a step back. "I haven't done anything! No one's been murdered! What are you talking about?"

"Chief Burke would like to talk to you in connection with the murder of Mr. Ian Meredith," Vern said. "It would be a lot easier if you came with us voluntarily."

"Oh, my God," she murmured. "He's dead?" And then she stood up straighter. "Well, I won't pretend to be sorry, but I didn't kill him."

It took a few more tries before they managed to coax her off our porch and into the back of Aida's cruiser. While Aida was reversing and making a U-turn, Vern ambled up the walk, and I opened the door to talk to him.

"I'm not sure whether to tell you to be careful or thank you for rounding up all our suspects," he said.

"Well, not quite all your suspects," I said. "There's still Cyrus Runk. I'm hoping he doesn't show up, though."

"We got an unconfirmed report that he might be hiding out with a cousin over in the mountains of east Kentucky," Vern said.

"I suppose that's good news," I said.

"Good news for us, maybe," Vern said. "Bad news for Kentucky. And maybe not great news for any of us when it comes to finding him. Pretty rough country down there. Easy to lose yourself in, and I know a lot of people will sleep better when he's behind bars again."

"Maybe he'll hear the news that Ian is dead and cancel any plans he has to spend Christmas in Caerphilly."

"News hasn't gone out yet," Vern said. "Ian's mother is traveling. We're holding off the announcement until his father can reach her to break the news."

"Understandable," I said. "I guess that's why Ms. Koenigslutter hadn't heard. But I hope the chief is able to release the news soon. Because as long as Ian's enemies think he's still alive and staying here, they're liable to keep showing up at our door."

"Yeah. We'll be doing extra patrols out here. And you take care of yourself."

"And you do the same. Hope the weather doesn't get too bad."

While we had been dealing with Ms. Koenigslutter, the scattered snowflakes had given way to a light but steady snowfall. Vern looked up, nodded, and strode back to his cruiser.

I went inside and locked the door again.

I stood there for a minute or so, just staring at the door. I reminded myself that Randall was sending two of his workers to deal with the bloody ice so we could open our rink. I should go out to my office to meet them. But I was having trouble letting go of the stress my last two visitors had triggered.

And for me, the best way to deal with stress was to do something. Take care of someone. Which wasn't all that easy to do at the moment, since Cousin Nora was the only other person in the house. Hard to think of anything I could do in the kitchen that would be more help than hindrance to her.

I glanced into the living room. The dogs were all curled up by the hearth—though since the fire was nearly out, it was more from habit than warmth.

I could fix that. I added a couple of logs to the fire. Then I poked it and blew air on it until the flames had taken hold. The dogs—Tink, Spike, and three Pomeranians—looked on with great interest. When the fire was going nicely, I sat down on the raised hearth and kicked my shoes off so I could stick my stocking feet under Tink's warm, furry body. The Pomeranians hopped up onto the hearth and climbed into my lap.

Even Spike shifted his position so he was ever-so-slightly closer to me and sighed with contentment.

Nice that I could solve someone's problems. I leaned back until my head was against the warm brick of the hearth and my view of the living room was obscured by all the stockings hanging from the mantel—so many of them that they overlapped and made a solid red-and-gold curtain of felt and velvet. It was a curiously restful sight.

Should I give up on trying to amuse the Canadians? With luck they'd be going home before too long. Still, no reason not to do what I could to make their life happier while they were here.

I rearranged the Pomeranians until I could reach into my pocket to pull out my phone. I called Kristyn.

"What's up, Meg?" she asked.

"I have another information-gathering mission for you," I said. "Any chance you could eavesdrop on the Canadians, or maybe start a conversation, and find out what foods they're missing? Not that what my cousin Nora has been serving isn't delicious, but I don't get the feeling it's what they're used to."

"Actually, I can tell you one thing already," she said. "Something called poutine. I've overheard half a dozen mentions of that—including one half-hour discussion about where's the best place to get it in Toronto."

"I've heard of it," I said. "I've never had it, though."

"Apparently it's French fries topped with cheese curds and a special gravy," she said.

"Doesn't sound appealing to me," I said. "Then again, I don't want anything on my fries but a little salt and a lot of fresh-ground pepper."

"Not even ketchup?"

"Tomatoes belong in salad and pasta sauce," I said.

"What are cheese curds, anyway?" Kristyn asked. "I don't think I've ever heard of them except in the nursery rhyme. You know, 'Little Miss Muffet sat on a tuffet, eating her curds and whey.'"

"I looked it up one time," I said. "Curds and whey is the old-fashioned name for cottage cheese."

"Seriously?"

"Yup," I said. "I always figured Miss Muffet was just as happy when the spider came along and gave her an excuse to go find something more exciting for dinner."

"Canadians put cottage cheese on French fries?"

"Maybe the gravy makes the difference," I said. "Or maybe without the whey the curds are a lot different. I'll let Cousin Nora figure it out. Thanks for the suggestion."

I could tell Nora. But not right now. I didn't want to disturb the sleeping dogs. And surely there was something useful I could do while sitting here?

I picked up my phone again and called Kevin. Normally he tended to let most calls go to voicemail. Should I feel flattered that he took my call? Or was it only a sign of how worried he was?

"What's up?"

"You're still at the Mutant Wizards office, right."

"Right."

"I won't interrupt you for that long," I said. "But I do have a mixed bag of good and bad news. What should I start with?"

"Surprise me."

"CatLady517 showed up here a little while ago."

"Oh, my God."

"That's the bad news," I said. "The good news is that she behaved badly enough that Horace and Vern hauled her down to the police station."

"Badly enough that they'll charge her with something?" Kevin sounded anxious—exactly what had CatLady517 been doing to spook him so?

"I have no idea," I said. "I'm sure they will if they can, because that would make it a lot easier to keep her around until the chief has had a chance to interrogate her. Maybe it's just a coincidence that she showed up here the day Ian was murdered, but I bet he'll want to make sure."

"Do they still do that thing where they lock people up until they can figure out if they're too crazy to be running around loose?"

"As far as I know, but these days I think you have to be pretty crazy to qualify."

"Trust me, she'll qualify. You should see the stuff she posts in our Facebook group and the message forums."

"Forget about me seeing it—maybe the chief should see it?"

"I've deleted a lot of the worst stuff," he said. "I could probably come up with copies of some of it. Maybe I should work on that tonight. And who knows what else she's posted in the last couple of days."

"You haven't looked?"

"I've been too busy with the AcerGen project," he said. "I've recruited an assistant admin who lets me know ASAP if Cat Lady posts anything really outrageous. And while I love our fans, sometimes settling their arguments and quashing the latest conspiracy theories is the last thing I need when I get home from a twelve-hour workday. So no, I haven't looked since—damn, since Sunday. I'll catch up tonight, if I have any energy left."

"I hear you," I said. "And not that I want to put any more pressure on you, but have you had any luck figuring out how Katherine Anne Koenigslutter and her lawyer knew Ian was here in Caerphilly?"

"Not yet. I can't find any mention online of him being here, so I don't think they found out that way. Best I can figure out is that maybe a disgruntled employee has been leaking Ian's whereabouts to people known to have an ax to grind with AcerGen."

"One of our Canadians?" I asked. "The ones staying with us, I mean."

"Doesn't have to be," he said. "I doubt if he's that popular with the ones back in Toronto, either."

"It would make me feel a lot better if we knew how people were finding out. Oh, by the way, I solved one mystery—Elias Boyd is the half brother Katherine Anne Koenigslutter didn't want to meet. Apparently he's trying to claim half of her inheritance."

"No wonder Koenigslutter is upset. I'll still see what I can find out about him when I have time. Anything else?"

"Isn't that enough?" I asked.

"Yeah. Later."

Reassuring that Kevin would focus on learning how Ian's enemies were finding their way to our door. But it sounded as if he'd already started trying to figure it out and hadn't found anything. That was unsettling. And it was downright annoying that the AcerGen project was keeping him so busy that he might not be able to get to it until he got home.

Nothing I could do about it. Well, I could always try looking online myself—searching for some mention of Ian and Caerphilly. But what were the odds I could find anything Kevin had overlooked?

I put the phone down and concentrated on doing Rose Noire's yoga breathing.

It was almost starting to work when the doorbell rang again.

Chapter 24

"Sorry, guys," I said, as I gently lifted the Poms off my lap. "Duty calls."

Now that they were awake, the Pomeranians decided to follow me to the door. Tink lifted her head and watched us. Reassuring.

I was relieved when I peered out the peephole to see Minerva Burke standing on our doorstep. And when I opened the door, I found her grandson, Adam, was also with her.

"Come on in," I said. "It's like a deep freeze out there."

"We can't stay," Minerva said. "We're just dropping off presents and such. Adam—you want to give Ms. Meg those presents for Josh and Jamie?"

Adam proudly held up two wrapped packages. They both were around three feet long, thin, and straight except for one end, which went off at an obtuse angle.

"I wonder if I can guess what's in that," I said, as I relieved him of the packages. The Pomeranians were greeting him with delight.

"Yeah," Adam said, over the heads of the swarming dogs. "I guess it's kind of obvious. I figured since Grandpa probably wasn't going to give Josh's hockey stick back, it would be a good present for him, and then he'd have a new one and Jamie would have an old one, so I thought he might like one, too. I picked them out myself. Well, Grandpa helped."

"And he's very knowledgeable about sports equipment," I said. "Want me to hide the packages so the boys won't guess too soon what's in them?"

Adam nodded vigorously.

"Give my best to your family," Minerva said. "Hate to run, but we've got two more stops to make before choir practice."

I had to pick up the sociable Pomeranians to keep them from following my guests out. I watched until Minerva and Adam were safely in their car before closing the door and setting down my wriggling armload of fur.

Later on I'd take Adam's presents over to Aida's house—we had a long-established tradition of hiding our outbound presents at each other's houses—at least those destined for our kids or other family members prone to snooping, like our two mothers. But for now I could probably stash them out of sight at the back of the coat closet.

I was a little taken aback to find four gaily wrapped packages of nearly identical shape already hidden at the back of the closet. Not to mention two large, flat boxes that did a better job of hiding the fact that they contained hockey sticks. Which meant we already had more than enough hockey sticks to equip the six players a team was allowed to have on the ice at any given moment. And I suspected other thoughtful friends and relatives might be planning similar gifts.

So maybe we'd be fielding a hockey team. Or hosting a

league. I'd worry about it later. I hid Adam's presents with the rest and went out into the kitchen.

"My covert intelligence operatives down at Mutant Wizards have come up with a menu suggestion," I told Nora. "Something the Canadians have been waxing nostalgic about."

"Well?" Nora's brusque tone might once have made me worry that I'd offended her. I'd come to realize that she had only so much attention to spare for mere humans when her mind was involved in delicate calculations involving yeast and flour, or internal philosophical debates about the optimal quantity of garlic.

"Poutine," I said. "It's—"

"Of course," she said. "I should have thought of that. Let me check which of my poutine recipes would be the best option. Can you make another grocery store run if necessary?"

"Just say the word," I assured her. Although I hoped she wouldn't, given the way the weather was heading. Or that she'd come up with any missing ingredients soon, before the roads got bad. Still, I could probably cajole Osgood or Beau into letting me ride into town and back on the snowplow if conditions got really awful. I'd done it before.

I was curious to see how Nora kept her recipes—would she pull out a recipe card file or a binder of some kind? So I lingered long enough to rummage in the refrigerator for a soda.

To my surprise, she pulled out a laptop and a handful of external hard drives. After examining the labels of the hard drives, she selected one, attached it to her laptop, and booted up.

I was already impressed with Nora, but after finding out that her recipe collection probably ran to terabytes of data, I was beyond impressed. I decided I could rest easy, knowing that the Canadians' poutine needs would soon be amply met.

"I'll be in my office, waiting for the Shiffleys," I said.

She nodded absently. I wasn't sure she'd even heard me, so I detoured back to the front hall to make sure the door was locked. I didn't want any more uninvited callers derailing the poutine project. Then I stuck the can of soda into my pocket and pulled on my gloves before heading out to my office.

An inch of snow had fallen by now, and it was coming down heavier. Or was that more heavily? And since my weather app predicted that the polar vortex—like my family and the Canadians—would probably be hanging around until well after the new year, it looked as if we would, indeed, be having a white Christmas.

The weather app had also changed, in the space of a few hours, from an 80 percent chance of snow to 100 percent, with a projected accumulation of four to six inches. When Janet and Fred Shiffley arrived I'd ask them what their family elders were predicting.

I was glad to get inside the barn. It wasn't heated very well, but it was a lot better than outside in the snow. Lurk poked his sleek, black head out of one of the stalls, so I tossed him a treat. He grabbed it on the fly and disappeared. He and Skulk were probably spending most of their time hanging out in one of the two cat shelters we'd set up in the hayloft, complete with heated floor mats. The floor mats were powered by one of the solar panels Kevin had installed on the barn roof, with a large storage battery to serve as a backup in case of prolonged cloudy weather. Kevin still hadn't followed through on his promise to install a similar system for the house. He hadn't even hooked up the rest of the barn to the solar panels. In case of a snowstorm that took out the power, Lurk and Skulk would have a lot better odds of staying warm than we would in the house.

In my office I turned on the space heater and decided to leave my coat on until it had taken the chill out of the air. The cold soda could wait, too.

I booted up my laptop and opened up a browser window.

I started by doing another search for Cyrus Runk. Nothing to indicate he'd been captured or even spotted. I found a topographical map of Virginia and zoomed in on the southwest corner. As Vern had said, rough country. Lots of mountains. Not many towns. And my eye was drawn to the Daniel Boone National Forest, just across the state line in Kentucky. It was bigger than most counties in Virginia. A great place to get lost in.

"Here's hoping Runk thinks the same thing," I muttered.

My phone rang. I glanced down at the caller ID. The chief.

"Hello," I said. "Should I apologize for overcrowding the jail or congratulate myself that I've assisted in the apprehension of so many potentially dangerous suspects?"

"Congratulate yourself," he said. "Most definitely. Just one thing—remember that you told me about Ms. Koenigslutter's lawyer showing up at your house earlier today?"

"Yes. Name of Alfred Sloan."

"Can you describe him? Hang on—let me put you on speakerphone. Okay. Go ahead."

Odd. Who else needed to hear my description of Sloan?

"He was tall—a little over six feet. Reasonably fit. Thirtyish. Blond hair, neatly cut. Gray pin-striped suit. Clean-shaven. Kind of on the pale side, as if he doesn't spend much time outdoors."

"Definitely not him," a female voice said.

"Alfred M. Sloan, Esquire, Ms. Koenigslutter's attorney, is short, round, in his sixties, and wears thick progressive lenses," the chief said. "And he's in Green Bay, Wisconsin, at the moment. I just spoke with him on the phone."

"Then who the heck showed up at our door looking for Ian?" I asked.

"It's Elias," the voice said—presumably Ms. Koenigslutter. "It has to be."

"Ms. Koenigslutter believes your visitor could be her half brother, Elias Boyd," the chief said. "Who sometimes now goes by Elias Koenigslutter."

"The nerve," the female voice muttered.

Since Ms. Koenigslutter was obviously still listening, I refrained from saying that I'd have stuck with my original name instead of taking on one that was so much longer and more difficult to spell and pronounce.

"We don't know if he's still in town," the chief said.

"He was staking out the Mutant Wizards parking lot a few hours ago," I said.

"I'll send someone to check," he said. "If he shows up again, call nine-one-one immediately and don't open the door to him."

"And don't listen to him, either," Ms. Koenigslutter said. "He can talk anyone into anything, and if he can't talk you into something he gets violent."

"According to Mr. Sloan—the real Mr. Sloan—there is considerable evidence to support Ms. Koenigslutter's assertions that her half brother is dangerous," the chief said. "The pallor you noted comes from his recent incarceration for a variety of fraud and extortion offenses."

"Maybe I should be glad Tinkerbell was with me when he dropped by earlier," I said. "And I got the idea she wasn't too keen on him."

"Tinkerbell?" Ms. Koenigslutter sounded puzzled.

"An Irish wolfhound," the chief explained. "Dogs have good instincts. I should go. I have a great deal more to discuss with the witnesses you helped us locate."

"Not till my defense attorney shows up," Ms. Koenigslutter said. "I'm not saying a word until I have proper legal representation. I know my rights. I don't care if it takes from now until Christmas. If you—"

Ms. Koenigslutter's voice continued, but suddenly got a lot

less clear, and I deduced that the chief had taken his phone off speakerphone, which also seemed to switch its microphone range from wide to close.

"As you will note," the chief said. "Ms. Koenigslutter is invoking her right to be silent."

"Very noisily," I said.

"Indeed." He sounded as if he was suppressing laughter. "Anyway—be careful."

"I will."

With that we hung up.

I turned back to my computer and did some searches on Alfred Sloan and his firm's name. Eventually I ran across a grip-and-grin shot of him accepting some kind of civic award from the mayor of Green Bay. Definitely not the man who'd given me his business card. Not that I doubted the chief. Maybe I just wanted to see if I could have unmasked the fake Sloan myself if I'd been less gullible.

And less busy. So since I now had a short space of time to fill while waiting for Fred and Janet Shiffley to show up. I should at least try to do something useful with it.

I spent a little time searching for combinations of words that would lead to pages that would have allowed Ms. Koenigslutter and her half brother to find their way to our house. I tried AcerGen and Caerphilly. AcerGen and Mutant Wizards. Ian Meredith with either Mutant Wizards or Caerphilly. Nothing. Which was probably what I should have expected. After all, Kevin had already taken a stab at this particular search and had cyber tools at his disposal that were a lot more powerful than ordinary search engines.

I decided to switch over to figuring out if CatLady517 was merely crazy or actually dangerous. Which required logging into the message boards Kevin had created for *Virginia Crime Time* fans. I'd done it once, a few months ago, when Kevin first created the message boards and needed a few volunteers to test them. But while I listened faithfully to their new shows every week, I hadn't felt the need to discuss the cases with other listeners who might be more immersed in the show or in the larger world of true crime. Or who, like CatLady517, might be quite a few ants short of a picnic.

So I consulted the secret hiding place in which I kept track of all the passwords modern life seemed to require—over two hundred of them the last time I'd counted, which wasn't all that recently. And I logged into the message board site, which Kevin had christened The Junkyard in what he'd had to explain was not an insult to the podcast's fans but a tribute to The Three Investigators, one of his favorite childhood book series. Although lately he'd been wondering if the name had somehow jinxed it.

I began paging down the topic folders—dozens of them. No, hundreds. And according to the home page, the message board had more than three thousand users.

Maybe I should be glad that only one of them had showed up and tried to intimidate me into revealing Kevin's and Casey's whereabouts.

So far.

I began dipping into some of the topic folders. Folders about cases I'd heard of, like Lizzie Borden and the Lindbergh kidnapping. Cases I'd never heard of. Cases the podcast had covered. Cases people thought they should cover in future. I tried to limit myself to scanning the posters' names, looking for CatLady517, but I kept stopping to read things. They had some extraordinarily thoughtful listeners . . . a lot of very enthusiastic ones . . . and a few real loons.

But I didn't stumble on any posts by CatLady517 until I spotted a folder called "Who's Hotter?"

Which turned out to be exactly what I thought it would be. Podcast listeners debating whether Kevin or Casey was hotter. Which was fairly amusing, since the debaters had never seen either of them and had only their voices to go by. Well, voices and their contribution to the content of the podcast.

CatLady517 was in the thick of it, and team Casey all the way. She'd be in for a shock if she ever met Casey, since he was an introverted Japanese American grad student and she was fantasizing him as a tall, redheaded Irish rogue. At least she had the tall part right.

And she used a little picture of a bouquet of red roses as her icon or avatar or whatever the current term was—the little picture that appeared beside all of her posts. No wonder she hadn't bothered to leave a card with the roses—she assumed Casey would guess they were from her.

By reading all of her posts in the Who's Hotter? folder, I picked up some clues to the cases and topics she was interested in. I looked up the folders on those cases, which revealed more posts from her. From what I could see, her approach to any case was to search out the wildest known conspiracy theory and then defend it doggedly against anyone who tried to argue from either evidence or common sense. I printed out some of her crazier posts. Were they enough to justify Casey getting a restraining order against her? Or would she need to have actually done something threatening in person?

And then I found a folder about the murder Cyrus Runk had committed. I hadn't recognized it at first, because whoever had created it had called it the Mary Brown case, after the woman he'd killed. Which was a good thing, I reminded myself. We should be naming the victims, not the lowlifes who killed them. I made a promise that I'd read all the articles about her life. But later. For now, I wanted to see if the folder contained any information that might help law enforcement track down her killer and see justice done.

The last thing I wanted to do was learn any more about what Runk had actually done. So I tried to skim posts that dwelled on that. By the third page of posts I ran across the first mention of AcerGen. Not unexpected. The posters were divided, some praising AcerGen for helping catch a cold-blooded killer, others bashing it for invading Runk's privacy.

About nine pages into the discussion, I came across an item that astounded me.

"No way AcerGen is getting out of the forensic DNA business," it read. "In fact, I hear they've come to the US specifically to work with a software company called Mutant Wizards to build a website to make it easier for cops and others to access DNA information."

The post was dead wrong, obviously. The site Mutant Wizards was building was supposed to make it easier for consumers to use DNA—to help them understand it and use it to make medical decisions or build their family trees by contacting DNA relatives. The ones who wanted to be contacted, of course.

But what if someone who already had a grudge against Ian and AcerGen read that? They could so easily look up where Mutant Wizards was located. And a little bit of eavesdropping around town would send them looking in one of two places for Ian—the Mutant Wizards office building, which had decent security, or our house.

I checked the date—the post had gone up two days ago. No wonder Kevin hadn't seen it. But it still left plenty of time for anyone eager to confront Ian to make their way here. Not just CatLady517. Cyrus Runk, Katherine Anne Koenigslutter, even Elias Boyd. . . .

Another forum member pointed out that maybe the *Virginia Crime Time* team would have some inside scoop on the case, since everyone knew about their connection to Mutant Wizards. I wasn't sure all that many people knew it before, but they certainly did now. Kevin and Casey's time out of the limelight might be coming to an end.

I was reaching for my phone to call the chief and let him

know when I heard a knock on my door. Presumably Janet and Fred.

"About time," I muttered. And then, more loudly, I called out, "Come in!"

I shut my laptop and turned toward the door as I stood up. But it wasn't Fred and Janet Shiffley standing in the doorway.

It was Cyrus Runk.

Chapter 25

I did my best to keep my visible reaction to mild surprise and try to act natural. My first instinct was to get out of the office and into the open air. I should pretend not to recognize him.

"Oh—I was expecting Fred and Janet," I said. "Did Randall send you instead of them? Let me show you where the project is."

I took a few steps forward, trying to look as if I expected him to step aside and let me out of the office. He took one step back, then reached inside his coat and pulled out a gun.

"We're not going anywhere," he said. "Not just yet, anyway. Where's Ian Meredith?"

"Ian Meredith?" I echoed. Did he not realize his attack with the hockey stick had been fatal? "Down at the morgue, I expect. Unless his father already took his body over to the funeral home."

Runk's mouth fell open slightly and he stared at me, as if

my answer had thrown him off stride and he needed to consider it for a while.

My mind was racing. Was he just doing a really good job of pretending not to know that Ian was dead? Or was he really surprised?

"What happened to him?" he asked finally.

"Someone killed him," I said. "Right out there on the skating rink. I can show you if you like—you can still see the blood on the ice.

"I listened to the local news on the radio today," he said. "Couple of times. They didn't say anything about a murder."

"They're keeping it quiet until they can track down his mother and notify her," I said. "So if you need to talk to him, I'm sorry. You've missed your chance."

He stared at me for a while with an expression of frustration and bafflement. I was beginning to get the idea that Runk wasn't particularly quick on the uptake. The eyes that had seemed so sad and baffled in his mug shot just looked dull and vacant now. He wasn't very tall—maybe a couple of inches shorter than me. But he was stocky. And possibly muscular—his heavy, slightly baggy coat made it hard to tell if his bulk was fat or muscle.

"I don't believe you," he said finally. "Tell me where he is."

"I saw him hauled away in the county ambulance," I said.

"Yeah, right." He was starting to sound irritable.

I was getting a bad feeling about this. After all, if I ever did convince him that Ian was dead, was he just going to say "thanks for the information" and leave? I wouldn't want to bet on it. He'd probably think shooting me was the best way to cover his tracks.

"Okay, how about if I show you where Ian was hiding the last time I saw him," I said.

"That's more like it." He took a couple of steps back and to the side, keeping his gun trained on me. Then he jerked his head as if signaling me to come out of the office.

I walked out into the main part of the barn as slowly as I could. If I could just drag this out, sooner or later Fred and Janet would show up to fix the ice. Not that I expected them to rescue me, but they'd provide a distraction that might let me get the drop on Runk. Or escape him. And come to think of it, being Shiffleys, they would probably feel obliged to rescue me, and would doubtless be reasonably competent at it.

"Stop dawdling," Runk said. "I don't want to—"

A hissing noise overhead startled both of us. I glanced up to see Skulk looking down from the rafters, his mouth drawn back in an expression whose ferocity would terrify any sane rodent.

"Gawd almighty!" Runk exclaimed. "What is that thing? A mountain lion?"

"Our barn cat," I said. "He's—"

Just then I heard a feline snarl. I whirled, and for a second I wondered when Runk had found the time to don a black fur hat. But it wasn't a hat, of course—it was Lurk, the smaller but feistier of the barn cats. He had landed on Runk's head. Runk was trying to pull him off, and Lurk was clawing and biting at Runk's face and hands.

Runk dropped his gun. I winced as it bounced off the bare wood of the barn floor, half expecting it to fire. But it didn't, and since Runk was still grappling with Lurk, I darted over and grabbed the gun.

Runk finally succeeded in dislodging Lurk—or, more likely, Lurk decided he'd done enough damage and leaped away to gloat over his victory. Runk looked frantically down at the floor, turning in a circle as he tried to find the gun.

I put a few yards between us before I said anything.

"Put your hands up," I said. "I have the gun."

Runk froze. He didn't put his hands up, but he didn't do anything else, like reach into his pockets for another weapon or charge at me. Still, those hands, away from his body, but held at waist level, much too near his pockets . . .

"I said hands up," I repeated.

He broke for the barn door.

"Stop or I'll shoot," I said. But he didn't stop—he was clawing at the barn door, trying to get it unlatched, and I realized that I wasn't sure I could shoot him. Not in cold blood. If he were running toward me, maybe. If he were running toward one of the boys or Michael, absolutely. In a heartbeat. I reminded myself that one of them could be just outside the barn, and even without his gun Runk could still be dangerous.

I could shoot to wound. At his legs, maybe.

In the seconds it had taken me to think this, he'd figured out how to unlock the barn door and was pulling it open. I took the stance Horace had taught me when he'd given me shooting lessons, holding the gun with both hands and aiming at what I hoped would be a nonlethal target, his upper right thigh. Skulk snarled overhead, causing Runk to look up as he stepped outside through the doorway—

And just then a large cast-iron frying pan swooped down and whacked his upturned face.

He let out a blood-curdling howl and crumpled to the floor.

I ran closer and found Cousin Nora standing just outside the barn door, holding the frying pan ready in case Runk tried anything. Though it didn't look as if he would—he was curled up in a fetal position on the floor with both hands clapped to his face and blood running out from under them.

"I saw him sneaking in here," Nora said. "Called nine-one-one, but it sounded like they were going to take a while, so I thought I'd come out and help."

"I owe you one," I said.

"You broke my nose," Runk whined

"Consider yourself lucky," Nora said. "I was aiming for a concussion. Meg—you got this? I have pies in the oven."

"Go tend your pies," I said. "I might not always win the family tin-can shooting contests, but I think I can manage to plug him if he tries anything."

Actually, tin-can shooting contests had never been a feature of Hollingsworth family gatherings, but Nora was smart enough to realize that my words were a precaution, intended to daunt Runk if he recovered enough to be dangerous.

Instead of heading back to the kitchen, though, she pulled out her cell phone and called someone.

"You want a scoop for that podcast of yours?" she said into the phone—from which I deduced she was calling Kevin. "Get out here to the barn. Your aunt Meg and I just caught the jerk who bumped off our houseguest."

"I didn't," Runk protested weakly from the floor.

"Well, come out here and help tie him up and you can ask him," Nora went on, obviously answering Kevin rather than Runk. "Unless you want me to burn those cherry pies you're so fond of."

With that she hung up.

"Kevin's on his way." She nodded to me and headed back to the house.

"I didn't kill Meredith," Runk said.

"The police will be here any minute now," I said. "You can make your highly unbelievable protestations of innocence to them."

"I didn't kill him!"

"Then why are your fingerprints on the hockey stick?" I asked.

"Oh, crap," he said. "They killed him with that?"

I wondered momentarily if I'd just accidentally spilled a bit of information that the chief was holding back to separate true confessions from false ones. Probably not.

And what did he mean by "they killed him." Was he just using *they* as the indefinite singular, or was he suggesting more than one person was involved in Ian's death?

"I'm still listening," I said. "Your prints, hockey stick."

"I touched it, sure," he said.

"How'd that happen?" I didn't have to work to make my tone sound cynical.

"I wanted to talk to him, and he was just skating up and down whacking a can of sardines with it."

"Water chestnuts, actually," I said. "Not that it matters. Go on."

"When I tried to talk to him he started threatening me with his hockey stick," Runk said. "So I took it away from him. Maybe I waved it at him a little. But I didn't kill him with it. He wouldn't talk to me, so I left. And tossed the hockey stick far enough away that he couldn't get to it and use it on me before I left."

"You can tell it to the police when they get here."

"They won't believe me either." He sighed heavily. "Damn. If only I'd given up smoking."

The non sequitur threw me for a moment.

"Maybe you should, if you're already craving a nicotine fix," I said. "Because our jail's nonsmoking."

"Smoking's the only reason I took my gloves off," he said. "I had on the thick padded kind that makes it really hard to hold a smoke, and he came at me before I finished it. That's the only reason my fingerprints are on the hockey stick."

His story did sound crazy enough that it might be true. Of course, even if he was telling the truth about taking off his gloves to make it easier to smoke, he could be lying about only threatening Ian and tossing the hockey stick away.

"You could do one of those anti-smoking ads," I said. "You could tell the sad story about how if you hadn't given in to your nicotine cravings you wouldn't have been convicted of murder."

"I told you, I didn't— Oh, never mind. I'll save it for the cops. Maybe they'll listen better."

I rather doubted it.

I heard a snicker from the doorway. Kevin was standing there, filming us with his phone.

"Get in here and tie the man up," I said. "There's a couple of dog leashes hanging by the doorway if you can't find anything else."

By the time Kevin had finished securing Runk, we could hear sirens in the distance. Kevin seemed intent on taking pictures of me and Runk from every possible angle.

"So I can document how we captured him," he said.

Since he had been reasonably quick to answer Nora's summons, I decided not to challenge the "we."

"Call nine-one-one and let Debbie Ann know we've got Runk secured," I said instead. "We don't want anyone running in here waving guns. And tell them our prisoner might need medical assistance for a broken nose and possible concussion."

"What did you do to him?" Kevin asked.

Kevin found my tale of Cousin Nora and the frying pan so hilarious that he had to hand the phone to me to repeat it to Debbie Ann.

By the time Vern stepped through the barn door it was obvious Debbie Ann had briefed him. He wasn't laughing hysterically, but he was grinning from ear to ear.

"The chief's going to be right pleased at having his main murder suspect in custody," he said.

"I didn't do it," Runk said. "I want my lawyer."

"I'm assuming you mean Mr. Morgan of Mason, Morgan,

and Friedman," Vern said. "Chief's already notifying him. Along with all the different law enforcement agencies that have been hunting for you."

Runk uttered a heavy sigh.

Vern turned to me.

"The ambulance is over at the far end of the county dealing with some tourists who skidded into a ditch," he said. "So I'm going to take Mr. Runk over to the ER, and your dad's going to meet me there to help check him out. I expect it will take a while before he's patched up and lawyered up—in the meantime, the chief would like to hear from you what happened— can you go downtown and meet with him?"

"If I can," I said. "How are the roads?"

"Beau and Osgood are keeping them pretty clear so far," he said. "And the snow's not supposed to get really heavy for a few hours."

"I'll go now while the going's good, then," I said. "Unless you'd find it more useful for me to stay here, where all the bad guys and weirdos keep showing up."

"I think you've pretty much reeled them all in," Vern said.

"That's good," I said. "Because I'm starting to feel like that goat in Jurassic Park—the one they tether out to lure in the T. rex."

"You're a lot less helpless than the goat." Vern chuckled as he said it.

"Then again, maybe it's more like a warped remake of *A Christmas Carol*," I went on. "Only instead of three ghosts I get three crazy stalkers."

"Lucky you."

"Yeah," I said. "I keep thinking of a line from Michael's one-man show. The part where Scrooge says 'Couldn't I take 'em all at once, and have it over?' I'm with him. Maybe if Runk, Koenigslutter, and Cat Lady had arrived at the same time, they'd have done some kind of Kilkenny cats number on each other."

"Ah, but if they did that we'd never figure out which one offed Meredith." Vern glanced down at his pocket, then pulled out his phone. "Update from the chief—can you meet him out at your grandfather's zoo? He's doing a few follow-up interviews out there with some of the Canadians."

"As long as we can get it over soon." I glanced up at the sky. "Before too much more of that white stuff comes down. I have a feeling it's not stopping anytime soon."

"Tell me about it," Vern said. "We'll be hauling tourists out of snowdrifts all night. Help me get this guy on his feet, will you?"

Kevin and I both pitched in to lift Runk to his feet, and Vern escorted him back to the road where his cruiser was parked. I was reassured to see that the roads were well plowed and not a bit icy. That was one good thing about the prolonged cold weather we'd been enduring—we were getting dry, powdery snow rather than the mix of wet snow and ice that could make driving conditions really treacherous.

I noticed that a Shiffley Construction truck had also arrived.

"Kevin," I called. He seemed intent on taking pictures of Runk being hauled off to the slammer, but turned around when he heard my voice.

"Any more excitement?"

"Let's hope not," I said. "Can you do something for me while I'm gone?"

"If I can," he said. "Pretty busy day, you know. The only reason I'm here instead of down at the office is that I came to collect some equipment that could be useful for a test we're running today, and—"

"Fred and Janet Shiffley just got here to clean the blood off the ice rink," I said. "And someone in the family needs to learn how to operate our new ice-resurfacing machine. Could you—"

"Cool," he said. "Sure thing."

"Text me when the blood's all gone," I said. "And Michael, so he can bring everyone home from the zoo to enjoy it."

"Awesome," he said over his shoulder as he hurried toward the road.

I went back into the barn to toss a few treats up into the hayloft for my rescuers. Then I grabbed my tote bag, locked up my office, and stuck my head through the back door to let Nora know I was headed for town.

"Fine," she said. "Can you ask your mother to shoo a few more family members home? We need more hands."

At the moment, in addition to her own hands, she appeared to have drafted three more sets belonging to newly arrived cousins. Evidently the task of the hour was peeling potatoes. The cousins looked a great deal more cheerful than I would if I'd been put on KP duty the second I arrived. In fact, they were singing along with the Christmas carols coming from the little speakers hidden in the evergreen garlands.

Then again, maybe Nora hadn't let them see how very many bushels of freshly washed potatoes were stacked in a far corner of the kitchen. Maybe I should make my escape before it dawned on Nora that I, too, could wield a paring knife.

Chapter 26

As I strolled out to my car I glanced toward the ice rink. I could
see Fred, Janet, and Kevin attaching a garden hose to something that looked like a collection of metal tubes arranged in
a trapezoid. Presumably the ice-conditioning machine. And—

I suddenly remembered something that Cyrus Runk's arrival had driven out of my mind: that people looking for Ian
might have found him here in Caerphilly through the *Virginia Crime Time* members-only message boards. As soon as
Kevin called or texted me to let me know the rink was ready,
I'd sic him on the project of figuring out if Runk or Ms. Koenigslutter had joined his message boards. Or should I interrupt him now? No—a few minutes' delay wouldn't make that
much difference, and we needed the rink back in shape so I
could get everyone to move the festivities back to the house
before the roads got bad.

I set out for the zoo. Michael had taken the Twinmobile, but
I didn't mind—in fact, I was glad to be driving my old Toyota,

with its lower center of gravity. The roads weren't bad—not yet, anyway. But that could change. I tucked my phone into the holder so I could glance at it periodically to watch for texts from Kevin.

As I reached the outskirts of town I started seeing more tourists on the road. At least I assumed most of them were tourists, since even when it was snowing the locals usually went more than five miles an hour, and were rarely seen hanging halfway out their car windows with cameras or iPhones in their hands, taking pictures of Christmas decorations, quaint houses, and just about anything they saw that was even marginally decorative. I was relieved when I could turn off the main road and take several side streets to reach Clay County Road without going through the tourist-infested heart of town.

The zoo parking lot was crowded, and tourists were still swarming through the front gate, most of them waving the brightly colored paper maps they could use to compete in the Creatures of the Bible scavenger hunt, a special holiday attraction at the zoo. Grandfather had started it a few years ago as Animals of the Bible, and it had been such a success that he expanded it every year. Anyone who successfully located all one hundred and thirty-one birds, mammals, reptiles, fish, and plants that appeared both in the Bible and somewhere in the Caerphilly Zoo would win a small reward and be entered into a drawing for a series of fairly substantial prizes.

I parked in the staff parking lot and used my all-access badge to let myself into the employees-only entrance. I found myself in a small courtyard between two of the administration buildings. Even here, I could hear the excited squeals of zoo goers.

"Look! A star! A star!" one of them exclaimed just outside the wall separating the courtyard from the public area of the zoo. She wasn't talking about the Christmas star, of course—

she'd spotted one of the small bright silver stars that marked the various items included in the scavenger hunt. Probably the one marking the row of now-dormant apple trees on the other side of the wall.

I was about to go into the main Admin building when I spotted a sign taped to the door.

MUTANT WIZARDS/ACERGEN HOLIDAY GATHERING: EVENT SPACE, SMALL MAMMAL PAVILION.

So I turned around and headed out into the public areas of the zoo.

The zoo's broad walkways were crowded with tourists, most well bundled-up against the cold. Although the holiday decorations were largely limited to twinkling lights, evergreen wreaths on the lampposts, and evergreen garlands looping between the lampposts, it all looked very festive, especially with the snow falling gently and adding a powdery dusting of white to everything. A band of carolers had taken up a position nearby, under a gazebo-like structure that served as a refuge from the sun in summertime, and had begun singing "The Friendly Beasts," a zoo favorite. Grandfather hired several bands of strolling carolers and musicians every holiday season rather than piping canned Christmas music over the zoo's loudspeaker system. The tourists seemed to find this warm and charming—we didn't tell them that Grandfather's real reason for doing it was so he could shoo the carolers away if they showed up near him when he was in a grouchy mood.

When I was halfway to the Small Mammal Pavilion, a voice came over the loudspeaker system, reading a weather report— obviously one customized for the zoo audience.

"The snow continues to fall here in Caerphilly," the voice said. "Accumulations of between four and six inches are predicted. After sunset, temperatures will plunge further and road conditions will continue to deteriorate. The front gate will be issuing return tickets to customers who need to cut their visit short due to weather conditions. Please be advised that only arctic animals will be visible in outdoor habitats at this time."

I didn't see a lot of people hurrying for the exits after that. Maybe I should suggest to Grandfather that a more strongly worded announcement would be advisable. Did we really want a repeat of the time that a freak snowstorm had made Clay County Road impassible before they'd shooed out all of the tourists? Fortunately the zoo had plenty of cots and sleeping bags on hand, thanks to its summer camp program for middle- and high-school students—Camp with the Cheetahs and Sleep with the Sloths! But the tourists hadn't all enjoyed the experience—in fact, some of the ones who'd been housed in the Reptile Pavilion or the Big Cat House had been downright traumatized.

I reached the Small Mammal Pavilion and hurried through its crowded hallways, averting my eyes from the naked mole rats and silently promising the meerkats that I'd come back and watch them later. When I opened the door to the event space a wall of sound hit me—overloud Christmas music mixed with the babble of many voices.

The Small Mammal event space was a big open room that could be put to many uses. Add tables and you could host a banquet. With booths, it could become an exhibit hall. Several sets of the kind of folding bleachers often found in high school gyms turned it into a good venue for Grandfather's nature talks. Michael had occasionally used it for a rehearsal hall, and the Caerphilly Garden Club now held its annual shows there.

Today, a series of long tables down one side of the room held a buffet, and a hundred or so people—mostly Mutant Wizard and AcerGen employees—were milling about holding plates of food.

The sight of the food made me realize that it had been a long time since breakfast. I headed for the buffet tables which, though visibly ravaged, still held more than enough food to keep me happy. And the menu was a delightful mixture of the coq au vin and Cousin Nora's other contributions along with some of the specialties of Grandfather's favorite local caterer.

I was still piling up my plate when the music halted, and Mother's voice came over the loudspeaker system.

"Attention, everyone," she said. "We have an important announcement."

People began shushing each other. I moved around the perimeter until I could see Mother standing on a small raised platform at one end of the room. Mr. Meredith and Festus were standing nearby.

And so, I noticed, was Chief Burke. Facing the audience, rather than Mother, as if interested in watching their reactions. I followed his gaze—he seemed to be marking down the locations of all the Canadians

"Thank you, everyone," Mother began. "First of all, I'd like to thank everyone here for all your hard work on this project. I know it's been difficult being away from your families at this time, with Hanukkah already going on and Christmas fast approaching. We appreciate your dedication."

These heartwarming sentiments were met with polite silence, but Mother went on unperturbed.

"I'd like to offer condolences from the Mutant Wizards team to Mr. Gordon Meredith and to all the AcerGen staff on the loss of Mr. Ian Meredith. And to assure you all that we'll be doing everything we can to help bring the person or persons responsible to justice."

Was it an accident that she glanced over at me when she said that?

The polite silence continued, although the mood of the crowd seemed a little warmer—probably because she'd avoided making any fulsome tributes to Ian's memory. I'd been more than half expecting a minute of silence, but luckily Mother read the mood of the crowd on that one.

"And finally, I'd like to announce that we are putting the project on hold for the time being."

That got a reaction. A buzz of comments rippled through the room.

"We know AcerGen needs time to regroup from the loss of its CEO. And since he was spearheading the joint project, now seems a good time to take stock of what we've achieved and make any necessary adjustments to our future plans. So we're asking team members from both companies to spend tomorrow wrapping up whatever work they're currently involved in, after which Mutant Wizards staff will be free to use their leave to celebrate the holidays, and we'll see what our Administrative Services staff can do to help the AcerGen staff book transportation home."

If Mother was disappointed in the reaction to her earlier remarks, she certainly couldn't complain about how the crowd reacted to this news. Cheers and applause filled the room and many Canadians and Americans exchanged high fives.

Mother smiled and left the small stage. I was about to walk over to let the chief know I was here when suddenly Grandfather appeared at my elbow.

"Meg," he bellowed. "What the devil's going on? Why is Mutant Wizards canceling that DNA-related project?"

His booming voice carried far too well. I could see nearby groups of people interrupting their own conversations to listen.

"Postponing, not canceling." I tried to make my voice loud enough so all the eavesdroppers could hear, and hoped that the elder Mr. Meredith had already left. "Didn't you hear what Mother just said? They need to regroup after Ian Meredith's death."

"Preposterous," he said. "It's not as if that idiot made any real contribution to the project. In fact, it will probably run a lot smoother without him going around interfering with the actual work."

"Good point," I said. "But come with me and I'll show you something."

I led him toward one of the staff-only doors and badged myself through. Mercifully, he followed. We were in a long corridor, brightly painted and lined with doors and the large, curtain-covered picture windows that could be used to observe the animals in the adjacent habitats. To our right was a small veterinary lab, empty but for a few four-legged patients. I led the way into it and closed the door behind us.

"So what is it you want to show me?" he said. "Not the *Didelphis virginiana,* I presume." He pointed at a nearby cage where a half-grown possum with a bandage on one of his forelegs was baring all fifty of his excessively pointy little teeth at us.

"Actually, I wanted to tell you something without the entire party overhearing," I said. "Since at the moment it's a corporate secret and all. Assuming you can keep quiet about it."

"Of course," he said. "I figured there must be some more logical reason for postponing the project."

"For canceling the project, actually," I said. "You were right on that part. But we don't want that to get out until we're ready to announce it. If you—"

"Canceling it? Why? Do you realize that DNA is—"

"Because we figured out that AcerGen doesn't know how to run it right," I said. "You heard about what happened with Cyrus Runk, right? And Katherine Anne Koenigslutter? Who knows how many more people are going to sue AcerGen for violating their privacy? And that could be small potatoes when the word gets out about the problems with mixing up samples and who knows what other shenanigans have been going on at DNA Gnostics, the lab they've been using to process people's test kits—"

"DNA Gnostics?" he bellowed. "You mean they've been using that bunch of charlatans? Who made that idiotic decision? Didn't they do any research?"

"Ian made the decision, and I don't think he researched anything but their low prices. So you've heard of DNA Gnostics?"

"Of course," he said. "All of us in the field have heard of them. They're completely incompetent and should have had their accreditation revoked ages ago."

"According to a conversation of Ian's that I overheard yesterday, their accreditation has probably been revoked and they're facing fraud charges."

"Excellent!"

"Which means AcerGen is scrambling to find someone willing to process DNA kits for what they can pay."

Grandfather nodded slightly.

"So that's why we're canceling the project," I said. "Not because we have any doubts about the importance of DNA. But because we do realize how important it is—and how vital it is to do it right. AcerGen isn't up to it. We realize that now. And so do they—at least Ian's father does."

Grandfather nodded slowly. He looked sad and defeated. And older. He suddenly looked his age.

"It was stupid of me," he said—words I couldn't have imagined ever coming out of his mouth. "I was so excited about Rob doing something in a scientific field. I thought maybe I could help out somehow."

"Maybe you still can," I said. "Now that we're terminating the contract with AcerGen, Mutant Wizards suddenly has a nearly finished and highly expensive program on its hands, with no interested buyer. A complex, interactive web-based program to help consumers understand and use their DNA test results—one that Kevin and Delaney assure us is a cut above what any other company in the consumer DNA market has to offer. You know everyone in the field, right? Maybe you can help Mutant Wizards find a more worthy buyer for all that fancy programming work they've already done."

He perked up a little.

"That's possible," he said. "Assuming it really is something that would be useful in the field. From what I saw of Ian—"

"He had no idea what he was doing," I said. "But Kevin and Delaney do. And they—and a bunch of other really smart people at Mutant Wizards—did a lot of research to figure out what would be useful. Get them to give you a demo."

"It's a plan," he said.

"But remember—don't tell anyone until we make the public announcement."

"Of course." He nodded and tried to look inscrutable. Then he gave that up.

"And you need to be more careful," he said. "I hear you've single-handedly captured three suspects for the chief. That should be their job. The police, I mean."

"I didn't really capture any of them," I said. "They just showed up and I managed to stall them all long enough that the cops could capture them."

Actually, I did play a part in capturing Runk, but Cousin Nora and the barn cats had done most of the work. I wasn't going to mention that and make him any more worried than he already was.

"Still," he said. "You should be careful. Especially if one of those creeps ends up getting bail."

"I will," I said.

We delayed our return to the party long enough for Grandfather to check on the well-being of the small mammals currently recuperating in the clinic. When we emerged into public view, Grandfather's face and body language clearly showed that he was gloating over being in possession of a secret. Dad was prone to the same thing. But at least Grandfather was reasonably good at keeping any secrets confided to him, if only because it prolonged his opportunity for gloating. Dad not only telegraphed that he had a secret, he almost always blurted it out. As a result, ever since my high school days, he almost always recruited me to pick out Christmas, birthday, and anniversary presents for Mother. Usually by the time I'd done enough research to select something she was sure to like, she had already figured out what she was getting. But since I was under orders not to tell Dad what he was giving her, lest he accidentally spill the beans, at least someone was always delightfully surprised.

Keeping the ice rink a secret from nearly everyone must have been an incredible strain on him. I looked to see if he was here at the party.

I didn't spot him, but I did see Chief Burke. I caught his eye, and he excused himself from the conversation he was in and headed my way.

Chapter 27

"Let's get that statement of yours," the chief said. "Your grandfather's given me temporary use of a small office near here."

He led the way back through the employees-only door and into the office. Clearly its regular occupant was a dedicated small-mammal keeper—the walls of the office were covered with smiling pictures of a tall, shaven-headed African American man proudly holding up meerkats, chipmunks, squirrels, moles, voles, rabbits, gophers, and a seemingly endless variety of mice and rats. I was momentarily distracted when I noticed that the foot-high Christmas tree on his desk was covered with a variety of meerkat-themed ornaments.

"So what are you doing here," I said in a mock stern tone as I took one of the absent keeper's comfortable guest chairs. "Here I give you three perfectly good suspects to interrogate, and I find you hanging around our party, looking for more."

"Ms. Fawn is over at Caerphilly General under psychiatric observation," the chief said. "And I can't very well interview the other two until they've lawyered up. Ms. Koenigslutter's attorney is still working on arranging local counsel until he can fly down here himself, and Mr. Runk's attorney is driving up from Richmond as we speak."

"Okay, I know Cat Lady probably isn't a prime suspect," I said. "But is Koenigslutter still in the running? I thought you found Runk's fingerprints on the hockey stick."

"We did." He pursed his lips, then sighed and continued. "But in some places they're smudged. In a way that suggests someone wearing gloves handled the hockey stick after he did."

"That's not good," I said. "Of course, he could have done that himself. What if he put on his gloves after killing Ian, and then picked up the hockey stick for some reason?"

"He could have," the chief said. "Or he could have had an accomplice who picked up the hockey stick after he dropped it. Or maybe his story is true—what little he said before shutting up and asking for his lawyer. Maybe he took the hockey stick away from Ian, and someone else came along later and killed him with it."

"It's possible," I said. "But not very plausible."

"A good defense attorney could make it sound plausible enough to raise reasonable doubt in the mind of a jury." His expression was grim.

And Runk had a very good defense attorney. I thought of pointing out that Runk was already convicted of one murder, and would be serving time for that. Unless, of course, his defense attorney managed to get the DNA evidence thrown out. In that case, the strength of the chief's case might be the only thing keeping a dangerous man behind bars.

"Once their lawyers get here I'll see what I can get out of the two of them," the chief said. "Who knows? Maybe they were in it together, and I can pit them against each other. Given the vehemence of Ms. Koenigslutter's antipathy for Mr. Meredith,

I certainly consider her a viable suspect, either for the role of his accomplice or as the actual killer. For now, while I'm waiting to talk to them, I'm trying to find out how both of them knew enough to come to Caerphilly in the first place. The Canadians seem like very nice people, all of them, but someone has been giving inside information about Mr. Meredith's whereabouts to people who aren't very fond of him. And they're the most likely suspects."

"Everyone at Mutant Wizards knew, too," I said.

"But the Mutant Wizards employees wouldn't know about Mr. Runk's connection to AcerGen," he said. "Or Ms. Koenigslutter's."

"They might if they were true crime aficionados—which a lot of them are, thanks to Kevin." I explained about the posts I'd seen on the members-only *Virginia Crime Time* boards.

"Interesting," he said. "That might explain how Jerosha Fawn found her way here. Not sure about the others. Has Kevin's podcast covered Runk's case?"

"No," I said. "At least not yet. But the members can start discussion boards about any case they're interested in. A lot of them are pushing for the podcast to cover the Runk case. And they might—when he has time, Kevin sometimes checks out the discussions to get ideas for future episodes."

"And he didn't see this?"

"It only went up a few days ago," I said. "He's been putting in long hours on the AcerGen project and hasn't had much time for eating and sleeping, much less going through the hundreds of messages the *Virginia Crime Time* fans post every day. But I see your point. If Runk is following everything said online about him—and if I were him, I would be—he might have seen from the *Virginia Crime Time* Facebook page that some of the fans were discussing his case on the members-only message boards, and then he could sign up for them. But that doesn't explain Ms. Koenigslutter."

The chief nodded.

"I might have thought that through if I hadn't been interrupted in mid-think by Runk," I said.

"It's still useful," he said. "If Ms. Koenigslutter was upset with AcerGen, she may have done some web searching to find out more about them. That could have led her to Cyrus Runk and Kevin's message boards. We can get him to look into his users."

"They all seem to use screen names," I said. "I don't know if he knows that much about any of them. The idea is to build a big community around the podcast, not to do a comprehensive background check on anyone who applies."

"He may not know much about them right now," the chief said. "But don't tell me he doesn't have ways of finding out about them if he needs to. Tracing their IP addresses and all kinds of things that I don't even know the name of."

"True," I said. "And if we're putting the AcerGen project on hold, he might have enough time to work on it. Let's get him started."

I pulled out my cell phone and called Kevin.

"Almost finished," he said, in lieu of hello. "And I think I've mastered the NiceIce machine."

"Great," I said. "Let me know when I can send everyone home. Meanwhile, Chief Burke has a request for you." I handed the chief my phone and listened in while he explained my find.

Maybe I should have told Kevin myself. From the chief's side of the conversation I gathered that Kevin was mortified that a key bit of information was lurking inside one of his own proprietary message boards. It wasn't often I heard either Grandfather or Kevin admitting to a mistake, much less both of them in one day. Then again, I doubt if I could have managed to do quite as good a job as the chief at reassuring Kevin that it was a perfectly natural oversight.

And by the sound of it, the chief definitely considered it

possible that Runk and Koenigslutter could be in cahoots. I was relieved to know that they were both safely in jail.

The chief finished his conversation with Kevin, signed off, and handed me back my phone.

"I'm assuming that if your prisoners are still waiting for their lawyers, the odds are they won't be getting out on bail anytime soon," I said.

"Not tonight, for sure," he said. "And not anytime soon if I can help it. Runk's definitely going back to Buchanan County when we're done with him. As for Ms. Koenigslutter, of course, there's no predicting what will happen in a bail hearing, but I have a hard time imagining any of our local judges turning loose someone who's suspected of bludgeoning someone with a hockey stick."

"Doesn't the fact that there are two of them complicate things?"

"It could," he said. "And as I said, when the case comes to trial, it will certainly make it hard to convict either of them if we haven't definitively cleared the other by that time. But for now, I'm optimistic. And I think we can all rest easy that the two of them will be spending some time in our jail."

"If you end up having to turn either of them loose, maybe you could do what Grandfather's been doing," I said. "He's been testing the next generation of his wildlife tracking devices by slipping them into the pockets of unsuspecting friends and family members. It would be nice to get a warning if any of them decide to visit our house again."

"In the unlikely event that we let any of them out on bail, I'll be pushing to have them wearing ankle monitors," he said. "Because, yes, I would like the whole department to have warning if any of them even head out of town in your direction."

"Grandfather will like that," I said.

"By the way, Kevin says he's finished with the NiceIce," he said. "Does that mean something to you?"

"It means we can send everyone home and let the small mammals catch up on their sleep."

My announcement that the rink was open was greeted with cheers, and everyone dashed out. Well, everyone except for a posse of relatives who stayed long enough to pack up any leftover food that needed to be taken back to the house.

And Mr. Meredith. He was standing in a corner, holding a white china mug of tea and nibbling half-heartedly on a cookie. A Norwegian Christmas cookie that I knew to be particularly irresistible, so the fact that he wasn't wolfing it down and dashing over to score a few more spoke volumes for his mood.

"You're welcome to come over to the house if you'd like to spend a little more time with your staff," I said.

"Thank you," he said. "But I think I will go over to the room your mother arranged, at the rectory. It's not as if I can be of any use to them right now. I was going to see if I could arrange a bus to take them up to Washington tonight, and put them up in a hotel there, but it seems the bus charter companies are as overbooked as the airlines."

"Don't worry," I said. "They're fine staying with us, and we'll find a way to get them home somehow."

"You're very kind," he said. "I'm changing the name back."

"The name?" I wasn't sure what name he was talking about, or what it had to do with getting the Canadians home.

"AcerGen." He was staring into his mug as if looking for answers. "It was Ian's idea. Silly one, if you ask me. I'm changing the name back to Maple Leaf Genealogy." He looked up at me. "Or does that sound disrespectful?"

"It sounds sensible," I said. "And maybe it will help people recover from their difficult stay here."

"Help them forget, you mean," he said. "Yes. So we will diminish, and go into the north."

Anyone who copes with heartache by paraphrasing Tolkien is my kind of people, and if he'd looked any less heart-broken I'd have responded with a quote of my own. "All you have to decide is what to do with the time that is given to you" came to mind. But while I was still trying to decide how he'd take it, he sighed, set down his mug and the half-eaten cookie, and shambled out.

I ended up chauffeuring a carload of elderly relatives who came from more southern climes and seemed to consider riding a few miles in a snowstorm in my Toyota to be as peril-ous as dogsledding in an Antarctic blizzard. Fortunately I dis-tracted them by starting a Christmas carol singalong. Music not only had charms to soothe a savage breast, it also worked brilliantly to distract nervous passengers. So I led them in "Jingle Bells" as we dashed through the snow, followed by all five verses of "Good King Wenceslas." At some point they fig-ured out that no matter how deep and crisp and even the snow lay round about, the county snowplows weren't leaving that much of it on the road. On the home stretch, they even got up enough nerve to venture "Let It Snow! Let It Snow! Let It Snow!"—bellowing out the recurring refrain with a great deal of bravado. Still, I could tell they were greatly re-lieved when I stopped in the loading zone at the end of our front walk to let them out. And luckily someone—probably Josh and Jamie—had already been busy with snow shovels, so the walk was beautifully clear. The walk, and the driveway, including the lane that led back to the Toyota's usual parking spot.

As I parked by the barn I couldn't help thinking that if we got enough coffee or hot chocolate into them, my nervous passengers might actually venture back to the rink to watch a little of the skating before bedtime.

Inside the festivities were going full blast. The crowd was smaller than last night, since most of the relatives who were lodging at Mother and Dad's or with friends in town had wisely stayed put. But though smaller, the crowd was just as merry—in fact, maybe a little more so, as if we were all doing our best to undo any blight Ian's murder had cast on our holiday spirits.

And Cousin Nora made a major contribution to the high spirits with her party menu. In addition to cakes, pies, cookies, ice cream, and crème brûlée, she had prepared a special treat for the Canadians.

"Oh, wow!" one of them exclaimed when he walked into the dining room with his plate. "Poutine!"

Soon the kitchen and the living room were filled with partygoers holding plates of poutine. Canadians closing their eyes with ecstasy at the first bite and assuring Nora that she'd gotten it perfect. Americans sampling it and either joining the Canadian enthusiasm or opting to switch to other, more familiar delicacies. Or doing what I did—after trying a small helping of poutine, just to see what it was like, I switched to plain old fries, seasoned with nothing more than sea salt and freshly ground black pepper. I wondered if there was any chance Nora could teach me to make fries as light and crisp and delicious as hers.

Chief Burke and Minerva had given their grandson Adam approval to have a sleepover with Josh and Jamie, and the three of them were out skating under the falling snow. As were several other young cousins and six or seven of the Canadians. We ended up having to make a rule against eating poutine—or anything else—on the ice, but Nora set up a satellite poutine-and-dessert station in the tent by the rink, so when hunger struck the skaters didn't have to come all the way to the house to fend it off.

The only long faces at the party belonged to a few of the Canadians, who had begun trying to book plane tickets for Toronto and were not having much luck.

"I can't find anything that doesn't cost a whole month's salary," I overheard one of the young Canadian programmers say to another. "And that's with two plane changes and the whole thing will fall apart if the first or second flight is even a few minutes late. I'm going to knock off for now. And I think tomorrow I'll see if I can get a group to go in on a rental car."

"Good luck with that, too," his friend said. "The car rental companies are just as overbooked as the airlines."

"Great," the first one said. "I hope our hosts are okay with putting us up over Christmas if it comes to that."

"No way," I muttered. They were going home if I had anything to say about it. Not that I had any objection to their company, and Michael and I were rather used to having a house full of people over the holidays. But it was Christmas, and they'd want to spend it with their families back in Toronto. I was determined to get them there, even if I had to chauffeur them myself. Although surely I could delegate the driving to someone else. Randall Shiffley might be willing to lend us a truck and driver. Or now that school was out, maybe I could borrow a school bus and recruit someone to drive it.

I'd worry about that tomorrow. It had been a long day—a day that felt like at least three very busy days all rolled into one. I was settled in an easy chair with one of the Poms in my lap, listening to Uncle Wes playing Christmas carols on his harp, and promising myself that in a minute I'd get up and go to bed.

I vaguely recall saying "not just yet" when Michael asked me if I was going up to bed now. And then I must have dozed off. I woke up still in the armchair with a lap full of Pomeranians and a stiff neck from falling asleep with my head at an odd angle. The living room was silent and dark except for the Christmas tree lights and the fading glow of the fire.

I shifted so I could pull my phone out of my pocket. Just past midnight. The witching hour.

Also time for me to go to bed. Past time.

I carefully transferred the Poms from my lap to the floor where they could cuddle up to Tinkerbell, and got up.

Michael had probably gone to bed, assuming I'd follow when the harp concert ended. And he'd probably have made the rounds, as we called it—checked all the doors and windows to make sure the house was secure.

Then again, he'd probably gotten just as little sleep as I had. And even if the chief's two prime suspects were safely locked up, they weren't the only bad guys in the world. Christmas was a prime season for burglary. I should make the rounds, just in case.

I went around the living room, checking the windows. Peering out, I could see that we had close to half a foot of snow, with flakes still coming down. A lovely night to be safe indoors. Then I checked the front door. The dining room windows. The kitchen windows. The back door. The library windows. The sunroom door.

"And all through the house," I murmured as I slowly trudged up the stairs. "Not a creature was stirring, not even a—"

Just then I heard an unearthly shriek.

Chapter 28

I wasn't sure whether the shriek came from a human being or an animal—I just knew that whatever creature had made that noise was in some kind of agony.

And it had come from somewhere upstairs. I hurried up to the second floor and stopped in the hallway, listening.

Maybe it had been a fox. When we'd first moved to the country, I'd been alarmed at how often I heard ghastly screams coming from the surrounding woods. I knew now that it was only the foxes' mating calls. But even knowing that I was sometimes alarmed when I heard them. If this was only a fox . . .

But no, it hadn't sounded as if it was coming from the wood. It had sounded closer. In the house.

There it was again, sounding even more agonized—and coming from the third floor. I raced up and stood at the top of the stairs, willing whoever had made the noise to do it again. Long seconds ticked by. I was about to go downstairs again, to fetch my main key ring, which had a master key. I could start opening all the doors and—

The shriek came again, and this time I heard a human voice, almost drowned out by the shriek.

"I think she's dying!" the voice said.

I recognized the voice—Rhea. And it seemed to be coming from the room now occupied by Maeve—the room with the excellent view of our backyard bird feeders.

I strode down the hall and knocked on the door.

"What's going on?" I said.

A pause.

"Nothing." Maeve or Angela, I wasn't sure which.

"Yeah, right," I said. "I heard someone screaming in agony. Let me in or—"

The door opened, and Rhea stood in the doorway.

"It's fine," she said. "We're only—"

I pushed past her into the room. Maeve and Angela glanced up, startled. They were both kneeling on the floor, one on each side of a copier paper box.

In the box was a cat. The pregnant yellow tabby who'd been hanging around the Methodist church. She was alarmingly tiny, and by contrast her pregnant belly seemed enormous. She looked up at me with an expression of helpless misery. Then her body tensed, and she yowled in agony—though not as loudly as before. She seemed to be running out of energy.

"She's having labor pains," Angela said.

"I figured that out," I said. "How long has this been going on?"

"A little while now," Maeve said.

"Two hours," Rhea said

"She only just started screaming," Angela said. "I don't think it's going well."

Understatement. From what I could see, the cat hadn't

even bothered to push with that last labor pain. Not a good sign.

"We need to take her down to the vet," I said. "Come on."

"Noooo!" Angela grabbed the box, and Maeve leaned over as if trying to put her body between me and the cat.

"We don't want her put down," Rhea said. "She's—"

"No one wants to put her down," I said. "I'm talking about saving her life. She's incredibly small. Way smaller than any other pregnant cat I've ever seen, which could mean the kittens are too large for her. And it looks as if she's given up trying. She may need medical help—possibly even a C-section. So let's get her downtown so our very skilled town vet can save her. Unless you want to stay here and watch her die."

Angela and Maeve exchanged a glance, then drew away from the box. I picked it up and headed for the stairs.

"If any of you want to come with me, run ahead and get your wraps," I said over my shoulder. "And get my coat. It's the—"

"I know which one." Rhea ran past me. Angela and Maeve followed.

By the time I reached the front hall, they were all ready to go. I handed the box off to Rhea, pulled on my coat, and led the way to the Twinmobile.

It was snowing more heavily now, and I could see that our road hadn't been plowed all that recently. Not surprising. Caerphilly only had two snowplows for the entire county. With this much snow Osgood and Beau, the drivers, were probably having trouble keeping up, and the more traveled roads in town took priority. I hoped we didn't get stuck in a snowbank on the way to town.

We set the box in the back seat, with Angela and Maeve on either side to steady it. Angela kept talking to the cat with a constant stream of soft, comforting words. Maeve appeared to be saying the rosary. Both good ideas, provided we accompanied them with a quick trip to see Clarence.

Rhea climbed up front with me, and I handed her my phone.

"Take this," I said. "I need to focus on my driving. Call Clarence Rutledge—the number's in my contact list. Tell him to meet us at his clinic."

Rhea nodded and began calling. I launched myself on the road, which was getting nasty. Surprisingly slippery.

Rhea reached Clarence, who was out at a farm at the other side of the county. He promised to head back as soon as he could.

"What if he doesn't make it in time?" Angela whispered.

"Call my dad," I told Rhea. "And tell him what's going on."

"Right." Rhea poked buttons until she found Dad's number and dialed.

"I thought your father was a medical doctor," Maeve said.

"He is," I said. "But he's also an animal lover. He helps out all the time, at Clarence's clinic and out at the zoo. He did an emergency C-section on a leopard once—I think he can handle this."

As I expected, Dad was eager to help out our pregnant cat—and he was already in town, having taken a hypochondriac aunt to the ER to reassure her that she wasn't actually having a heart attack.

"I'll meet you at Clarence's clinic!" he said.

"Thank goodness," Angela breathed from the back seat.

"I wish you had told me sooner that you had her," I said. Which would probably make them feel guilty—well, maybe they *should* feel guilty. Maybe they'd have more common sense the next time something like this happened. "Given how small she is, and how close to her term, we could have had her under observation at Clarence's all evening. Much safer for her. Especially since Clarence would probably have realized how close she was to giving birth, and would have stayed up with her."

"We weren't sure if we should tell you," Angela said, "since we figured out you don't exactly like cats."

"Why on earth would you think that?" I asked. "We have two of our own—on top of five llamas, several dozen chickens, four resident dogs and any number of visiting ones. We're not exactly averse to animals."

"Yes, but you exile your cats to the barn," Rhea said.

"Skulk and Lurk are ferals," I said. "Clarence rescued them and neutered them, and we adopted them as our barn cats because he thought at their age they were too set in their ways to be good candidates for house pets."

"Oh." Maeve looked chastened. Angela was crying softly.

"I'm sorry," she sobbed. "We misjudged you."

"Don't worry about it," I said.

Maybe I should have let them keep worrying. Half a mile farther on we came to a dead stop. A rental car full of tourists and Deacon Washington's farm truck were tangled up together in the middle of the road, totally blocking traffic. Clearly this was one reason Beau and Osgood hadn't been able to plow our roads recently.

The deacon was standing and shaking his head at the truck. Nearby was his grandson, the one who had been driving him around since his eyesight got too bad to drive.

"Can't you get by on the shoulder?" Rhea asked.

"There's not really much of a shoulder in this stretch of the road," I said. "Just really deep ditches. Stay here."

I set the emergency brake, jumped out, and strode closer to the wreck.

"Anyone hurt?" I asked.

"We're all fine," the deacon said. "But I'm blessed if I know how I'm going to get home."

"I'll carry you if I have to, Gramps," his grandson said.

I glanced back at the Twinmobile. Rhea and Maeve were staring out with stricken looks on their faces. Angela was still crying.

Just then a police cruiser pulled up on the far side of the accident. Vern Shiffley stepped out.

"Vern!" I called. "Veterinary emergency! Can you take me and the patient into town?"

"Hop in," he said.

"But what about our car?" one of the tourists wailed.

"The tow truck is right behind me, ma'am," Vern said. "And if any of you have any injuries you want treated, I can run you into town right quick."

I ran back to the Twinmobile, grabbed my tote, and opened the driver's side passenger door.

"I'll take the cat," I said. "Rhea, can you run Deacon Washington home? He can show you the way. At his age he shouldn't be standing around in the cold. By the time you do that they will probably have cleared the accident and you can join us at Clarence's."

"Okay." Rhea jumped out and began circling around to the driver's side.

"I'll come with you," Maeve said.

Carrying the cat's box we carefully picked our way around the perimeter of the accident—there was barely enough room for pedestrians to avoid the ditch—and hopped into the back of Vern's car. Which reeked of vomit. I saw Maeve's nose wrinkle.

"Sorry about the smell, ladies," Vern said as he began turning his car around. "Picked up a pair of drunks earlier this evening."

"It's not really that bad," Maeve said in a brave tone.

"Yes, it is," I said. "Vern, can you crack the windows?"

Even with all the windows open it was still a smelly ride,

and a wild, cold, windy one to boot, but Vern got us to the front steps of the Caerphilly Veterinary Hospital a lot faster than I could have managed in the snow. Dad and Lucas, Clarence's assistant, ran out the front door as soon as we pulled up in front of it. Vern carried the box inside, and waited with us while Dad and Lucas examined the cat. Actually, Dad, Lucas, and Grandfather, who must have come along for the ride to keep Dad company.

"I'm not sure we can wait for Clarence," Dad said. "She might not make it. Lucas, can you prep the operating room?"

Lucas nodded and ran into the back part of the clinic. Vern and Dad followed, carrying the cat's box. Vern emerged a few minutes later, looking a little green around the gills.

"They're prepping her for surgery," he said. "Keep me posted, will you?"

"Will do," I said.

Vern left. Maeve and I looked at each other, then sat down side by side in the waiting room. Grandfather must have decided to enact the role of surrogate expectant father. He began pacing up and down.

"Whose cat is that, anyway?" He had stopped in front of us and was eyeing Maeve suspiciously.

"Feral," I said. "Maeve and a couple of her friends rescued her."

"Ah." His expression changed to one of approval and he resumed his pacing.

Maeve began crying softly. Few things rattled Grandfather, but seeing women cry was one of them.

"Fine looking orange tabby," he said, obviously trying to distract her. "I prefer the term yellow, actually, and you'll also hear them called red, ginger, marmalade, or even butterscotch. Orange cats are always tabbies, and males greatly outnumber the females."

"Until I met this one I thought they were always male,"

Maeve said. I suspected she was just being polite rather than fascinated by these bits of feline lore. She kept glancing at the door that led back into the main body of the clinic.

"The gene for the yellow or orange color is carried on the X chromosome." Grandfather was in full lecture mode now. "A male cat who inherits it will be yellow, but a female has to inherit the gene from both parents to be yellow, like this one. So male yellow cats outnumber females approximately four to one."

Grandfather continued to dispense bits of lore about feline genetics, including the differences between the classic, mackerel, striped, and ticked tabby patterns, the reason for the extreme rarity of male calicos, and the fact that the domestic cat shared 96 percent of its DNA with tigers. And it did seem to have the effect of distracting Maeve from her stress—at least enough that she didn't shed any more tears. Although she was shivering, as if still feeling the bitter cold outdoors. Evidently Grandfather noticed. He went back to check on how surgery was going, returning with two steaming cups of coffee.

"Going well so far," he said, as he handed Maeve one of the cups. He offered me the other, but when I declined, he began sipping it. It would take a lot more than a slight chill to make me interested in drinking a cup of coffee.

Grandfather was just getting started on sex-linked traits in humans, such as hemophilia and red/green color blindness, when Dad burst through the door from the back area. The sight of his face, beaming with obvious delight, was immensely reassuring to all of us.

"It's a litter!" he exclaimed. "Six of them! All reasonably sized, and perfectly healthy, as far as I can tell. Want to take a look?"

He led us back through the door into a room that served as Clarence's main examining room, and then to one of the small side rooms for patients that were staying at the clinic. Clarence preferred small rooms to the large open room full of cages you saw in so many veterinary hospitals—he felt that the small rooms contributed to animals' faster recovery, since they let him separate dogs from cats, and cats from rodents, and aggressive or noisy creatures from timid or shy ones. The formerly pregnant cat was in a large crate in a small room with no other patients. Lucas was sitting in a stained and battered beanbag chair beside her crate, obviously planning to keep a close watch over her. The cat was purring, and the kittens were nursing—all six of them: three yellow, one calico, and two that would either be black or tortoiseshell—it was hard to tell when they were still slightly damp.

"Mother and kits are all doing fine," Lucas said. "And I'll be staying with them until we're sure she's recovered from the anesthetic."

"But what will happen to them?" Maeve looked anxious. Clearly she didn't know Clarence. Or Caerphilly.

"Don't worry," Dad said. "We've had a bit of a kitten shortage lately—which is a good thing, actually, since it means our spay and neuter campaigns are working well. And it also means that Clarence has a list of fully vetted potential adoptees for any kittens he comes across. And we should have no problem getting this little lady adopted, either." He reached in and scratched the mother cat behind the ears. She lifted her head to meet his hand.

"Obviously not a feral," Lucas said. "Some creep must have decided he didn't want kittens and dumped her off in the town square. There oughta be a law. But Clarence and I know a couple of people who have lost cats recently and might be ready to adopt a new one. They'll be fighting over her. For now, we're calling her Merry—as in Christmas."

"A lovely name," Maeve said.

We all stood in a circle for a while, gazing at Merry and

her kittens, and it struck me that we were rather like a slightly off-kilter live reenactment of the Nativity scene. Lucas made a sturdy, protective Joseph, with Dad hovering in character as the guardian angel. Maeve, Grandfather, and I could fill the role of the shepherds. Although Grandfather would probably prefer being thought of as one of the three kings. The boss king, if there was such a thing, and if there wasn't, Grandfather would invent it.

"They all look quite vigorous," Grandfather said in a satisfied tone. He preferred fierce animals to docile ones, which meant he tended to approve of most cats on general principles. And even he probably realized that the kittens were too young to be fierce, so vigorous would do for the time being.

That broke the spell, and we all began talking logistics. Dad planned to stay at the clinic until Clarence arrived and he could hand off his patients—then he and Grandfather would head home. Maeve begged to be allowed to stay overnight and help Lucas keep watch over his charges, and no one had any objection. I checked with Debbie Ann and learned that the accident with Deacon Washington's truck was still being cleared up.

"But don't worry," she said. "It won't take much longer. Just stay there at the clinic, and as soon as the road opens, I can ask one of the deputies to run you back home. Probably Horace—he'd enjoy the chance to check on Watson. Or maybe Vern, when he finishes cleaning up his patrol car."

I thanked her and hung up.

Everyone else was focused on the various animals staying here at the clinic. Grandfather was trading stares with an ailing iguana. Dad was talking soothingly to a pit bull as he examined its teeth. Lucas and Maeve were hovering over the kittens.

I suddenly realized that the clinic was way too hot. Which was good for all the ailing or recovering animals, but it was starting to feel oppressive. And the smell was getting to me, disinfectant with a faint undertone of animal waste.

"I'm going to get some air," I said.

No one argued with me—I wasn't even sure any of them noticed when I left the back part of the clinic for the waiting room. I donned my coat, hat, and gloves. Then I made sure the front door was unlocked, so I could get back in if everyone continued to be preoccupied, and stepped outside into the snowy night.

It wasn't snowing all that hard at the moment. But it was a pretty snow, with the flakes spiraling down, glittering in the clinic's outside lights. I took deep breaths of the clean, cold air and basked in the sudden equally refreshing sense of solitude. The Caerphilly Veterinary Hospital was on the outskirts of town, well away from the tourist-filled environs. In fact, there was even a small woods behind it—only a couple of acres, but that was enough to make the neighborhood much quieter, and the woods made a nice place for exercising the dogs.

Someone had obviously plowed or shoveled the parking lot in front of the building fairly recently—there was only about an inch or so of snow on it. Still, enough to dampen any sounds. I listened for the sound of snowplows, cars, or even shoveling in the distance, but there was nothing to disturb the snow-muffled stillness.

And it was darker now. A few of the nearby houses left their holiday lights on all night, but most had turned them off. A few were enough to add a touch of holiday spirit, I decided, without disturbing the peace and quiet of the winter's night.

Peace and quiet. No one was asking me to do anything. I'd get plenty of that tomorrow, no doubt—helping the Canadians find their way home, clearing out their rooms so family members staying elsewhere could move in. Thank goodness Nora was here, so my contribution to meals would be limited to grocery runs and other menial chores. And the skating rink should make entertaining our visiting relatives much easier—the skating rink and everyone's ongoing fascination with finding out which of the chief's two suspects had committed the murder. But still. It would be busy, noisy, and tiring. Enjoyable. I could feel my holiday spirit returning. Another five minutes and I'd start humming "Joy to the World."

I was about to turn and go back inside the clinic when something poked me in the back.

"Don't move," a voice said. "And don't scream. If you do, I'll shoot."

Chapter 29

I recognized the voice. Elias Boyd, who had been pretending to be Katherine Anne Koenigslutter's lawyer when he showed up at the house. And who might or might not be her half brother, depending on how badly AcerGen's lab had screwed things up.

"Get moving," he said. "And put your hands in the air."

"Moving where?" I asked, hoping I could get away with not putting my hands in the air—maybe I could manage to turn on my phone and use it to notify someone that I was in trouble.

"I said hands in the air!" He shoved me roughly, and I instinctively pulled my hands out of my pockets so I could break my fall if I couldn't keep on my feet. I stumbled forward a few steps and managed not to fall.

"Keep going," he said. "And bear left."

We were going along the side of the clinic now. It didn't have a lot of windows, and what few there were had their blinds tightly drawn against the cold and dark. I kept looking for something I could stumble against, something that would cause enough noise to make someone inside curious. But we weren't going anywhere near the Dumpster or the chain-link-enclosed exercise yards, and Clarence had done an annoyingly good job of keeping the premises neat and free of junk.

The section of parking lot along the side of the building hadn't been cleared as recently as the front, making it slower going. I tried to exaggerate how much it hindered my steps.

And then I hit the patch of open land behind the building and no longer had to exaggerate how much the snow slowed me down. It was like in one of those dreams where you're in slow motion and every step takes an eternity.

I welcomed the obstacle. Every step took us closer to the woods. Closer to the point when no potential rescuers could see me.

Boyd wasn't happy about our slow pace.

"Get a move on." He emphasized this with another shove from the gun. I stumbled again, and fell to my knees, but I couldn't figure out any way to leverage this into an escape attempt or a feint for the gun, so I settled for getting up as slowly as I could manage.

"You're not helping, you know," he said.

"Why don't you just tell me what you want from me?" I asked.

"Right now, I just want you to keep walking."

And now we were in the woods, with the visible holiday lights rapidly fading behind us. The snow wasn't as deep under the tree canopy, and you could hardly see any falling. Then we reached a small clearing where the snow was at least half a foot deep and we could see the flakes coming down heavily again.

"This'll do," he said. "Take your coat off."

I turned to look at him. He didn't object—he just took a few steps back and stood there, smirking at me.

"You want me to do what?" I asked.

"Take your coat off," he said. "And your hat and gloves, too. *Now!*"

I shed my wraps as slowly as I could and dropped them nearby, where I could grab them again if I got a chance. Although I suspected he wasn't planning to give me one.

"You can sit down if you like," he said. He followed his own advice, dusting off a section of a nearby fallen tree and half sitting, half leaning against it.

"So you're just going to sit there and watch while I freeze to death?" I asked.

"Pretty much," he said. "Doesn't take long in this kind of weather. Once you're unconscious, I'll arrange it so it looks like you wandered out here by accident."

"You don't think the fact that I'm not wearing a coat will be a dead giveaway?" I asked.

"Happens all the time with hypothermia victims," he said. "It's called paradoxical undressing. For some reason, when you get really far along, your body tricks you into thinking you're burning up instead of freezing, and you start shedding clothes."

"Still, this is going to take a while," I said.

"Not as long as you think." His wolfish grin was not reassuring. Especially since I was already having a hard time not shivering.

"Then maybe you should distract me." I said. "So I'll forget about trying to figure out how to get the drop on you while we wait. Tell me: How did you find Ian? Who told you he was going to be here in Caerphilly?"

"He did."

"Yeah, right."

"Of course, he didn't know it was me he was telling. He thought he was talking to the detective in charge of the Cyrus Runk case. I set up a Gmail with a variation on the guy's name and told him I was using that because of leaks in the department."

"You catfished him."

"Worked like a charm. And then I figured out how to leak his whereabouts to a couple of other people who had it in for him."

"Cyrus Runk and your half sister," I said.

"Yeah. I figured the cops would think one or the other of them had done it."

"So you steered them toward the *Virginia Crime Time* message boards and leaked Ian's whereabouts there."

He wasn't expecting me to know that—I could tell from his quick frown. He recovered almost immediately and pretended nonchalance.

"Yeah. Like I said, it all worked like a charm. Aren't you starting to feel sleepy yet?"

"Not yet. And of course we've figured out why you wanted to kill Ian."

"Yeah, right."

"Because he knew you weren't really Katherine Anne Koenigslutter's half brother."

It was only a guess, but from the expression of shock and anger on his face I knew I'd guessed right.

"Beep! Wrong!" he said. "Try again."

"It's the only thing that makes sense," I said. "You assumed that with Ian gone, AcerGen would do its best to hush up the quality control problems with its DNA testing program. Maybe even work out some kind of settlement with Ms. Koenigslutter to compensate her for what you'd taken away from her."

"Compensate her." Boyd snorted. "She's rolling in dough.

Been living high on that great big farm all her life, in the lap of luxury. She can afford to give me a little."

If Ms. Koenigslutter had been living on a farm all her life, chances were she'd been working hard rather than living high. I'd come to know a lot of farmers since moving to Caerphilly, and not a one of them lived in the lap of luxury. But I didn't think Boyd would understand that. And besides—

"That argument might work if you actually were related to her," I said. "And had even the slightest claim to her inheritance. But you don't."

"Good thing I'm getting rid of you," he said. "You've figured out way too much. And here I thought all I had to worry about was you seeing me running away from the skating rink."

"Actually, I didn't."

"Yeah, right. Then why did you say you did?"

"I was bluffing," I said. "To chase away anyone who might be there. I did see something, but only out of the corner of my eye, and it could just as easily have been an owl or a fox. So it's not as if I can identify you."

"Uh-huh," he said. "That's what you say now. Bet your eyesight would improve pretty miraculously if they put you on the witness stand. Plus you took a picture of me when I was running away."

"I did what?"

"Don't pretend you didn't. I saw you holding up your phone."

"I was talking to the nine-one-one operator," I said. "And even if I had tried to take a picture, how recognizable do you think you'd be in an iPhone photo taken in the middle of the night at fifty or sixty yards?"

"You'd be surprised what they can do these days, those prosecutors," he said.

"There is no photo—let me get out my phone and I'll show you."

"Keep your hands out of your pockets," he said. "I'll get your phone and delete the photo once you're out of it."

I racked my brain for something else I could do. Maybe the cold was starting to affect me. Over Boyd's shoulder—behind his back—did I really see someone approaching? Or was it only wishful thinking—maybe even a hallucination. Hard to see anything given how heavily the snow was falling by now, but it looked like a cloaked figure. I'd given up the battle to keep my teeth from chattering. Yes, definitely a cloaked figure. And carrying a staff. It looked like Gandalf at the Pass of Caradhras. Obi-Wan Kenobi striding across snow instead of the Tatooine desert. Father Merrin the exorcist looming out of a foggy Georgetown street. Were hallucinations another symptom of impending death from hypothermia?

"You're not fooling me, you know," Boyd said. "I know damn well there's no one sneaking up behind me, so stop pretending—"

That was when Grandfather hit him over the head with his hiking staff.

The blow knocked Boyd unconscious, and he sprawled limply on the snow. Grandfather darted over to him, bent down, and then retreated back to a safe distance.

"I've got his gun," Grandfather announced. "I'll keep him covered while you tie him up."

"I'm not sure my fingers are working well enough to tie him up," I said. "And tie him up with what?"

"Well, then, put your coat back on." I was already doing that. "And we'll figure out something. Reinforcements should be turning up soon anyway—I called nine-one-one to tell them which way I was heading."

"I gather you saw him capture me." Having my coat, hat, and gloves back on was helping, but I was still shivering and trying to keep my teeth from chattering.

"No," he said. "Maeve remembered you saying you'd gone

outside to get some fresh air, but I didn't figure anyone would want all that much fresh air in weather like this, so when I didn't find you nearby, I pulled out my phone and checked on the little GPS thingie I hid in your coat."

I should have known.

"When did you manage that?"

"Earlier tonight, out at the zoo," he said. "While you were in talking with the chief. Seemed to me that with the two main suspects locked up, everyone was getting a little smug and complacent. And you were the one who might be in the most danger. So I slipped one into the lining of your coat. Aren't you glad I ignored your telling me not to do that anymore?"

"Very glad." And I was, even though I knew we'd never hear the end of this. "Thank you. You saved my life."

"Oh, you'd have figured out a way to deal with him sooner or later," he said.

Meanwhile I'd cautiously moved closer to Boyd.

"It looks as if he's got those really heavy-duty unbreakable boot laces in his boots," I said.

"The kind with Kevlar in them?"

"I don't know," I said. "They really make Kevlar boot laces?"

"Of course," he said. "Standard equipment these days if you're going on a real hike."

"Well, even if these aren't Kevlar, they look pretty strong," I said. "If you keep the gun on him, I'll take them out of his boots and tie him up."

"Good idea." Grandfather nodded his approval. "If they break, we're no worse off than we are now."

"Maybe better off," I said. "I'll take his boots off while I'm at it. I doubt if he'll want to do much walking in his stocking feet in this weather."

Boyd remained unconscious while I untied his boots and pulled them off. He only moaned slightly when I pulled his hands together and tied them behind his back. I was a little alarmed when I saw a small pool of blood flowing over the snow, but it turned out to be a nosebleed,

"It looks as if he broke his nose when he fell," I reported.

"Here." Grandfather handed me a more-or-less clean handkerchief. "You can staunch the bleeding with that."

I wadded the handkerchief against Boyd's nose and then stepped back, out of his reach. If he needed more than cursory first aid, he'd have to get it from someone he hadn't tried to murder.

He was starting to come around—and cursing a blue streak—by the time Vern and Aida appeared. Closely followed by Dad and the chief.

"Here comes the cavalry," I said. "If you need me for anything, I'll be inside where it's warm."

I was so cold I was actually looking forward to having a cup of Clarence's wretched coffee.

Chapter 30

"Silver bells, silver bells,
It's Christmas time in Caerphilly . . ."

I leaned back against the hearth and took another sip of my
hot cider. Ever since last night's ordeal in the snow with Elias
Boyd, I'd been having trouble feeling warm. Dad had dragged
me down to the hospital that night to have me checked out by
every relevant specialist on staff, and they all assured me that
I was in tip-top shape and had suffered no damage from my
time in the cold. Dad informed me that I was experiencing a
psychological reaction to trauma that would wear off before
too long.

He was probably right. But meanwhile, I was mainlining
hot chocolate, hot cider, and mulled wine. And spending an
inordinate amount of time sitting with the dogs by the fire.
As if sensing my need for warmth, Tinkerbell and the Pomeranians had spent much of the day glued to my side or lap.
Even Spike hovered nearby, and on those occasions when I
had to leave to visit the bathroom or grab a plate of food, he

guarded my favorite spot on the hearth with a fierceness he usually saved for defending his own food.

"And on every street corner you'll hear
Silver bells, silver bells . . ."

"Such a lovely version of the song." Maeve came to sit by me, and Angela and Rhea perched nearby.

"Even though Caerphilly isn't where you were hoping to be at Christmastime?"

"It's impossible," she said. "No one has been able to find a flight except for Seth, and when he realized it was going to cost more than a month's salary, he decided to pass on it. I'm afraid you're stuck with us."

"Not a problem." I thought of mentioning that with the single glaring exception of Ian, they had all been perfectly lovely guests. I decided they'd probably already figured that out.

"It won't be that bad," Rhea said. "That huge monitor Kevin set up in your library will make Zoom visits with our families much nicer."

"And I'll probably manage to regain my long-lost skating skills," Angela said.

"And it will be nice to drop by Clarence's clinic and visit the kittens," Maeve said. "And—ooh! There's your grandfather. He's taking us owling tonight, you know—are you coming?"

"Some other time," I said. "When it's warmer."

Grandfather was beaming as if he'd done something marvelous. And heading our way. I braced myself. Grandfather's marvelous ideas sometimes turned out to be exhausting. When he reached the fireplace, he nodded to Maeve and me and stepped up onto the hearth.

"Let me have your attention please!" he bellowed. His voice was hard to ignore, and the furor immediately began to abate, replaced first with shushing noises and then with an expectant silence.

"As you all know, the decision was made yesterday to postpone the DNA website project so our Canadian visitors could go home for Christmas," he said. "Except that the decision was made so late that it's almost impossible for any of them to get plane tickets and they're even having trouble finding rental cars."

"Gee, thanks for rubbing it in," Rob said from the back of the room. "We were actually hoping this bash would help distract everyone from that."

"I wouldn't have brought it up if I didn't have a proposed solution." Grandfather scowled at Rob briefly, then favored him with a brief smile before continuing. After all, this was the grandson who had at least displayed some interest, however superficial, in his beloved DNA. He turned back to his audience and continued. "Manoj Batra, one of my staff members, has a commercial driver's license—which is what you need if you're going to drive the bus I use for expeditions. At least the tame sort of expedition that doesn't involve camping. And Manoj would be overjoyed at having a chance to spend the holidays with his parents. Who just happen to live in a suburb of Toronto."

An excited buzz swept through the room.

"It's a long day's drive—ten to twelve hours, depending on traffic and road conditions," Grandfather went on. "So anyone who wants to ride along with Manoj, pack your stuff tonight and be ready to take off from here at Meg and Michael's house tomorrow at eight a.m. sharp."

A cheer went up, and Grandfather acknowledged it by raising his mug and taking an appreciative gulp of its contents.

"And the owling expedition will take off in"—he glanced at his watch—"precisely one hour."

He stepped down from the hearth and began strolling

toward the hallway, somewhat hindered by the half dozen Canadians who had rushed over to thank him.

"How wonderful," Rhea said to me. "Your grandfather is so generous."

"It will be a long day," Angela said. "But when you consider how much time even a direct flight always takes—and at least this won't involve nearly as much walking."

"I'm not fond of bus rides," Maeve admitted. "But even a bus ride's better than missing Christmas with my family."

"A ride on Grandfather's bus isn't exactly a hardship," I said. "This is the bus he's fitted out to be as comfortable as possible for when he goes on the road, with or without some of his major donors. Big, comfy reclining seats with extra legroom, decent-sized lavatory, bar, kitchenette, multiple TV screens, Wi-Fi—if you can think of any reasonable feature it's missing, let Grandfather know and he'll probably insist on adding it for the bus's next run. The video library's almost entirely nature films, including a lot featuring Grandfather, but he can be pretty entertaining."

They exchanged looks, and then smiled.

"I knew I liked your grandfather," Maeve said.

"We should go and thank him," Angela said.

"And find our wraps for the owling!"

They hurried off.

I closed my eyes and basked again in the warmth of the fire.

"You look relaxed."

I opened my eyes to see Chief Burke.

"So do you," I said. "I deduce that things are going well down at the station."

"They are," he said. "Vern took off an hour ago to drive Cyrus Runk over to Appomattox County."

"Appomattox? I thought he'd committed his murder in Buchanan County."

"He did," he said. "But two days ago, on his way up here, he committed an armed robbery at a gas station in Appomattox County. Buchanan County has kindly consented to let Appomattox have him first."

"That was nice of them," I said.

"Well, Buchanan probably won't be needing him for a while. The Virginia Supreme Court has agreed to take the case of whether his conviction should have been overturned because of a confession from a man who has spent more than half his life in a high-security psych ward. And now that Runk has demonstrated that he's both a flight risk and a danger to the public, I don't think anyone's going to let him out on bail anytime soon."

"What about his lawyer's challenge to the DNA evidence?"

"No telling what will happen with that." He sighed and shook his head. "But even if that goes sideways, there's still the armed robbery. If Vern were here, he could tell you for sure, but if memory serves, there's a minimum of five years for armed robbery."

"Five years seems short to me."

"That's the minimum," he said. "It can go as high as life if the circumstances are bad enough. There's also an additional penalty of three years, minimum, for the use of a firearm in a felony. Odds are he'll be behind bars for a good long time."

"Assuming Appomattox has a good case against him," I said. "Do they have DNA?"

"They won't need DNA," the chief said. "They got fingerprints, plus unusually clear video footage from the gas station's security camera."

"Yeah, but couldn't it be useful for the Buchanan County murder case?" I asked. "As I understand it, Runk's lawyer is saying that if it weren't for the DNA information from Acer-Gen, they wouldn't have had any reason to suspect Runk and test him—so the DNA match to the murder scene is fruit of the poisonous tree and should be thrown out. But what if they do DNA at the armed robbery scene, to make the case against Runk that much stronger, and then put that DNA in CODIS . . ."

"Then his DNA in CODIS would match the DNA from the Buchanan County murder," the chief said. "I'm no lawyer, but I think that might pass muster as inevitable discovery. At the very least, dealing with it will help ensure that Mr. William Morgan earns whatever fame or fortune he's getting from this case. I'll pass the word to Appomattox. Maybe you should have been a lawyer."

"I'll leave that to Festus," I said. "What about your other two prisoners?"

"Ms. Fawn's family are driving down from Long Island to collect her," he said. "They promise they'll try harder to keep her on her meds. And since we have no evidence that Ms. Koenigslutter is guilty of anything, we turned her loose this morning. Actually, we told her she was free to go late last night, but given the weather and the fact that there wasn't a hotel room to be had this side of Richmond, she opted to stay overnight as our guest. And now, with your permission, I'm going to go out there and watch my grandson skating."

"Enjoy."

For a moment I contemplated joining him. But it was still in the twenties outside. The ice rink wasn't going anywhere anytime soon. And I'd have plenty of chances to watch the boys skating on it.

I closed my eyes and basked in the warmth of the fire.

"Meg, dear." I opened my eyes and looked up to find Mother gazing down at me. She looked unhappy. "Can you speak to your grandfather?"

"Yes, I can," I said. "In fact, I do, pretty often, and sometimes he even lets me get a word in edgewise. Is there a subject you'd like me to bring up the next time we're conversing?"

"Perhaps you could ask him why he brought *that woman* to our lovely festivity." Although politely phrased, it was clearly an order. Having delivered it, Mother sailed away, head high.

That woman? Had Grandfather brought an unsuitable female companion to the party? From Mother's tone I half expected a brazen hussy—although actually if the hussy dressed with a bit of panache Mother wouldn't really mind. She'd be much more apt to disapprove of someone who chewed with her mouth open. Or called this year's Christmas decorations "over the top."

I glanced around until I spotted Grandfather—his height usually made him relatively easy to find in a crowd. He was holding forth to a small audience, gesticulating wildly with a gravy-soaked fry.

At his elbow I spotted Katherine Anne Koenigslutter. She was beaming with happiness, which I found a little unnerving. I realized that Elias Boyd's arrest for the murder would clear her of suspicion, and the chief had already told me she was out of jail. But why was she here? And smiling. Surely anything that made her that happy would turn out to be bad news for the rest of us.

I strolled over to where Grandfather was standing.

"Can we talk?" I asked.

"Of course." He beamed at me with the proud, self-congratulatory expression that had become habitual since he'd rescued me.

"Privately." I plucked him by the sleeve and managed to drag him far enough away from Ms. Koenigslutter that she wouldn't hear us over the noise of the crowd. At least I hoped so.

"What's she doing here?" I asked.

"She didn't do it," he said. "Elias Boyd's the killer."

"Yes, I know," I said. "But she might still not be all that happy with us, since she probably thinks we were aiding and abetting Ian."

"She's pretty happy with me," he said. "Since I was able to tell her that Boyd isn't her half brother."

"That's not proven yet," I said. "We suspect it, from things both Boyd and Ian said, but we don't know for sure."

"We do now," he said. "Remember that handkerchief of mine you used to mop up Boyd's nosebleed? I reclaimed it once your Dad and I got him down to the hospital. Called in my DNA experts to do their thing with it. And then I went around to the jail before they let Ms. Koenigslutter go. When I explained what we suspected, she was more than happy to give me the necessary samples. And we've got our processing time down to five hours. We had the good news for her well before noon."

"That's great," I said. "But will those tests hold up in court? Since there was no chain of custody or anything like that."

"They don't have to," he said. "Ms. Koenigslutter's lawyer can now push to do new, official, court-ordered tests, knowing what the outcome will be. And since Boyd's lawyer now also knows those tests will torpedo any claim that his client has on Ms. Koenigslutter's assets, he'll probably cut his losses and drop the case. It's not as if he won't have plenty of work on his hands, defending the guy against a murder charge. So Ms. Koenigslutter is pretty pleased with us right now."

"You're full of good ideas lately," I said. "First figuring out how to track me down after Boyd kidnapped me, and now helping solve Ms. Koenigslutter's problems."

He beamed for a second or two, and then a shadow crossed his face.

"Tracking you down wasn't entirely my idea," he confessed. "As a matter of fact, it was your grandmother who suggested it."

"Cordelia?" I asked.

"Of course, Cordelia." He scowled at me. "Do you have any other grandmothers I haven't heard about?"

"I'm just trying to figure out when she could have suggested it," I explained. I didn't add "since the two of you usually avoid even being in the same room."

"Called me up special to give me what for about planting a bug on Caroline," Grandfather said. "She didn't seem to understand that Caroline was okay with it. In fact, Caroline knew I was going to do it, or should have if she'd been paying attention."

Given another day to think about it, he'd have convinced himself that Caroline had asked him to plant the little GPS tracker on her.

"I bet Cordelia didn't approve of your tracking Dad, either," I said.

"Luckily she doesn't know about that," he said. "And we should keep it that way. No sense upsetting her. She's not a young woman. Anyway, after she finished yelling at me for spying on Caroline, she asked why I didn't do something useful with my fancy gadgets, and I said 'like what?' and she suggested planting one on you so we could track you down if you insisted on going out and doing something dangerous. So I did."

He beamed at me and the satisfied expression returned to his face. No doubt he was thinking that Cordelia might have suggested planting the tracker on me, but he was the one who had succeeded, against all odds, in carrying it out.

"I probably owe my life to the two of you, then," I said. "You should cooperate more often."

He frowned and looked thoughtful.

"Using my bus to send the Canadians home was her idea, too," he admitted. "She does have a few good notions sometimes."

He frowned slightly, as if giving credit where credit was due had slightly dimmed his pleasure in the good deed.

"But her suggestion would have been pretty useless if you didn't happen to have the bus available to carry it out," I said.

"So you both made an important contribution. And you're the one who will have to give up use of the bus for a few days."

"That's true," he said. "But Manoj should be back with the bus in plenty of time for our January birdwatching trip to the Dismal Swamp."

He looked cheerful again, and beamed at the nearby friends and family. Including, wonder of wonders, Cordelia. Who was so surprised to find him beaming at her that she started and frowned. Her expression suggested that she suspected him of being up to something.

I should probably reassure her that he wasn't. That he was merely uncharacteristically full of Christmas cheer. And— also uncharacteristically—actually saying nice things about her. Maybe this was a turning point. Unlike Rose Noire, I was under no illusions that my grandparents would patch up their differences and become a couple again. But if they could co-exist peacefully—which might actually happen if Grandfather could manage to stop deliberately doing quite so many things to annoy Cordelia—life would be easier. Especially at the holidays. I vowed to do everything I could to bring about this new, improved state of affairs. Peace on earth and goodwill to all humankind.

"Your grandmother's being quite civil lately," he said, as if reading my thoughts. "Makes for a nice change. Maybe I'll ask her to join us for the sleighing party tomorrow."

"Sleighing party?"

"I sicced Randall Shiffley on it," he said. "The man's a marvel. He's rounded up three sleighs, and enough horses to haul them. So as soon as we wave goodbye to your Canadians, we'll start with the sleigh rides."

"Dashing through the snow," I said. "I like it."

"Well, we won't be dashing all the time," he said. "We'll be taking it slow much of the time, so we can get in a little bird-watching along the way. Bring your binoculars."

I had a feeling that if Josh and Jamie were involved, there'd be a lot more dashing than bird-watching. But he'd find that out in due time. Right now, he was smiling benignly at the crowd and tapping his foot in time to "Deck the Halls."

"Sing we joyous all together
Fa la la, la la la, la la la
Heedless of the wind and weather . . ."

"Come on," I said to Grandfather. "Let's go join the caroling."

Acknowledgments

Thanks once again to everyone at St. Martin's/Minotaur, including (but not limited to) Lily Cronig, Hector DeJean, Stephen Erickson, Nicola Ferguson, Meryl Gross, Paul Hochman, Kayla Janas, Andrew Martin, Kelley Ragland, Sarah Melnyk, and especially my editor, Pete Wolverton. And thanks also to the Art Department for yet another glorious cover.

More thanks to my agent, Ellen Geiger, and to Matt Mc-Gowan and the staff at the Frances Goldin Literary Agency for taking care of the business side of things so I can concentrate on writing.

Special thanks this time around to my Canadian accuracy consultants, Jane Burfield and Pam Thomson—anything I got wrong about Meg's visitors must be something I forgot to ask them about. Thanks—for the umpteenth time—to retired police officer Mark Bergin, who takes time from his own crime writing to advise me (and so many of his friends) on police procedure.

I'd like to give a shout-out to David and Kristen Mittleman of Othram—I follow their cutting-edge forensic DNA work with a fascination that helped inspire part of the plot of this book. Anyone who wants to learn more about—or support—their work of solving crimes, can visit their website, DNA solves.com.

Many thanks to the friends who brainstorm and critique with me, give me good ideas, or help keep me sane while I'm writing: Stuart, Aidan, and Liam Andrews; Deborah Blake; Chris Cowan; Ellen Crosby; Kathy Deligianis; Margery Flax; Suzanne Frisbee; John Gilstrap; Barb Goffman; Joni Langevoort; David Niemi; Alan Orloff; Dan Stashower, Art Taylor; Robin Templeton; and Dina Willner. And thanks to all the TeaBuds for two decades of friendship.

Above all, thanks to the readers who make all of this possible.

Read on for an excerpt from
Let It Crow! Let It Crow! Let It Crow!—

the next Meg Langslow mystery,
coming soon in hardcover from Donna Andrews
and Minotaur Books!

Chapter 1

"You can still change your mind, you know."

I closed my eyes and counted to ten. Then I opened them again. I crawled out from under the rough-hewn medieval-style trestle table I'd been repairing and looked up. Alec Franzetti was staring down at me with a pleading expression on his broad, bearded face. Both of his enormous, hairy hands were clutching a clipboard that held an untidy, inch-thick sheaf of paper. He gripped it tightly enough to turn his knuckles white. He looked so stressed that the temptation to snap at him vanished. I made sure my tone was gentle. Gentle, but firm.

"No, Alec," I said. "I'm very happy doing what I'm doing."

His face fell, and he sighed loudly.

"Is there anything I can help you with?" I stood up and gestured at the clipboard.

"Probably." He flipped through a couple of the top papers. "Let me think."

He glanced down at the clipboard, then wandered off, looking distracted and lost.

"Change your mind about what?" came a voice from behind me.

I jumped at the sound. Alec's anxiety was rubbing off on me. I turned and smiled when I saw my old friend Caroline Willner.

"Sorry," she said. "Didn't mean to startle you. Merry Christmas."

"Merry Christmas to you." I gave her a quick welcoming hug.

"And you don't have to apologize. How long have you been in town?"

"Only just arriving," she said. "Haven't even been to your house yet, because your dad said you were out here at Ragnar's farm, and could I drop by and try to rescue you? He wouldn't say from what. So who is this Alec person, and what does he want you to change your mind about? And for that matter, what is all this?" She made a sweeping gesture.

I glanced around, trying to see our surroundings through her eyes. We were in an enormous outdoor tent, the kind you'd get to hold a small circus or a really large outdoor wedding reception. We stood in the end that had been designated as the banquet hall, featuring the enormous oak table, four matching backless benches, and half a dozen tall, branching wrought iron candelabras. In the middle of the tent, taking up more than half of the floor space, was the forge area, featuring six assorted blacksmith's workstations, each complete with a forge, anvil, worktable, and a tall metal locker for tools, coats, and anything the director didn't want to see on camera. Beyond that, at the far end of the tent, was the production area, in which workers were setting up the lights, video cameras, microphones, and other tech gear needed to film what went on in the other two areas.

"Alec's an old friend," I began.

Not entirely accurate. But what was I supposed to call him? He certainly wasn't an old enemy. We'd never been all that close, and yet he was more than an old acquaintance. We'd known each other since our college days. He was someone I knew well enough to spend time with when we were thrown together, at craft fairs or blacksmith gatherings. Someone I rather liked when he wasn't being a complete pain in the neck. I vividly recalled that long-ago day when I'd met Alec, although I could no longer remember if it was in my sophomore or junior year of college. I'd ridden my bike from the UVA campus to the tiny, rundown building where William Faulkner Cates, my blacksmithing teacher, had his forge. I'd dashed inside, fired up for my next lesson, only to find that Faulk was working with another pupil. A much more traditional blacksmithing pupil—Alec was tall and burly like Faulk. He had brown hair to Faulk's blond, but apart from that they could have been brothers. I'd watched for a few minutes, unseen, as Faulk calmly guided Alec's faltering first attempts at blacksmithing. And felt a pang of—what? Jealousy, perhaps? Not sexual jealousy—even before I figured out Faulk was gay I'd realized we were meant to be friends rather than lovers. Still, I was more than a little resentful that someone else was taking up a part of my mentor's time and attention.

But it was more than that. Alec's arrival seemed at first as if it might slam the door I was trying to open—the door into a profession that wasn't exactly welcoming. Women blacksmiths were relatively rare, and the old guard treated us more as curiosities than colleagues. And apart from Dad, my own family members hadn't exactly been supportive. Oh, they were very encouraging about my taking lessons, but they seemed to see blacksmithing as a unique and interesting hobby to occupy my free time, once I'd taken up a suitable career as a doctor, lawyer, or professor. Something white collar and professional.

Faulk's forge was the only place where I could feel free from all those pressures—free from the disapproval of chauvinistic blacksmiths and the expectations of my family. And Faulk was, back then, the only person who really took my work seriously.

And then this intruder showed up. I was tempted to slink away, never to return. Clearly Faulk had only taken me on as a pupil because he hadn't found any men who wanted blacksmithing lessons. Alec would take my place and—

Just then Faulk noticed me, and his face took on such a look of welcome and relief that my urge to flee vanished.

"Meg," he said. "This is Alec Franzetti, our new pupil. Come show him how to tell when the iron's ready to work."

Our new pupil. My world fell back into place. There was a new pupil. But I was still the senior pupil—that post was mine to hold on to, if I could.

And I did. Alec might have looked more like most people's idea of a blacksmith, but he wasn't exactly Faulk's star pupil. He was a bit of a klutz, and bad at taking directions. Especially from me, which was unfortunate, since Faulk's original idea was to have me cement my knowledge of the blacksmithing basics by imparting them to Alec. We gave that up after a few weeks, and Faulk was more than half expecting Alec to quit his lessons entirely. But he never completely gave up, and over the years, Faulk eventually turned him into a competent blacksmith and then a bladesmith. But not a master at either.

I'd been overjoyed when Faulk and his husband, Tad, moved to Caerphilly, but relieved when Alec relocated to California. He was fond of bragging that "Cates taught me everything I know." Faulk tended to wince at this, and at least once I'd heard him murmur, "But unfortunately, not everything *I* know." Alec was much less annoying as an occasional visitor to the East Coast, and his change of career from journeyman bladesmith to TV impresario seemed like a good thing to me—as long as he stopped trying to drag me into it.

"An old friend who moved to California and has gotten involved in television," I went on. "They're making a TV series," I said. "*Blades of Glory.*"

"Ooh," she said. "So Michael's acting again? Some kind of swashbuckling heroic fantasy, I assume."

I could have pointed out that my husband had never exactly given up acting—although these days, as a tenured faculty member of Caerphilly College's Drama Department, he spent more time teaching and directing. I could have added that, since in his salad days he'd played a sinister though sexy wizard on a low-budget cult-hit TV show, appearing in yet another swashbuckling heroic fantasy was not a career move that would interest him. But I stifled the urge.

"Not that kind of TV series," I said. "This is one of those reality-TV competition shows. They start out with six blacksmiths—correction, bladesmiths; it's all about weapon making. Each episode, the judges will assign them a different weapon—a two-handed sword, or a Viking battle-ax, or whatever. And all the competitors have to go and make one. Then the judges test it for strength and sharpness and assess how aesthetically pleasing and historically accurate it is, and whoever does the worst gets kicked out of the competition. So by the last episode, they're down from six competitors to two and both the winner and the runner-up get nice cash prizes."

"Sounds interesting," Caroline said. "And you're going to compete?"

"No," I said. "Not really my thing."

"You're a blacksmith," she said.

"But not primarily a bladesmith," I pointed out.

"You've made plenty of weapons."

"Not compared to these guys." I waved at the forge area, although at the moment none of the competitors were there. "They're all specialists. Most of them members of the American Bladesmith Society. And Faulk *is* competing."

"And you don't want to show up your mentor." She nodded as if that explained everything.

"Since everything I know about making weapons I learned from Faulk, I'm smart enough to know better than to try to compete with a master bladesmith," I said. "And besides, although reality-TV competition shows aren't exactly my cup of tea, I've seen enough of them to know I don't want to be on one. I'm just helping out with some of the backstage stuff."

"Oh, you're no fun," she said. "Is there a reason they're planning to film here in a tent in Ragnar's goat pasture?"

"Ragnar invited them to film here," I said. "And offered to put up all the cast and crew during filming."

"Very generous," she said. "And just what you'd expect from him."

I nodded, although I wasn't sure if Ragnar was being generous or whether he thought the filming would be a lot of fun and wanted a ringside seat. Ragnar had retired from a lucrative career as the drummer for several heavy-metal bands that had evidently been wildly successful—although I'd never heard of any of them. He'd bought a large estate in the Caerphilly County countryside and was busy turning what had started out as a sprawling mansion into a veritable castle, complete with stone walls, towers, a moat, and enough wrought iron to keep both Faulk and me busy for the rest of our careers.

"But for some reason, none of the hundred or so rooms in the castle quite works for filming the main blacksmithing scenes," I went on. "So here we are."

"Hope they get some space heaters for this tent," she said. "It's a bit chilly now, and the temperature's going to get colder, not warmer, over the next few days."

"I've suggested that," I said. "And the forges will help warm things. Here's hoping the snow holds off."

"And the arctic polar vortex. And— Wait. No. That would doom us all to not having a white Christmas. I take it back. Let it snow! They can just cope with it."

"If you have any influence with the snow, please tell it to hold off until Friday afternoon," I said. "They're going to film the first episode this week, then take next week off."

"That's nice," she said. "Everyone can celebrate the holiday and then pick up again in the new year."

I nodded. Actually, I doubted if the production team would have time for much celebrating. I'd overheard enough to know that they'd spend the holiday creating a rough cut of the first episode and showing it to some of the higher-ups in their company—higher-ups who, if not sufficiently impressed, might pull the plug on the whole project. Which meant Alec wouldn't be doing much celebrating, either, since he'd invested more money in this crazy project than he could afford to lose. He'd spend the whole Christmas break worrying, and I was afraid he'd go bonkers if the show didn't get green-lighted. Bonkers, and maybe even bankrupt. But I kept this to myself, since I only knew any of it from the eavesdropping I'd done while helping to set up the six blacksmithing stations. So far all of the production people tended to overlook my presence, as if I were merely a non-stationary part of the set. I wanted to keep it that way.

"Will you be here much longer?" Caroline began to sit down on one of the benches, but I grabbed her arm just in time to stop her.

"Don't sit on that just yet," I said. "The idiots who assembled the furniture didn't bother to tighten any of the bolts. That one's safe."

I steered her to the one bench I knew could hold the weight of even a small, roundish person. It had collapsed about an hour ago, spilling the assistant director onto the straw-covered floor of the banquet area. I'd reassembled it, making sure the hidden bolts were good and tight, and was now working on ensuring that the table and the rest of the benches were structurally sound.

"Thanks for the warning," she said. "And if there's something you need to be doing, don't let me interrupt you."

"You can amuse me while I work," I said.

So while I made sure the other three benches and the table were safe to use, she chatted away, relating some of the recent happenings at the wild animal refuge she ran. She was in the middle of telling me about the success she was having raising several orphaned Virginia big-eared bat pups when an officious young woman in a mustard-colored mini-skirted suit and stiletto heels strode over. Her clipboard was much tidier than Alec's. Jasmyn, the production assistant, was organized—I liked that in a person—but she never brought good news.

"Those simply won't do." She pointed toward the two folding tables we'd set up for the judges. "They're not in period."

"They're not finished yet," I said.

"But they need to be finished today!" Jasmyn sounded stressed. "We start filming tomorrow at eight!" She proceeded to rant and rave on the subject, and I'd have cut her short except that I spotted something happening behind her back. Ragnar had appeared, carrying what looked like an armload of star-spangled darkness. Unfolded, the darkness was revealed as two large expanses of black velvet, embroidered in silver. While Jasmyn continued to revile me, he spread the velvet over the tables, and then stood back to admire the result.

"You're right," I said, finally interrupting my tormentor. "They need to be covered with something, so they look in period. I'll take care of that immediately." I snapped my fingers, then pointed to the tables. "How's that?"

She turned to look. I saw her nod slightly. Then, clearly in the mood to continue venting at someone, she turned back to me, frowning.

"Well, why wasn't it done already?" she asked. "What are we *paying* you for?"

"You're not," I said. "I'm one of Alec's people. The guys you're paying went on break an hour and a half ago, and I have no idea where they are."

She pursed her lips, and I suspected she was trying to think up a sufficiently snide reply. But just then a large splotch of gooey white liquid landed on top of her sleek auburn pageboy. I looked up to see a crow sitting on one of the guy wires near the ceiling of the tent. He cawed raucously.

It took Jasmyn a second or two to realize what had happened. Then her face crumpled.

"Oh, gross!" she screamed. And then she ran out of the tent, shrieking. The other workers in the production end barely looked up in spite of her noisy exit.

"He must like you." Caroline was staring up at the crow with an expression of approval. "Have you been feeding him?"

"Only helping Ragnar," I said. "He feeds them all the time."

"Crows notice," she said. "They're very intelligent."

"Yes, I know," I said quickly. Caroline, like my grandfather, was fond of sharing little tidbits of information about her favorite creatures. Little tidbits or great long lectures. And they were both particularly fond of corvids—crows, ravens, and even jays. Caroline had been a nurse before retiring to found her wild animal sanctuary and often put her medical knowledge to good use rehabilitating injured creatures—including corvids.

"I'm worried about this one, though," she said. "It's starting to get dark outside. He should be out finding a good place to roost for the night. Getting his rest. Not in here where some idiot who doesn't like corvids might try to chase him."

As if he'd heard us, the crow cawed twice, then took off and flew out through one of the tent openings. Caroline nodded in satisfaction.

"Caroline! Have you come to watch the filming?" Ragnar loomed over us, six and a half feet tall and looking almost as wide in a bulky down coat. He hugged Caroline. Given the foot-and-a-half difference in their heights, he had to bend over almost double to do so.

"I've come to spend Christmas with Meg and her family," she said. "But I'd love to eavesdrop on the filming if it's allowed."

"Of course!" Ragnar exclaimed. "You can even stay here at the castle if you like. Plenty of room. And arriving today—perfect! You can help with the Christmas decorations. I've been too busy to put them up!"

"But Mother's coming over today to take care of it," I reminded him.

"Yes." Ragnar beamed. "And I know she would love to have Caroline's sharp eye to help her."

"Sounds like fun," Caroline said. "Do you—"

Just then the crow flew back in, cawing. He headed directly

for where the three of us stood. He circled us three times, still cawing, and then flew out the tent opening again.

"He must want us to see something." Ragnar began striding after the crow.

"Either that or he flew around us three times as part of casting a spell on us," I said, falling into step behind him. "What if we suddenly transform into crows?"

"Then Ragnar will feed us until we figure out how to change back." Caroline sounded out of breath. Even though at five-ten I have long legs, I had trouble keeping up with Ragnar. She was flat-out running behind us.

When we emerged outside the tent, we found three or four crows circling overhead, seeming to indicate something on the ground. No, someone.

It was Faulk. He lay on the close-cropped grass, clutching his right arm to his side and breathing heavily. Enough light fell on him from the tent opening that I could see that his face and his shaggy mop of blond hair were streaked with blood.

"Call nine-one-one," Caroline said as she scrambled to Faulk's side, all of her retired nurse instincts kicking in. "And get me a first-aid kit."